THE THIRD FATHER

angela j. phillip

lC

Lame Crow Press

First published in 2020 by Lame Crow Press.

Book design by Paul Way-Rider.
Cover based on photo by Rosario Janza from unsplash.com

ISBN 978-1-913669-06-5 (paperback)
ISBN 978-1-913669-07-2 (ebook)

www.lamecrowpress.com

For Jay McAlbus

1

After that first session with Darius, the rest of the weekend passes in a dream. I know what it means to walk on air. I get up, sit down, get up again and my feet hardly touch the ground. I can hardly believe what has happened and that my writing problems can be solved at last. Everyone thought I was stupid because I couldn't put pen to paper. Or pencil to paper.

Daniela, you're not trying. Try harder, Daniela. Try harder!

They were sure that I was being lazy. I could read so why couldn't I write? I thought I'd be thrown out of school. It felt so bad that I'd started to bite my arm. One pain takes away another. It does, you know. Just for a little while. My biting wasn't serious, but when they found out about it, they thought I was mad. Thank God that's over.

I didn't know why I couldn't write when everyone else could, but now I do. I've got a problem called dysgraphia. I'm not mad. There are reasons for the problem and ways to help. On top of that, Steve, my beloved Steve who had lived with us for ten whole years is back in the house. I'm nearly fourteen so that's almost the whole of my life that Steve has been my Dad. Not my real dad, but like a real dad. Maybe better. It was the only good thing that happened when Mum thought I was mad and wanted to save me from self-harm. She asked Steve to come home. I love him.

I'm down in the cellar trying to work on my second bike, feeling pleased every few minutes. I keep smiling. Keep sitting down on the old wobbly bus seat and then I stare at the grubby-looking whitewashed walls in a happy daze instead of getting on with building Mandy's bike. Just sit here looking around at my neatly organised tools and parts, then out of the window at the bottom of the wall and the garden higher up. Mum's upstairs in the kitchen and she's pleased. I can hear her banging about. And singing. She's so happy for me. That there is a name for my problem and ways to help. It's brilliant.

I stand up again and go back to the bike but still can't concentrate. It doesn't matter. I could do with a better back wheel. Sometimes I find just what I'm looking for on the tips (I build bikes out of abandoned pieces) but then at other times I look and look and I still can't find anything that's quite right. In fact, I'm stuck at the moment until I can find some more parts that fit properly. Or until I can buy some, but that would be expensive and I've got no money. I hope when I finally start selling these bikes that I will be able to make enough so that I can buy some of the parts new. You need new brake blocks, for instance, and there are some other parts that are better bought new. I start to hum as I begin to clean the rust off the handlebars.

In the afternoon I set off for the park, hoping that Jaffa will be there. Hoping that, like me, he'll have some good news but when I get there, I see someone sitting on the bench who isn't Jaffa. It's another person. I look again willing the man on the bench to turn into Jaffa but it doesn't work. I ride around the park for half an hour and it feels a bit stupid because the park is quite small and I go round and round it so many times. I nearly go home but decide to wait a bit longer. The man has gone and I sit on the bench. Our bench. I suppose it is our bench, mine and Jaffa's, but he doesn't come. I get cold because it is nearly winter. Should have put my scarf on. Start to shiver but still Jaffa doesn't come so finally, I give up and go home. I hope he'll be at school tomorrow.

On Monday morning even though Jaffa's not back, I can't help feeling cheerful because I keep thinking about my writing problem and the fact that it's no longer a problem. Solved at last or it will be once I manage to learn how to type. Mandy's back recovered from the 'flu so I tell her about my writing session and she smiles and says it's good. She doesn't understand but it doesn't matter.

We arrange to do another round of the tips probably tomorrow night to get some more bike parts although it won't be easy because Mum says I can't go. Not in the evening anyhow. She's worried about the Yorkshire Ripper. He's still out there and she's convinced that he's in Leeds somewhere and probably near where we live. One of the murders happened in Reginald Terrace and that's not far from here. I'm not worried because he doesn't seem to attack girls of my age but Mum says that Jayne MacDonald was only 16 and that's not that much older than I am. He hasn't killed anyone in Leeds for over a year but Mum says that means we have to be extra careful because he's probably back in the neighbourhood again. The police think he's in Newcastle, but Mum doesn't.

Mum's contradicting herself by not letting me go out in the evenings because she claims to believe in female rights. Believes in 'reclaiming the night for women'. Always says she's not going to stay in just because the Ripper is out there, but she doesn't think that applies to me. I'm too young to be out when it's dark she says. Thinks I'm too young for everything. But I'm not. She doesn't know that I'm not a child anymore and neither is Mandy but her mum thinks more or less the same. They mean well so basically we just don't tell them what we do or where we go.

At lunchtime, I go to see Miss Smith for the five minutes report session I've had to do since they discovered that I was biting my arm. I had thought it would be an awful thing to have to do. Report to the teacher every day but it's been almost pleasant. It's because Miss Smith is nice. Towards the end of last week, I even started wishing that the sessions were longer. I can't wait to tell her about what happened at my writing session with Darius. As soon as I get inside the room, I gabble it all out and can't stop talking for the whole five minutes. All Miss Smith can do is smile. She's very pleased for me

It's my day for the library. I always go to the library after school on Mondays so I set off. It's not far and I need another couple of books to read. Dysgraphia is a writing problem, it's nothing to do with reading. I've never had any problems with reading and I've always read a lot. That's why they called me lazy when I couldn't write. *Daniela, you're not trying. You can do it, but you won't. Daniela, you're lazy. You just don't care, do you!*

Over the years, it got worse. They thought that I couldn't be bothered. But I'm not lazy. Just awkward, stubborn and difficult. Not always, of course. Only when I need to be but I have to survive. You know how it is. School can be dog eat dog but Mum doesn't know that even though she's a teacher. Teachers never know. It must have been different in their day.

I'm waiting to cross over opposite the police station and it's cold. I wish the lights would change so I could get across and into the library where it's warm. But people are not dogs, I think, they're worse. The dogs I know wouldn't eat each other so maybe dog eat dog isn't right. I like them. Dogs that is, and people, too. Some dogs, I mean, and some people. It's only the scared dogs that are vicious. Poor things. I keep thinking about dogs and their similarities to people while I'm waiting to cross the road, but my thoughts are freezing up. It's getting colder and it's windy. Terrible traffic. Pedestrian lights on everlasting red.

'Hey, Blondie,' somebody shouts. A boy's voice but it's not Jaffa. I half turn but the lights change so I finally make it across the road and into the library. Out of the wind, I take my rucksack off and my coat. It's warm inside almost too warm. I'm about to go straight to the fiction section as usual when I remember my writing problem and decide to go and look up dysgraphia. It takes ages to find a book on reading and writing problems, but at last, I find what I'm looking for. It's got entries for dyslexia, dysgraphia and dyspraxia. It's in the reference section in a book on education. Aha, so dysgraphia does exist. Darius hasn't made it up and I feel a wave of satisfaction. I find an empty table in the corner and take the book so I can sit down to read.

First of all, I read about the symptoms and find out that, yes, they do fit. Then I read the description which says that people with dysgraphia don't usually have problems with reading. Excellent. It is all just as Darius told me. Then I start on the section marked Causes. It says there are five causes of dysgraphia and I stare at the list:

- Brain damage
- Mental confusion
- Deformity or physical illness
- Writing badly with intention
- Inadequate teaching

I read it through three times and by then, I am sure. The only possible cause is brain damage. The one at the top of the list. I'm brain damaged. The words repeat in my head and won't stop. Brain damage. Brain damage. Brain damage. So much for telling me that I have a high IQ. I have dysgraphia and it's caused by brain damage. I close the book and leave the library. Walk home like a robot. What a fool I've been. A stupid bloody fool.

2

Esme is out of breath from jumping off the motorbike and rushing up the steps to the front door. She looks fit but she isn't. Should stop smoking. It's Monday, Dani's library day, the one day in the week when Esme gets home before her daughter. She gets the key in the lock and almost falls through the door into the living room of her back-to-back house in Potter Terrace. Leeds is full of redbrick back-to-back houses. She's never seen them anywhere else. Joined on all sides except at the front where the sun shines in whenever it can. Esme loves her house because it's easy to heat and full of light. Windows all the way up the front. Two rooms on top of two rooms on top of two rooms. And a cellar, too.

It's cold out. Nearly winter. Windy and overcast. She takes off her outdoor clothes and turns on the gas fire which heats the living room in a matter of minutes. Sits down to roll a ciggie.

The phone rings.

'Are you back?' It's Suzi, her friend from down the street.

'Only just.'

'Is Dani home? Why don't you come round? I've got some news.'

'No, it's her night at the library. I'll come round later. What's your news?'

'Not big news. Tell you when you come.'

'Is it what I think it is?'

'I'll tell you later,' Suzi repeats. Esme hopes that it's baby news. That's what Suzi's been hoping for. Normally, they talk about Dani and worry about her problems, but not anymore Esme thinks with satisfaction. Dani's problems are on the way to being solved. At last.

For years, it hadn't sunk in that her daughter really couldn't write. Dani could copy slowly with pain in her hands, but a sentence would take hours. Said that when she tried to write her own thoughts the pain was so bad that she forgot what she was trying to say. But everybody thought she should just try harder. Esme, too, had kept thinking that things would surely improve if only Dani would try a bit harder. And then she'd been sure that her daughter was struggling at school because she was upset about Steve leaving.

Dani loves Steve. He's been like a father to her for almost ten years, but Esme had asked Steve to go. Now she has messed things up because she's invited Steve back to live with them again. She shouldn't have done. She had invited him back for Dani's sake, but it's not working between them. Esme knows that her original decision was the right one.

Still no sign of her. It's getting late. Dani is usually back by now. Esme goes to the sofa and picks up Friday's *Evening Post*. The last one to read it was Steve. She knows because it's folded over neatly and smoothed down. Who folds a newspaper that carefully? And why does it irritate her? Esme takes it to the table and opens it out. Another analysis of the Yorkshire Ripper. Another double page spread. He still hasn't been caught and he's much too close for comfort. Esme worries more than she cares to admit. Not for herself but for Dani.

It's windy outside but Esme still hears the gate click. Good. She looks out of the window and sees her daughter climbing slowly up the steps. Looks weary. Shoulders hunched.

'Hi, Dani,' she opens the door to let her in, but Dani barely looks at her. Doesn't speak. Walks past and opens the stairs door. 'What's the matter?' Esme asks but Dani shakes her head.

'Nothing. I'm tired. Going to bed.'

'It's only just gone six o'clock!'

'I'm tired,' her daughter repeats and is gone. Esme considers following her but changes her mind. She'll be down later. Goes into the kitchen to start the dinner. Mince with loads of onions and tomatoes. And pasta made with egg. What's wrong with Dani? She's been bouncy all weekend. Hasn't stopped talking and singing since she came back from the session with Darius.

'Dysgraphia,' Dani had announced with triumph on Saturday, 'is a condition that affects writing but not reading.' And she had proceeded to give Esme a blow by blow account of her writing session ending with the news that all she had to do was to learn to type and then she, too, would be able to write all she wanted.

'So,' Esme had said. 'Just another couple of sessions to get familiar with the typewriter and you'll be writing a novel, will you?'

'Ha ha,' Dani had replied, but nothing could dampen the bounce.

'So was Darius all right?' Esme couldn't help asking when Dani came back from the session and had seen Steve look away. He knows how she feels about Darius. So does Dani and she saw a flicker of annoyance cross her daughter's face.

'Yes, Mum, he was fine,' Dani said and had gone straight down to the cellar to work on the bike (or to get out of the way, Esme thought) but still, she could hear Dani humming as she walked down the steps. Her happiness was overflowing. Couldn't be contained.

Esme knows that she shouldn't have asked about Darius but she couldn't help herself. Even though the man didn't seem to be interested in her, she still hoped. Her relationship with Steve was over. It had been finished long before Darius turned up. All through the summer, Esme had run around Chapeltown flirting with one man after another trying out her freedoms until it all went wrong and she got beaten up. Then she had stopped. Brought to her senses, at last, Steve had muttered but he'd been kind about it. The onions are making her eyes water and Esme keeps going to the sink to hold her hands under cold running water. It always works.

She thought she'd made the best decision when she separated from Steve but now she's gone backwards and is not sure how she's going to fix it. Dani will be distressed if Esme asks him to leave again. More than distressed. Esme stops to listen. What is Dani doing upstairs? There's no sound at all. Not even the music that she usually listens to non-stop. Surely there can't be anything seriously wrong. Something must have happened at school. She hopes that Dani will talk to her about it over dinner, but it's unlikely.

Her daughter is more likely to say nothing at all until she's sorted out whatever it is that's bothering her. Dani is awkward and frustrating. How can Esme help her if she never says what's wrong?

The food smells good. Ess stirs the pot with the mince and onions and drops the pasta into the second pan. The water's boiling now and Esme jams the lid on to push the spaghetti down. Her thoughts return to Darius. Why didn't he get in touch with her after their meeting in the cafe? She's sure that he felt the attraction as strongly as she did. It doesn't make sense. And now he's seeing Dani about her writing but he's asked to see Dani alone.

Everything is cooking nicely. Esme turns the flame down under both pots and goes to sit down. Rolls a cigarette, sighs and draws the smoke into her lungs. Once more she's failing to give up. Next week, she promises herself. Next week, she'll try again.

'Fifteen minutes,' she shouts up the stairs to Dani. 'We won't wait for Steve.'

No reply from above. Esme goes to check the pots once more, stirs both then sits down again. Esme realises that she is waiting. Waiting for Dani to come down and tell her what's wrong. Waiting for Steve to come home so she can find a time to talk things through with him. And she's waiting for Darius. Even though there is no indication that Darius will ever get in touch with her again.

She stares out of the window but can't see much. It's dark now. There's still no sound at all from upstairs and the street outside is quiet. Not many people have cars. A motorbike goes past. Too loud. Needs a new exhaust. Her own motorbike is a little Honda 70. At least, her friend

Howard calls it little. It's parked on the short path between the street and the house. She's been sharing Steve's car for a long time, but he'll take it with him when he goes. And he will go. Esme will somehow manage to ask him again to leave but it won't be easy. Steve is a good man and she's loved him for a long time. Hurting him feels dreadful.

It's more than two hours before Steve gets back and Dani still hasn't come down. Despite frequent entreaties, she has remained stubbornly silent. As soon as Steve has taken his coat off, Esme tells him that Dani came home upset and has shut herself away in the bedroom.

'Why don't you go and talk to her,' Esme suggests thinking that Steve might have more luck in getting Dani to talk.

'OK,' he says obligingly but comes back only minutes later to report that Dani says she's tired and that she's gone to bed. Esme serves out the steaming tomato pasta while Steve goes into the kitchen to fetch a bottle of wine. 'Do you want a drink?' he asks as he sits down. Esme nods. 'Thought you might have gone to see Suze,' he says.

'Yes, I would have done, but I was worried about Dani.'

'She's been on a cloud all weekend. Must be something that happened at school,' he says. 'Probably be fine tomorrow.'

3

Next morning Dani refuses to go to school. Steve has been working at home and when Esme gets home after work, he informs her that Dani has stayed in bed all day. Wouldn't talk and only came out of the bedroom twice.

'At the weekend, it was like getting the old Dani back,' he says as he goes into the kitchen to make a pot of tea, 'But it didn't last long, did it?'

'Did you do the washing?' Esme asks.

'Yes,' he says. 'I've spread it about upstairs. Some of it's hanging over the bannisters.'

'We ought to get a washing line. There's room enough outside for a short one.'

'Yes, we keep saying that,' he says. 'One day, we'll remember to buy one.'

'And she didn't say anything at all to you?'

'No,' he confirms.

Esme rolls herself a cigarette and remembers that she'd almost given up a couple of weeks ago. She sighs. Even when Dani hadn't done her homework, she still went to school. There must be something terribly wrong.

The next morning it's the same again and when Ess gets home from work, Steve says they need to talk about Dani.

'Where is she now? Is she still in her room?'

'No,' Steve says. 'She's gone to see Mandy. I talked to her and she's agreed to go back to school tomorrow so I thought it wouldn't hurt if she went out for a while.'

'Well, that's a relief,' Esme sighs. 'So what was wrong?' She takes off her coat and settles down on the floor with her back against the sofa, gets as close to the gas fire as possible and reaches for the ashtray.

'She told me she's got brain damage.'

'What?' Esme says and begins to laugh as she lights up and draws the smoke into her lungs. 'What do you mean she's got brain damage?'

'Dani went to the library to look up dysgraphia,' Steve says. 'She found a list of causes. The first one was brain damage and she said that none of the others could possibly fit.' Esme's thoughts whirl into action.

'And what did you say to her?'

'I told her it was nonsense, but she wouldn't listen.'

'Did you persuade her that she was wrong? Something must have changed her mind if she's decided to go back to school again'.

'No, she's still upset. Convinced it's true and that Darius lied to her. I think we need to phone him and tell him what's happened. Ask him to talk to her.'

'All right,' Esme agrees, 'but will you do it?'

Steve shrugs his shoulders and looks uncomfortable. 'It was you who went with her to the writing session. It would be easier if you called him.' Steve doesn't look keen but picks up the phone.

'What's his number?'

'I don't know if he's got a separate line. I've only got Joe's number. That's where he lives, you know, at Joe's house.' As she says this, she remembers that of course Steve knows where Darius lives. It was Steve who first introduced him to her. She sees that Steve is looking irritated. 'Sorry,' she says. 'You know all that. The number is in the book somewhere.' Ess points to the notebook that is lying next to the phone then picks it up, finds the page and hands it to him.

Steve dials the number, but it's Joe's sister who answers. Sorry, she says, but Darius is out. She'll leave him a message to ask him to ring back.

'Just have to wait then,' Steve says and walks over to give her a hug, but Esme turns away.

'Sorry,' she says. 'I'm sorry, Steve. Can't help it. I'm feeling tense.'

When Dani gets back from Mandy's, there's another row. Says she can't believe it. How could Steve have told Esme what she'd said? Ess tries to reason with her but Dani rushes off upstairs. Esme sighs. All evening she waits for a call from Darius but the phone doesn't ring.

Next day Dani goes to school as promised. A relief of sorts and when Esme gets back from work, Steve tells her that there was a phone call. Darius had apologised for not getting in touch earlier and suggested that he could speak to Dani on the phone.

'OK,' Esme says,' Is she in the cellar? Have you asked her?'

'No,' he replies.

'Will you?'

Steve shrugs then nods. Goes to talk to Dani and when he comes up again says that she has agreed. She will talk to Darius so long as he and Esme go out when Darius rings. Not out of the room. Out of the house. She wants to be alone when she talks to him.

'I said that would be all right, Ess,' he says. 'What do you think?'

'Yes, of course,' Esme agrees and Steve rings Darius to confirm.

It is half-past seven and they've already eaten when Darius calls so Esme and Steve set off for a walk as promised. They stay out for more than half an hour.

'What happened?' Esme asks as soon as they get back.

'Nothing,' Dani replies but she grins. 'We just talked.'

'Is Darius going to come here?'

'No,' Dani says. 'Why would he?' Ess heaves a silent sigh of relief. Her daughter is contradicting her and beginning to look bouncy again. 'I'll go and see him on Saturday morning at the school,' Dani says.

So that's that. Things seem to be getting better almost back to normal. Dani is going to school and spending time with Mandy again but what did Darius say to her? Esme asks Steve to try and find out and he half agrees. But only if Dani feels like talking.

Esme desperately wants to know what Darius has said. More than anything, she wants to know what has caused Dani's dysgraphia and tries to shut out of her mind the terrible suspicion that she can't quite face. What if Dani's dream is based on a memory and her father did try to suffocate her?

She had wanted her daughter to have good memories of Andreas. Had tried to stop Dani saying *Daddy kill Dani* and putting cushions over her face. She had refused to believe what Dani seemed to be saying. But there was always a doubt. Part of her can't believe it, but another part of her can. Maybe he really did put a pillow over her face.

Grandma had been the last person to see Andreas alive. He had fetched Dani and shouted that he was taking her to Leeds to teach Esme a lesson. Andreas had been beside himself that day. Drunk and angry. He had found Esme in bed with another man.

Esme was full of guilt so she couldn't bear to hear a bad word about him. But she could have been wrong. The terrible thought hits that if it were true, then temporary suffocation might, just might, have caused the dysgraphia.

***

The rest of the week drags. Dani seems more or less all right, but she isn't chatty. Steve is back to normal working on his research, but Ess feels miserable. She wants to know what Darius has said and she wants to know why he won't speak to her. Dani is her daughter so she has a right to know what's going on, but that's not how Darius sees it. He has always insisted on dealing directly with Dani. Has always insisted on discussing things with her, not with her teachers or with her mother.

The need to talk to Darius is beginning to drive Esme mad. It's not just the wanting to talk about Dani's writing, it's the need to find out how he feels. Ess is sure that he is drawn to her in the same way that she is drawn to him. He had watched her at the party when they first met. When they saw each other again, he had asked her out and spending time with him had been good. More than good. They had talked all afternoon. Couldn't stop. They belong together, she is sure of it. So why hasn't he been in touch?

***

The kitchen sink is full of bubbles because she's used too much washing-up liquid. The weekend here at last but not much to look forward to. Ess stares at the froth on top of the water which is warm and comforting. Slowly she swishes the dishcloth backwards and forwards. Another squirt of washing up liquid then she turns on the tap again to make more bubbles.

It's dark outside and brightly lit where she stands at the kitchen sink in front of the window. She looks at her reflection in the black pane of glass and pulls a face then grins. Stop it, she tells herself, get on with the job or you'll be here all night. Steve is upstairs working and Dani is at Mandy's, allowed to stay out until ten when Esme will go and fetch her. Ess finishes the washing up and goes back into the living room to roll a cigarette. Still hasn't managed to stop smoking.

Time to make a decision she thinks. Otherwise, life will go on like this forever. It's time she faced up to the fact that Darius is not interested in her. Is it because she's still with Steve she wonders? Her thoughts ramble on until they come to a sudden halt. Whether or not Darius wants her, she can't stay with Steve. Esme finishes rolling the cigarette and goes upstairs to tell him.

4

I was in a strange state after my shock at the library and I nearly walked in front of a car that I didn't see at all. I'd been so pleased to find out that I'd got dysgraphia because it explained, at last, why I've had so much trouble trying to write. But now I know what having dysgraphia means. It means that I have brain damage. A moron. Thinking I might be stupid because I could hardly write had felt dreadful but being brain-damaged is on another level, as Steve might say.

I thought that Darius had lied to make me feel good. They had all lied to me. All my life, all of them had lied to me to make me think I was OK. Esme had even made me think I was clever. And Steve. And Grandma. They must have known and never told me. That's what I thought as I lay upstairs in my room. But after a while, I thought that perhaps Steve could be trusted and that he had not lied. Maybe Steve just hadn't known.

In the book, it said that brain damage happened when the brain was deprived of oxygen. The book said it often happened at birth. Steve wasn't there when I was born but my mother was, obviously. If it happened, it must have been when I was small because I can't remember any accident when my brain could have been deprived of oxygen. It must have been when I was so small that I couldn't remember. Probably at birth like it said in the book.

When I told Steve about what I'd found out, it was clear that he didn't know about anything happening to me. He was sure that I didn't have brain damage and he persuaded me to go back to school but he knew I was still upset. He told me that I should talk to Darius. I wasn't keen, but then I thought that maybe I should. Darius ought to know that I'd found the information he didn't want me to have. To be honest, I was scared of talking to him. Scared of even thinking about having brain damage. I like to seem tough but I'm not really. That's why I wanted Mum and Steve to go out while I talked to Darius.

He didn't ring until after seven. I'd hardly been able to eat for worrying about his phone call.

'Hi, Dani,' he said and his voice sounded the same as before. Slow and deep. Nice. I tried to remember that I was angry with him, but all I felt was misery.

'Hi, Darius.'

'Steve tells me that you think you've got brain damage,' he said. Just like Darius. No messing about. Always talks directly so I told him about the book I found in the library. About what it said. And about what I'd thought about since then.

'Yes,' he said. 'Brain damage is the primary cause of dysgraphia so you probably do have some brain damage.'

How could he say that? I didn't think he would say that. How could he say it? There was a long pause because I couldn't think of what to reply. My thoughts were spinning. Then Darius continued.

'Why does it matter?'

This time I almost exploded.

'Of course, it matters,' I said. I could barely speak. It's not me that's mad, it's Darius I thought. 'What a stupid question!'

'No,' he replied, 'it's not a stupid question.' All our brains have slight differences he said. And our bodies. If I'd read that dysgraphia was caused by a damaged wrist, would that have upset me? We are as we are. All different. None of us perfect. We have to make the best of what we've got and he said that he would expect me to be grateful for the excellent brain that I've got.

'What do you mean I've got an excellent brain? It can't be damaged and excellent both at the same time!'

'Of course, it can, Dani. You know very well that you've got an excellent brain,' Darius paused for what seemed like ages. 'Don't you!'

It was hardly spoken as a question. Darius was sure that I did know.

And I suppose he's right. In some ways, at least, he's right. He has no sympathy with me at all and somehow that feels good. I'm still trying to work it out, how I feel and all that and what I think. But I've said that I'll see him on Saturday and carry on with the writing sessions. I don't tell Steve and Esme what Darius has said. I need time to think it through, but I do tell them that I'm going to carry on with the sessions. They are surprised and pleased and gradually, I find myself feeling cheerful again.

***

Well, I did feel cheerful until my life fell apart again. To begin with, everything was all right except for Jaffa. Where was he? Not in school all week so I was anxious about him. I made up my mind to find out where he lived so I could contact him and try to help. But everything else was just about back to normal. I was feeling hopeful about my writing. Bike building coming on fine. But then it happened. Mum and Steve fell out again. I knew I shouldn't have thought that Steve was back for good but that's what I did think because it was what I'd hoped. It was what I wanted to be true. When I listened to Mum's thoughts, I knew things were not all right with her and Steve, so I shut them out. Couldn't bear the truth. Oh, bugger, shit and hell.

This is the second time that Mum has thrown Steve out and I start to wonder whether it's worthwhile believing in anything. Working at anything. Hoping for anything. Maybe it will be me who gets thrown out next. I daren't say this to Mum, but it's what I fear. One minute I'm up, then I'm down, but at this moment I'm deep down. It feels like I'm carrying a lead weight, crawling along the ground. Surprising to see that I look the same as usual.

Worse still is the fact that my weird dream is happening again and it always wakes me up, usually towards morning about five a.m. and then I can't get to sleep again. My father pushes a pillow over my face and then says he loves me and leaves. Always the same but I don't understand it. I've told Mum and Grandma about the dream. Except how it ends. I haven't told them about the end of it. About how I always want my daddy to come back.

It doesn't make sense. Why would I want anyone who had tried to kill me back again? It makes me scared. In the dream there's a feeling of longing for my father and the longing is mixed with fear. It's not about Steve because he isn't my dad. Not in real life and definitely not in the dream. Even though I never see the man in the dream, I know it isn't Steve.

***

I'm sitting in Mandy's attic bedroom, and we're eating crisps.

'What do you think I should do?'

'There's nothing you can do,' Mandy says. 'Is there?'

'There must be something.' My hand goes in and out of the crisp packet eating automatically. My hand comes out with nothing but a few broken bits. I peer into the bag. Can't believe it's finished. 'They don't put many crisps in these days.'

'No,' Mandy agrees.

'Why has she done it again?' It's a question with no answer, but it still keeps hammering in my brain. 'She threw him out before, then she asked him to come back and now she's thrown him out again.'

'How do you know?' Mandy asks. 'How do you know that it's all your mum's fault.' After a slight pause, Mandy adds that according to her mother, there are always faults on both sides.

'That's what people say,' I agree, 'but in this case, there's no fault on Steve's side. He's always nice and he always wants to stay. But Mum won't let him.' I feel miserable because Mandy doesn't understand. How can she? She's never known what it's like to have her mother tell her father to leave. Then I feel guilty. Her mother has just had an operation for cancer and that's terrible. But at least she's now clear. Mandy says that her mum will have to have regular check-ups and treatment for some years, but still, the news is good.

Mandy doesn't understand what it feels like to have what you thought was your family that would last forever suddenly falling apart. I suppose it's not suddenly. It's been coming for a while. I rip open the crisp packet, turn it inside out and lick the inside.

'Are there any more?'

Mandy shakes her head.

'I asked Steve what had happened between him and Mum.'

'And what did he say?'

'Not much,' I reply. 'I kept asking him why he'd gone, and at first, he wouldn't say anything. It wasn't until I asked him if it was my fault that he started talking.'

'And what did he say?' Mandy asks again.

'He said of course not. It wasn't anybody's fault, so I asked him why he was leaving. Eventually, he said it was because Mum wanted to live by herself.' I remember his exact words 'Your mother wants to live by herself.' No mention of me. Did that mean that I was going to be thrown out along with him? But I don't say that to Mandy. It feels shameful to admit that I'm not sure whether my mother wants me or not. I sigh and stretch out on the floor and wave my legs in the air.

'Can you do a backwards roll?' Mandy asks.

'Of course,' I reply. 'Watch.' I turn around, check the space behind me and roll neatly backwards. 'Your turn.'

'Can't do it,' Mandy says. 'Only forwards. I can do forward rolls.' She sits up and looks at me. 'I want to ask you something.'

'What's that?' I ask.

'What do you think about David Williams?'

'The new boy?'

'Yes.'

'He seems all right,' I say. 'But what's happened to what's-his-name? Breally? Have you gone off him?' Mandy looks uncomfortable.

'It's not his real name,' she says. 'Just a nickname. Something to do with Be Really.' I make no comment. 'I went for a walk with him,' she goes on, 'and I decided I didn't like him.'

'Hmmm,' I say and have a sudden intense longing to see Jaffa. There's been no sign of him and I haven't heard from him at all since I saw him in the park when he told me about his mum being in hospital. 'What happened on the walk?'

'He kissed me and I didn't like it.'

'OK,' I say, 'so that's the end of him.' I have a sudden vision of Jaffa kissing me and wish that he would. 'Do you fancy David Williams now?'

'I was put in the same workgroup,' Mandy says and blushes. 'I thought he was nice. Easy to talk to.' She gathers up the empty crisp packets and puts them in the bin. 'Do you want some?' she asks holding up the half-empty Coke bottle. I nod and hold out my hand. Wipe the top and drink out of the bottle. Leave some for Mandy and hand it back.

'Are you still going for the writing sessions?' Mandy asks, changing the subject.

'Yes,' I say. 'I'm going every Saturday. I'm learning to type. I can take the typewriter home with me but have to take it when I go for the sessions. It's got a case which is good but it's heavy.'

'What's it like?' Mandy asks.

'What? The typing or the sessions?'

'Both.'

'All right,' I say. 'Both all right.'

'What's your teacher like?'

'He's not a teacher,' I tell her. 'He's a consultant.'

'What's your consultant like then?'

'All right,' I tell her. 'And interesting. He's from Papua New Guinea.'

'Where's that?'

'It's a country near Australia. Takes about three days flying to get there. He's going back for Christmas. To see his family.'

'But what do you do in the sessions? Is it just you and him?'

'Yes, just me and him. Steve always goes with me, but he just sits at the back and reads a book.'

'Doesn't your Mum go with you?'

'No. I don't want her there. I prefer to go with Steve.' I do another backwards roll and then go back to sitting where I was before.

'Do you know what's happened to Jaffa?' I ask her.

'Oh yes,' she says. 'Didn't you know? His mum died and he's gone to live with his sister in Hunslet.'

'Oh my God.'

Mandy looks at me and I can see that she suddenly realises that I like Jaffa. That I really like Jaffa and that I'm shocked at the news.

'I'm sorry,' she says. 'I thought you didn't like him. You always said it was a drag when he followed you around.'

'I started talking to him,' I tell her. 'He's nice.' I feel my legs begin to tremble. Now I know why he hasn't been in school. He must be feeling dreadful. I'll have to find him. The realisation sinks in that I can't imagine life without Jaffa. Can't imagine what it would be like never to see Jaffa again. He's my friend. He drew a picture of me. 'Do you know where his sister lives?' I ask her.

'Yes.' Mandy says. 'Hunslet.'

'I'm going home,' I say. 'I know what I'm going to do.'

'What's that?' asks Mandy.

'I'm going to move out. I'm going to go and live with Steve.' It might be easier to find Jaffa if I move out, but I don't say anything about that. I look at Mandy and see that she doesn't think much of the idea. 'Don't you think it's a good plan?' I ask her. Perhaps I'm clutching at straws.

'Not really,' Mandy replies. 'How will I see you?' She stops to think. 'And where does he live anyway? And what will you do if he won't have you?'

'He will have me,' I tell her. 'He told me he would always be my family.' I remember looking at him when he said it. Always, Steve had said. Whatever happens? I had asked. Yes, he had said, but then I remember him saying in Scarborough that my place was with my mum. That I couldn't go and live with him. Mandy's right and I feel ashamed. He doesn't want me. I'm stuck.

'But Steve's not really your family, is he? He's not your Dad.'

'No, he's not my Dad,' I have to agree.

'But your Mum's your real Mum.'

Mandy's right again, but not entirely. Steve has definitely been my real dad and I think he always will be. It all depends on what 'real' means. Steve's gone from the house but I'll still see him. I'll always love him. And Jaffa's my friend so I'll have to find him because we need to be together. To cheer each other up. To watch tennis together on that bench next to the tennis courts. Even if no-one is playing. Like they usually aren't if you know what I mean. It's one of the things we do together while we talk.

5

Mandy is right and I know that running off to Steve's won't work. He wouldn't have me, and if I'm honest, I would miss my mum. I love my mother but can't understand why Esme doesn't want Steve to live with us anymore. For years she told me that Steve was part of our family. That he wasn't my dad but was like a dad and he has been. Has been? Is it over now? No dad? What has happened to make her change? She doesn't seem to have anybody else. No boyfriends. She isn't going dancing or anywhere else. She likes Darius but he's not interested. (Good!) Her decision doesn't make sense and I desperately want Steve to stay and life to go back to how it was before.

It was the dancing that started it. Before then, everything was fine. My mother used to say that we were a family, the three of us. Why did she change her mind? And if my mother suddenly doesn't want Steve, will she soon feel the same about me? I remember that she didn't want me around over the summer. Mum had wanted me to stay at Grandma's. Then I think about what Mandy said about Steve. I know what she means when she says that Steve isn't my real dad. But what does 'real' mean? For years I've thought of him as my dad.

'Dani! Are you down there? You'll turn into a mole one of these days.'

It's Mum shouting down to me. Says I'm spending too much time down here but it's a relief. It's where I can think.

'Are you coming up? I've made you a cup of coffee.'

I go and get it and come back down, don't want to talk to Mum. I'm finding it almost impossible to concentrate on bike building or anything else. Wish I was back at Mandy's. At least I can talk to her and she doesn't freak out at anything I say. Keeps me down to earth.

I was shocked when she told me about Jaffa's Mum. I had no idea. I try to think what it would feel like if your mum died, but it's too awful to imagine. I'll have to think of a way to find him. I have to tell him that I will help in any way that I can. That I'll stand by him. I've thought of looking in the telephone directory to see if I can find his sister. I know her name is Annie. But her surname won't be Johns. She will have a married name. My second idea is to ask Miss Smith. I'll tell her I want to send Jaffa a card and then ask for his address. That's a better idea and it might work, but I won't see Miss Smith until next week because we've got a day off tomorrow. An unexpected Friday treat.

Steve is coming to pick me up to take me to Ilkley. The day off is because the school heating system is being overhauled. A letter was sent out about it a week ago, and a lot of the parents complained. Too short notice, they said, but there was nothing they could do. Luckily Steve's work is flexible so he's going to take me walking on Ilkley Moor. I'm going to take a sleeping bag and stay the night at his place when we get back from the hike.

I take a sip of the coffee and pull a face. Mum's trying to cut down on my sugar intake. I set off up the cellar steps back to the kitchen to put in another spoonful. Taste it after one heaped. Nearly all right. One more flat one should make it drinkable. It's only half full but I still manage to spill some on the way down. Not much. No mop needed. Doesn't take long before I'm back in the cellar. I get the rags and the chrome cleaner and carry on with the handlebars. There's so much rust on them, it will take weeks to get it all off.

Steve's place is actually his friend, Paul's place so that's where I'll be staying. Steve hasn't got a flat of his own yet. I know that he is hoping that Mum is going to change her mind and that he will be able to come back, but I don't think it will happen. I believe that my mother's decision is final this time because I asked her. She says that she and Steve are incompatible. Tells me that she is sorry, but that yes, it's final.

How can you be compatible one minute and not the next? How can you love somebody for ten years and then change your mind? Ten years! More likely she's fallen for somebody else. That's what I used to think before. I thought it was Darius. I worried that my mother wanted to replace Steve with Darius. I rub harder while I'm thinking this. Try to rub the thought out of my mind but it won't go.

Mum liked Darius right from the start and when she went to meet him the day Steve took me to Scarborough, she was like a kid.

'Do I look all right, Dani?' she asked me that morning, as though she was nervous before going on a first date. It felt as though I was the adult and she was the child. I hated her for that. How dare she worry about looking good for Darius when she's thrown Steve out. Steve! And back in the summer when Darius had been supposed to come to dinner with Joe, Mum had told me about Papua New

Guinea and shown me where it was on the map. She was excited about him even then. But Darius didn't turn up for the dinner and apart from having coffee with her that day when she'd shunted me off with Steve, they hadn't met again. At least, not to my knowledge.

I'm going to run out of chrome cleaner soon and it's expensive. Can't believe how much I use all the time. It's the most expensive part of building a bike, the stuff I need for cleaning. Sandpaper is cheap but I need loads of it. That's what I use before applying the chrome cleaner. I shake the tin. There's still some left. Should be enough for tonight. Look for a clean bit of rag. Hardly any left.

Keep thinking about my mum. I can't be sure about who she sees or where she goes when I'm not there. I used to think I knew about her life, but I was wrong. She was warned to stay away from Jackson but she still went to visit him and got herself beaten up. None of us knew about that until afterwards so it's quite possible that she's been out to meet Darius. But I don't think so. Mum has changed since Jackson's woman belted her. I'm almost positive that my mother hasn't been seeing anyone because she doesn't go out at all and I think I can cross Darius off my list of threats. He doesn't seem interested in my mother and he never comes to our house. Not even now that Steve has gone.

When I'm not worrying about Darius getting together with Mum (and most of the time, I'm not), I like him. The writing sessions are hard work but gratifying and often fun. I enjoy talking to him because Darius treats me like an intelligent human being and listens to what I have to say. One of the best things is that I am gradually learning to use the typewriter that he lent me. When I first tried, it was harder than writing by hand. That was depressing, but Darius told me that I had to stick with it. And I have. And it's getting easier.

'When you can type,' he said, 'then you can decide whether or not it's useful. Not before.'

I have worked at it. I can be both stubborn and determined when I'm working at something that interests me. I won't stop until I succeed. My mum says that I'm like my father. He was the same. Always wanted perfection and wouldn't stop whatever he was trying to do until he achieved it. It had not made him easy to live with she said. I get a funny feeling when I think about my father. My real father. It's because of the dream. It's weird that I end up longing for someone who has just tried to kill me and it happens every time. Does that make me mad? And why doesn't my mother take me seriously? I only tell her about the part where he tries to kill me but she tells me to forget it. It's just a dream. I shiver.

It's true that I'm a perfectionist, but whether I get it from my father or not is debatable. I'm certainly hard-working despite what Mrs Richards used to think about me. I look at the handlebars and see some rusty bits next to the rubber grips and reach for the sandpaper. I rub hard and think about my writing. At least that's getting easier as I learn how to type. Grandma has been very encouraging. Apparently, a long time ago, she thought she might become a secretary and taught herself shorthand and typing from a book she had. *The Pitman Course.*

'And did you ever work as a secretary, Grandma?'

'No, but I did the lessons,' she said, 'and I've still got the book. Shall I send it to you?'

'Yes, please,' I said so the book was sent. It's old-fashioned with a dull grey cover, a bit like a school exercise book but it's useful. Darius is good at diagnosing writing problems and recommending solutions, but he has no idea how to teach typing. He can't even type himself except with two fingers. (Soon I'll be faster than he is!)

I am determined to learn how to touch type. That means doing it without looking at the keyboard like my mother can. When I was little she used her typing skills to earn money. I can remember her sitting with an old typewriter surrounded by papers. She used to type for hours late at night when I was going to sleep. It was noisy but a comforting sound. Mum says that typing is one of the most useful skills she ever learned.

It seems that there's nothing Mum can't do. Anything she tries, she's immediately brilliant at it. Unlike me. I need more time to learn than she does (except for the bike building stuff which doesn't count), but I manage everything in the end. And I'll manage the typing, too. At the moment I do it slowly and make a lot of mistakes. A word takes quite a long time. I find that typing a sentence on the typewriter can still take longer than for me to copy it out although it depends on the word. I can do some words a lot more quickly than others.

'It will get easier,' Darius tells me and he's right. One thing though is very different from how it used to be. I am beginning to enjoy working on my writing. Not as much as I like working on the bike, but I find that it's satisfying learning to type. I'm starting to concentrate on what I want to say instead of feeling angry with my hand for not working properly. When I make a mistake, I have Tippex to save me from having to type out the whole lot again. My mum bought the Tippex for me. I can white-out the mistake and type over it. Miss Smith has arranged for me to submit my homework on typed sheets in a special folder rather than in my exercise book. And Darius is right. I am getting faster. Not much. But a bit. I'm tired. Time to go to bed. I wonder where Jaffa is and how he's coping. I pray that the dream doesn't come tonight.

6

I get up early but Mum has already left for work. She shouted up before she left. It's cold all through the house and I make porridge to warm myself up. Get the Lyle's Golden Syrup tin out of the cupboard. It's a bit sticky but not too bad. Get a dessertspoon and dip it in. Watch the treacle fill the spoon and overflow as I lift it out carefully to pour on to my porridge. Stir it in and watch the satisfying golden whirls and smell the sweetness mix into the steam. So good. I look at the lion on the side of the tin and read the words underneath. *Out of the strong came forth sweetness.* I wonder for the hundredth time what lions have got to do with treacle or sweetness.

I've only just finished eating (and washed up!) when Steve turns up. He's early but I'm ready. Sleeping bag and typewriter packed. It makes me feel good having a typewriter. It feels purposeful. Almost glamorous. My mother says that she, too, would like to have a typewriter again. It's an envied possession even though it is only on loan.

It is cold outside. It must be the wind. It's the very end of November and bits of old verses run through my head.

The cold wind doth blow
And we shall have snow
And what will cock robin do then, poor thing?

The sun comes out so it's bright and windy. Steve says it's perfect hiking weather. I think it's icy but don't comment. I've been walking on Ilkley Moor before but not for a few years. We are going to walk to the Cow and Calf which is about three miles away. Not very far, I think. I tell Steve that I could do a much longer walk, but he laughs and says that the aim is not to walk as far as possible but to enjoy ourselves. OK then, I expect it will be fine. Steve wants time to look around the town and have some lunch there.

Ilkley is fairly busy but once we get up on the moor, we see hardly anyone. The wind is blowing a gale and we lean into it pressing forward.

'There aren't any trees,' I say.

'Well, no,' Steve agrees.

It is bleak and wide and empty. The sun shines and the wind blows. We walk without talking because if we try to say anything, the wind blows our words away. It seems to take hours but eventually, we reach the Cow and Calf rocks and I have a good look at them.

'Why are they called the cow and calf?'

'Well, the big rock's the cow, and the little one is the calf,' Steve says.

'They don't look much look a cow and a calf to me,' I mutter. 'More like just rocks.' Steve laughs and tells me the story of the giant Rombald landing on the rock to split the cow from the calf as he runs away from his enemy. I'm not impressed.

'Who was his enemy?'

'His wife, I think,' Steve says.

'His wife?'

'It was his wife who dropped the rest of the stones out of her apron. They're supposed to be her skirt full of stones,' he says, pointing.

Not much of a story in my opinion. 'Why was she his enemy?'

'I don't know,' Steve admits. 'But somebody must have thought the stones looked like a cow and a calf. They've been called that for a long time.'

'How long?'

'I don't know, Dani,' Steve replies and looks at me. 'You're very argumentative today.'

'Sorry,' I say. He's right. Don't know what's wrong with me, but I do like it here. It's spacious.

The time with Steve passes quickly. We walk some more. Admire the view. Wander around the town and eat a large meal of fish and chips with fruit pie (unspecified type) for pudding.

In the evening, I go with Steve and Paul to a club attached to a pub and have my first game of pool. I wonder if I have to be sixteen to be there and feel pleased that Steve thinks I look old enough, but apparently it doesn't matter because it's a club not a pub.

I had planned to talk to Steve about him and Mum but when I try, he says he doesn't know what will happen and changes the subject. There isn't another opportunity and it doesn't seem worth trying again. Steve doesn't seem to want to talk. Maybe there isn't much point in talking anyway. I can't think of anything Steve could do to make things better. It is my mother who needs to change and she won't. The rest of us are powerless.

The next morning, I wake up feeling stiff and miserable and can't shift my mood. There seems to be no way to keep Steve in our house. We get to the bottom of Roundhay Road where the Self-Help School is and he drops me off for my writing session. I climb the uneven stone steps up to the door clutching a bag in one hand and the typewriter in the other. I won't let Steve carry it for me. Prefer to be independent. I'm strong and I'm tough. Ha ha. He tells me that he's going to see my mother and will be back later to pick me up. Is that all right? Fine, I tell him. But don't hope for anything he mutters as he drives off. I do though. I always hope for something.

When I reach the classroom, I see that Darius is already there.

'Morning, Darius.'

'Hello, Dani. Where's Steve?'

'Gone to see my mum,' I tell him. 'He's coming back later to pick me up.' Darius nods and reaches into his briefcase to get out the notes he keeps on my sessions. He allows me to read them and says I can look at them anytime. I find that comforting. It feels threatening when people write notes about you that you're not allowed to see. I place the typewriter on the table and lift it carefully out of its case. I am normally cheerful when I come for the writing sessions especially now that I'm making good progress so Darius notices that I'm looking depressed.

'What's wrong, Dani?' His voice is kind.

'It's my mum,' I say before I can stop myself. 'She's sent Steve away again, and I miss him. I don't know why she's done that and I can't make her take him back.'

43

'I'm sorry,' Darius says as he helps me feed paper into the typewriter. I watch him sorting it out and suddenly I have a brainwave.

'Can you make her change her mind?'

'Me?' Darius asks looking surprised. 'Why would your mother listen to me, Dani? And it's not my business.'

'Because she likes you,' I tell him. 'She was excited when you were coming to dinner that time but then you didn't come. And she was excited when she went to have coffee with you.' I see that Darius looks confused and a little uncomfortable, but I carry on trying to explain. 'I understand that you don't like her much,' I say. 'She waited for you to invite her out again, but you didn't. And that's not your fault.' Once again, I look at Darius and see that the man looks embarrassed. 'It doesn't matter that you didn't invite her out,' I tell him. 'But maybe she would listen to you if you talked to her about Steve.' Darius doesn't reply so I decide to have one last try.

'Could you tell her that I'm desperate for Steve to come back and live with us? I miss him.'

I have to turn away so that Darius doesn't see the struggle I have with my face. I'll have to work harder at being tough. I'm sure I used to manage better than this.

7

Esme dismounts and wheels the bike through the gate. Parks it as usual in front of the house and wishes, as usual, that there was somewhere else to put it. She takes the books out of the plastic box on the back, bangs her leg on the bike pedal as she walks past it and climbs wearily up the steps. A whole evening to herself she thinks, but what she means is a whole evening without Dani who is staying the night with Steve at Paul's. Luxury. Esme has arranged to meet Joe at the pub later on. Wants to talk to him about Darius.

He is still on her mind. Her brain is like a broken record. Round and round with the same question. Dani sees him every Saturday but he sends no message and he never drops in.

Ess drops her bag on the floor and struggles out of the blue plastic cagoule and over-trousers. She would like something more glamorous but can't afford it. Dreams of leather as she switches on the gas fire and goes to make a cup of coffee. She can accept that there are plenty of men who aren't attracted to her, but it is rare that she gets the signals wrong. Maybe Joe will be able to explain things although it might be difficult to ask.

Much better to write a letter to ask Darius directly. She could ask Joe to give it to him. Ess takes a pad of paper out of her school bag and settles down at the table. First, she rolls a cigarette and lights it. That's better. She should have given up by now she thinks as she stares at the blank page.

Dear Darius

I shouldn't write this letter, but I've waited so long to hear from you. I would be grateful to know why you haven't contacted me. I was sure there was something special between us.

No, that won't do.

Dear Darius

How are you? Just wanted you to know that you're very welcome if you feel like calling in some time.

No, that won't do.

Dear Darius

I had hoped to see you in person to thank you for all that you're doing for Dani.

No.

Dear Darius

I would like to thank you for all that you've done for my daughter. As you probably know, Dani struggled with her writing for years. We tried to help her but failed, and it wasn't until you diagnosed the problem that things started to get better.

Steve tells me that you won't take any payment for the sessions that you run with her but I would very much like to show my appreciation. I would like to invite you for

dinner next weekend. Either Saturday or Sunday would be fine. Could you let me know?
With very best wishes
Esme

Yes, that will have to do. At least she will get an answer and with a bit of luck get the chance to speak to Darius in person.

***

In the pub with Joe, Esme sits down and looks for somewhere to put her bag. There is no space to pull the chair out properly and the table is very small. Music blares out from the speakers above her head. Cheerful music, good beat, but too loud. Not many here yet. Esme likes this place but had forgotten how cramped it was although it doesn't seem to make any difference to its popularity. Later on, the place will be crowded. She looks over to the bar where Joe is getting the drinks.

'Here you are,' he says. Joe puts the pint of lager in front of her. 'It's nice to see you, Ess,' he grins. 'I would have got in touch before, but I knew you were with Steve and didn't like to intrude.'

'I'm not with Steve anymore. He's left.'

'Yes,' Joe says, looking interested. 'I'd heard that Steve had left. Is it over then?'

'Where did you hear that?' Esme asks and Joe shrugs.

'Can't remember,' he says and grins. 'What went wrong?' he asks, but she hesitates. 'Or shouldn't I ask?'

'It's all right. Steve's a good man, but we just weren't right for each other.'

'How has Dani taken it?' Joe asks. Esme feels her stomach clench.

'Not too badly,' she replies. 'She misses him, of course. But she still sees him regularly. In fact, she's with him now.'

'That's good then,' he says. 'And how are her writing sessions going?' Esme looks at him in surprise. Wonders why Darius hasn't said anything.

'Fine,' she tells him. 'Dani is getting on very well.' She watches Joe try to stretch out his long legs. 'Not much room, is there?' she says. 'I can't even find enough space for mine.'

'You're right,' he says. 'Bring your glass and let's go into the other room and see if we can find somewhere more comfortable.' Esme follows as Joe leads the way into the back room which is smaller but quite differently arranged. It looks a bit like the padded benches in the Palace dance club, but the cubicles are smaller, more intimate. 'What about in here?' he asks as he ushers her into a space in the corner at the back. This time he sits next to her instead of opposite.

They talk about this and that and *Wuthering Heights* plays through the speakers. Esme listens to the voice rise and fall. A thrill every time. No-one sings like Kate Bush. She starts to relax and realises that it is a long time since she's been out in the evening.

'Shall we have another one?' Joe asks. 'We're not driving, and it is Friday night.'

'Yes,' Esme says, 'but it's my turn. What are you drinking? It looks like Guinness.'

'It is, but I'll get them.'

'No,' Esme insists, 'You're a student and I'm working.' She sets off to the bar. Crisps as well, she thinks and wonders what kind to buy. Cheese and onion she decides. Two packets. It's her second pint, but she's been drinking so much wine lately that she can hardly feel the effects. When she gets back, she takes a long drink and asks casually, 'How's Darius these days?'

'He's fine,' Joe says. 'Seems to be working very hard. Often doesn't come home until late.' Joe settles back and stretches out. His left leg touches Esme's and she pulls away as though she's been shot. Joe grins and apologises. 'Darius says that he has to get through as much work as possible so that he can go home for Christmas.' Esme waits to hear more, but that's it. Joe doesn't offer any more information. Esme gets the letter out of her bag, puts it back and then gets it out again.

'Will you give him this?' she asks. 'I just wanted to write and thank him for the work he's done with Dani.'

'Of course,' Joe says.

Next morning, it's hard to get out of bed. After a short deep sleep, Ess had woken up in the middle of the night with a dry mouth and a headache. A glass of water didn't help and she lay awake thinking first about Darius, then about Steve. Dani misses him. Esme knows that but she can't go back to how they were before. Eventually, she manages to drop off again but when she wakes her head still pounds. Dani will be back at lunchtime. Better get up. Ess drags herself out of bed. Orange juice and coffee.

Nothing to eat she decides as she thinks of her mother. *It's the most important meal of the day, Esme.*

It was good to go out and have a drink. She should do it more often and Joe is good company. He didn't say as much about Darius as she'd hoped but she couldn't keep asking questions. Joe had flirted with her a little. He probably flirts with every girl Esme thinks and wonders if he will ever settle down. Joe seems very young despite being more or less the same age as she is. He must be nearly thirty.

Dani won't be back before lunchtime. They usually finish at half-past eleven. A whole morning to herself. Esme ought to go and get the shopping done. Or clean the house. It could certainly do with it but she doesn't feel like shopping or cleaning. What about getting the marking out of the way? Esme gives a little shudder. That feels like an even worse prospect than shopping or cleaning.

In the end, she decides to lie on the bed and read but doesn't open the book. She stretches out and keeps imagining Darius opening the envelope and reading what she's written. Suddenly she jumps up. She'd better go and sit downstairs in case Darius rings, but as she's settling herself on the sofa, Ess realises how stupid she is. Darius is with Dani so he won't be ringing this morning. Perhaps he'll send a message with Dani.

At least he'll have received the note and will be in touch before long. Esme stretches out as much as their short sofa will allow and places a cup of coffee and a packet of chocolate biscuits on the little table next to her. She'll just have a couple and save the rest to share with Dani. There's a knock at the door and Esme feels her heart start to flutter erratically. It can't be. It might be.

'Steve,' she says as she opens the door, 'I thought you were with Dani,'

'She's having her writing lesson,' he says. 'Can I come in?'

'Of course,' Esme says and goes to put the kettle on. 'You can have a cup of coffee and a chocolate biscuit as well.' As he takes off his jacket and sits down, she asks him how yesterday's hiking trip had been.

'Great,' he says. 'Really good.'

'So how are you?' Esme asks and then wishes she hadn't.

'Not good,' he says. 'That's why I've come.' He picks up the cup that she's put in front of him. Esme rolls a cigarette and lights it. She waits to hear what he's got to say, but she shouldn't have done. She should have stopped him from speaking.

'I can't manage it, Ess. I can't manage without you. I want to come home.'

Esme looks at his face and searches frantically for the right words. For a kind way to say no. But she has hesitated too long and Steve has started speaking again.

'I'll do anything,' he says. 'You can do what you want.' He stops again and then says with an effort. 'You can go with other men.' He turns away then turns back again. 'I'll stay in and look after Dani. I miss her dreadfully. It's not just you, Ess. It's Dani.'

'Oh, Steve,' Esme says. 'I'm sorry, but I can't. It's over. I can't go back to how we were before. I'm so sorry.' Steve puts his head in his hands and sobs.

'Please.'

'No,' Esme replies and hurries on, desperation hardening her tone. 'Don't do this, Steve. It's over. I want you to go.' She rolls another cigarette and lights it from the one she is still smoking. She watches as he jumps up, grabs his jacket and leaves the house.

8

I've never seen Steve so upset. He usually says that he's fine but when he comes to pick me up at the end of the session, he can hardly speak. He doesn't have to tell me what's happened. I can see. He doesn't come in when he drops me off and I feel like hitting my mother, thumping her and hurting her until she knows what she's done until she knows what Steve feels like.

I stop for a minute on the steps and think. Whatever I do, she still won't know. Still won't know how Steve feels. Even I don't know how he feels because I'm not him, but I saw his face. I rush in and grab her but instead of trying to hit her, I hold her tight and hug her close, feel tears rising that I can't stop. I don't know what to do or what to say so I let her go again and turn away. She's hurt Steve so badly and there's nothing I can say.

'I'm going to Mandy's,' I say as I dump my typewriter and my sleeping bag in the corner of the room. I open the door and go out.

'Make sure you're back by six,' my mother calls after me. She doesn't try to stop me from going. I stand by the hedge and look back to see her standing in the doorway, watching me go. My mother's face is white. Good. She deserves to be upset. I remember the drive home with Steve. He was shaking. I have never seen him shake like that before. Couldn't stop his hands from trembling. Had to keep them on the wheel to keep control. I didn't need to ask what was wrong but I asked him anyway. He told me that we were not a family anymore. Our family was finished.

I feel tired. Bone weary. I didn't sleep very well on the sofa in Paul's living room. It doesn't feel right sleeping there. It is lumpy and uncomfortable and I woke up twice wondering where I was. And then I remembered. And remembered why I was there. I wanted to be at home with my family around me but there's no family left. Just my mum. I've never had any brothers or sisters, so my family was just me, Steve and my mother. The three of us. Now we are only two and my whole being longs for the time before. It was only a few months ago, but it is beginning to feel like another lifetime. I can't bear Steve's misery and although he tries, he can't hide it.

Perhaps I shouldn't have said anything to Darius, but my mother won't listen to me, so I thought it was worth a try. She might have listened to him. Anything is worth a try. I felt that I needed to find someone who would talk to Esme. Someone who would make her take notice. I've tried to get Grandma to talk to her but it hasn't worked. At least Darius was sympathetic but he told me there was nothing he could do. Just like Grandma, I suppose. Who else can I turn to for help? Who is capable of making my mother change her mind? I asked Darius because I know my mother admires him. Had really believed that he might be able to help. Suzi is another possibility. My mother listens to Suzi and respects her but mostly she doesn't do what Suzi advises. Still, Suzi is a possibility. I am almost at Mandy's when I hear a familiar voice.

'Hello, Dani, want to come for a walk?'

It's Jaffa. I turn around and there he is, pushing his bike up the road, just like before. Hadn't expected to see him on a Saturday and especially after he hasn't been to school. Especially after the news about his mum. Oh, Jaffa. I'm so glad that you're here.

'Jaffa,' I say and fall into step beside him as we head for the park. My bike's at home but it doesn't matter. 'Jaffa,' I say again. 'I'm so pleased to see you. Are you all right?'

'Sort of,' he says and we walk in silence until we get to the bench, the one opposite the tennis courts where as usual nobody is playing. 'It's the time of year,' he says, nodding towards the empty court, but we like it like that. We like watching nobody play.

'I'm sorry about your mum,' I manage. That's all I can say and he nods again. He'll tell me about it when he's ready. Another time. He can't talk about it now. 'Are you still in Hunslet?' I ask him. He tells me that he's back in their old house. He's living with his dad, but Granville is going to stay with Annie. He'll be back at school next week.

I tell him about Steve and it seems less bad when I look at Jaffa and think of what's happened to him. He's gone thin and he doesn't walk in the same way. His swagger's gone and I miss it. Maybe he will change again. Maybe the old Jaffa will come back but I can see that from now on, he won't ever be quite the same.

I look at Jaffa and think of Steve. Steve's still there. Miserable but still there. Jaffa's Mum has gone. Forever. Impossible to understand that. Steve is only moving out of the house. He will be somewhere. Jaffa's Mum won't be anywhere. I push these thoughts away and tell Jaffa about my writing and biting my arm. It's somehow easy to tell him things that I can't say to anyone else. Feel as though I can't stop talking as though I've got to fill the space between us until he, too, can talk again.

'Show me your arm,' he says and I pull my sleeve up. It's healed now but you can see the scars. He lifts my arm very gently and kisses it then pulls my sleeve down. 'That's to make it better,' he says and smiles at me then gets up and lifts his bike out of the bushes 'See you soon, Dani,' he says and rides off.

I get up and start walking back towards home. I think of my arm and smile. It feels different where Jaffa kissed me. My first kiss. An arm kiss. I can't tell you how I feel. I can't tell anybody because it's too good for words. I'll go to Mandy's another time. I'll go home now but when I get to Suzi's house, I hesitate. The lion door knocker hangs there waiting for someone to bring him to life. I don't have the energy for my usual tattoo to rock the street. I'm still tired. I knock so softly at first that I'm sure no-one will have heard so I knock again a little louder. You have to be happy to beat a drum I think. Or angry. But not tired. I'm happy because of Jaffa but I'm weary. Suzi appears at the door before I've finished the second knock.

'Dani,' she says and grins at me. 'Come in.'

What a relief to go into Suzi's house. It is orderly. Familiar. The same. Like Grandma's house only completely different. I take off my shoes and collapse onto the sofa. I'm aware of the kiss on my arm but nobody can see what has happened. It's my secret.

'How are things?' Suzi asks.

'Good and bad,' I reply thinking first of Jaffa, then of Steve. 'Very good and very bad.'

'Then maybe you need a drink and some toasted cheese?'

'That would be brilliant,' I say. 'I haven't had any lunch and I'm tired.'

'I can see that,' Suzi says.

'Where's Pete?' I ask.

'At the office.'

'As usual,' I say and Suzi nods.

After I've eaten, I tell Suzi what has happened. Not about Jaffa and my arm. I tell her about Steve and the way Mum's told him he can't come back. I tell her that I've asked Grandma and I've asked Darius but neither of them can do anything.

'What about you?' I ask. 'Can you do anything? Can you talk to Mum and persuade her to let Steve come back?'

'I'll try,' Suzi says. 'But I think your mother has made up her mind. I don't think anyone is going to make her think or feel differently.'

'But you will try, won't you?'

'Yes,' she says, and I feel grateful. I know that Suzi is sometimes able to influence my mother. There is a faint hope I think.

'I'm off now,' I tell Suzi. 'I'm going home to talk to Mum. Thanks a million for the toasted cheese.'

'You're welcome,' Suzi says.

I arrive home just before six to find my mother unloading shopping bags and putting the groceries away. Mum looks tired. We're both tired. When everything is put away, Esme sits down and tries to talk to me. She says she is sorry that I'm so upset. Sorry that it is over between her and Steve. My mother is sorry for him. She hadn't wanted it to be like this. It just is.

I thought I wanted to talk about things but find that I don't. I can't. I've had enough. Too tired. Can't talk anymore about Steve moving out or anything like that. Can't talk about anything. But she doesn't understand. She won't shut up. Keeps going on and on.

'Shut up' I finally yell at her and then I speak quietly. 'Please, Mum, I'm tired.'

After this, a quietness settles on the room, but it's a miserable empty silence. Mum looks hurt. She never seems to understand me these days, but she tries. She has cooked one of my favourite meals, spaghetti cheese (even better than macaroni cheese), but as we sit down to eat there is no pleasure in it. No comfort in the nice long spaghetti which she's been careful not to break with the fork when she stirred in the sauce. It's just the way I like it but I can hardly taste it. I eat automatically and I don't offer to wash up. For a change, my mother doesn't insist. I tell her that I'm going to bed while she is clearing away the dishes.

'But it's only eight o'clock.'

'I'm tired.'

I lie in bed with mixed feelings. The arm that Jaffa kissed feels warm, almost hot. It's as though there's an imprint of Jaffa's mouth that is still there but the rest of me feels empty. No energy left to feel upset about Steve. About anything. It's been a terrible day but a good one, too. Unexpectedly special and I shiver with pleasure. What a strange person Jaffa is. One day I'll kiss him back.

9

As she wakes, Esme's nightmare seems more vivid than the reality around her. In the dream, she was looking for Steve. Funny. She remembers that she used to have nightmares about Dani and always, always, she was looking for her, searching for her daughter. Could never find her. In last night's dream, she did find Steve but it was his dead body. She found his corpse wrapped in newspaper, pushed under the bed. She can see it still. Can feel the soft body through the newspaper as her foot touched it. In the dream, she remembers thinking that he must have been dead some time. First comes rigor mortis and then the corpse goes soft as far as she knows.

She tries to hold it back but the memory of the dream forces its way into her consciousness. The image is clear in her mind as well as the feel of the body. That's what is worst. The soft feel of the body and a faint smell of rot (although you're not supposed to be able to smell in dreams). Time to get up she thinks but feels exhausted. She remembers Steve's pleading face when he sat at the table. Before he rushed out. Must try not to think about him.

Esme pushes one foot out of bed but it's cold. She changes her mind and pulls it back under the covers. The bedroom is freezing. She snuggles down, shuts her eyes and tries to shut out all the thoughts, the images, Steve's face, his words, the memories of the dream. She has to stay strong. Whatever she does, she can't change things again.

Hold on, she tells herself. It's time for a new start. She pulls the bedclothes tightly around her ears, but it's no good. Time to get up.

Dani needs looking after. Esme hasn't heard her daughter get up but when she gets downstairs, she discovers that Dani has been up for hours. Has already eaten breakfast and is down in the cellar working on the bike. She's always down there. Esme switches on the gas fire and turns it up full then goes into the kitchen. As she's putting the kettle on, Dani comes up to ask to use the phone. Privately she says. She needs to speak privately Will Esme please go back upstairs?

'Of course, I will,' she says. 'Just let me make myself a cup of coffee. Do you want one?'

'No, thanks,' Dani says but Esme notes with relief that her daughter doesn't look quite as upset as she did yesterday.

'Let me know when you've finished.'

Ess picks up her coffee and takes it upstairs. Looks for a space to put the mug down. The bedside cabinet is full of books, papers, all sorts, but she pushes the papers to one side, puts it down and stretches out on the bed. The heat rising from downstairs is already warming the room. The whole house heats up when the gas fire is on downstairs especially when the stairs door is left open. She listens to the dialling sounds coming from below. Surprisingly loud, but it sounds as though Dani is not getting through. She'll be ringing Paul's house so she can speak to Steve. The dialling goes on for ages until finally, Esme hears her speaking to Grandma.

Hello, Grandma, it's me. How are you? Esme gets up and quietly pushes the bedroom door and wedges it open with a shoe. Goes back to lie on the bed. Then she hears something that sounds like Dani saying that she needs help. Another long pause. Then she hears Dani speak again.

It's Steve, and then *Mum says it's final. She won't have him back*, and *he's terribly upset.* Then there's another silence before Esme hears Dani say *he told me that we're not a family anymore.* Esme's heart aches and she strains to hear the rest of the conversation but it's difficult. Seems as though Dani is asking Grandma to make Esme change her mind and take Steve back.

I'm sorry, Dani, Esme whispers into the pillow. I'm so sorry, Dani, but it won't happen. Steve is not coming back.

The conversation downstairs goes on for a while longer and finally, there is silence. Esme gets up and picks up her mug to take down but Dani must have heard her moving because she calls up the stairs.

'I haven't finished yet.'

'All right,' Esme replies, 'but I'm coming down in a few minutes whether you've finished or not. It's nearly lunchtime.'

There are more dialling sounds and another conversation. Dani must have got through to Steve, at last, or to Paul. Well, that's a relief. When Esme finally goes down, Dani has disappeared into the cellar and spends most of the day down there. Esme is sure that Dani hasn't done any homework but can't bring herself to mention it. Instead, she makes Dani's favourite food and offers her orange juice, but nothing works. She is unreachable.

When her daughter comes home from school on Monday, Esme looks at her face and wonders if she got into trouble over the homework but it's impossible to tell and she daren't ask. Dani is home early.

'No library today?' Ess asks, but Dani doesn't answer and barely shakes her head. 'Are you going to Mandy's?'

'No,' Dani replies. 'I'm waiting for a call from Steve.' She takes off her jacket and sits down next to the phone. Doesn't even go into the cellar. Esme, too, is waiting for a call from Steve. She wants to hear that he's OK, but even more she's waiting for a call from Darius. He still hasn't replied to her letter. She waited all weekend but there was no call. She tells herself she should give up hope but some stubborn part of her just won't. At a quarter to five, the phone rings and Dani grabs it before Esme gets anywhere near but it's a wrong number. Esme sees Dani looking at her and knows that she'd like to be alone so Ess picks up her tobacco tin and goes to see Suzi.

By the time she gets back, Steve has called. Seems that he's all right. Esme feels relieved. She didn't think that he would do anything stupid but the call is reassuring. At least he's spoken to Dani.

'How was he?' Esme asks but Dani shrugs and then says that he didn't sound good. His voice sounded strange and slow. Steve had told her that he'd been out last night because there wasn't much space at Paul's so he'd been working in the library. Esme doesn't think the library stays open late in the evenings but thinks it's better not to mention this.

'Have you arranged to see him?' Esme asks, but Dani shakes her head and says that Steve is going to get in touch in a few days' time. He'll see her soon.

***

In the days after Steve is first gone, Esme manages to stay fairly cheerful. At least there has been a resolution, a clearing of the air, but as the days go by, depression begins to set in. Dani is miserable. Darius hasn't been in touch and Steve seems to be at rock bottom. Not much cause for optimism. Worst of all, Esme feels worn out and can't shift the tiredness that won't lift. She hopes she's not ill. The atmosphere in the house is flat and miserable.

At first, she tries over and over again to talk to Dani, but her daughter turns away, won't listen and won't talk. By this time, Esme herself doesn't feel like talking and has gone as silent as her daughter. Hardly speaks. Just spreads out the exercise books on the table and says she has to get on with the marking. At the slightest noise, which is usually from next door on Vee Jay's side, (although they're fairly quiet for such a big family) Esme jumps, and whenever the telephone rings, she lunges towards it like a drowning woman towards a life raft. She sees Dani look at her when she goes for the phone., but each time it is Grandma. No-one else rings. It's nearly always Grandma. Occasionally, Suzi.

The second week without Steve passes as slowly as the first, but Friday night arrives at last. It should be a good night for both of them since it's the end of the school week, but Esme feels irritable as usual and Dani's face is grim.

She watches Dani switch on the tv then switch it off again and Esme doesn't feel like watching anything either. Dani says she's going up to her room to read and Esme does the same. It's been happening more and more, so the house has an empty living room and two people lying on beds in separate rooms reading (or pretending to read). Dani has said she's going on the bus to her writing session tomorrow. Steve is not available and she won't let Esme go with her. She doesn't want her mother there. The bus will be fine she says.

'How will you manage your bag and the typewriter by yourself?'

'I'll be fine.'

In the morning Esme watches her daughter set off carrying the typewriter in one hand and a bag in the other. Stubborn. Just like her father. Esme doesn't think of him often but as Dani leaves the house Esme notices that her daughter walks like he did. Her blonde head bobs up and down with the same bounce. Dani leaves looking fairly cheerful but when she returns, there is more bad news. Darius has stopped the writing sessions.

'Why is that?' Esme asks with a sinking heart.

'I'm too good,' Dani replies with a hint of her old grin but it's clear that she's unhappy about it. Esme feels miserable, too. Seems like her links to Darius are being gradually severed and he still hasn't been in touch. At least he has told Dani that she can keep the typewriter on loan. Esme supposes that's something.

'Darius said that he's enjoyed working with me. And that I can get in touch with him at any time if I need help.'

'That's nice. That's nice of him, Dani.'

'Yes,' she replies, 'but I'm disappointed, Mum. I should be pleased, I suppose, but I'm not. Maybe I shouldn't have worked so hard at my typing. I wanted to impress him, but I've impressed him too much.'

Esme's mood matches the weather. Cold and grey. Dani spends the afternoon at Mandy's while Ess tries to get on with her school work. Marking. Lesson preparation. In the evening Dani asks if she would like to play chess but Ess says she doesn't know how. Dani offers to teach her but Esme doesn't feel like it so Dani shrugs and goes upstairs to read.

'Why don't you stay down here with me? You can stay here and read. Why don't you stretch out on the sofa?'

'Because it's short and lumpy. Why don't you?'

She's right, Esme thinks, it is short and lumpy. In the end, they both go to their bedrooms to lie down and read.

It's late, gone eleven o'clock when the phone rings and Esme races downstairs to answer it. She's hoping it might be Darius, but it never is. Not this time either. It's Paul and Esme's heart starts to race when she hears the tone of his voice. It's Steve. He's had an accident. He's in hospital. Has cut his hand. Needed twelve stitches. Twelve stitches! As she puts the phone down, Dani comes flying down the stairs.

'Who's not all right? What's happened? Is it Steve?'

'Yes,' Esme tells her. 'He's had an accident. But he's all right now.'

'What kind of an accident?'

'I think he cut his hand on a glass while he was washing up,' Esme says. 'But he's had it stitched up and he's going to stay with his parents for a while.'

'Oh, Mum,' Dani says and they hug each other for the first time since Steve left.

Later, when she is in bed, Esme prays for both Steve and Dani. Please let Steve be all right she prays to the God she doesn't believe in. And please keep Dani safe and don't let her start biting her arm again. At the end, she can't help adding one final prayer. Please God, make Darius get in touch with me. Please, God.

10

I don't believe it was an accident and Mum doesn't either. I know what happened and so does she, but she won't admit it.

'He tried to commit suicide, didn't he?' I say to her over and over again but she just looks sad and turns away. I really believed this might be the turning point but as the days go by, I see that she's still not going to invite him back.

'Shut up, Dani,' she says when I keep asking her to get him back. 'You're not helping.'

'You could make everything all right,' I tell her. 'All you've got to do is take him back. Tell him he's still got a home and a family. Ask him to forgive you.'

Mum gives me a funny look but she won't budge. It's unbelievable. Such an easy solution but she won't do it. I don't tell Grandma about Steve's 'accident' because I think it would upset her too much but when I go and talk to Suzi, I find that she agrees with Mum.

'I thought you liked Steve,' I say. Isn't there anybody who can see sense? I feel like hitting her. Punching someone. I look at my arm and ache to bite hard. I need the pain. As much pain as possible to make me forget.

'I do like him,' Suzi tells me, 'but Esme wouldn't be able to help.'

'Of course, she would,' I say.

'No, Dani, she wouldn't. Steve's a grown man. He has to sort himself out.' I take my jacket and go. There's no point in talking to her. Don't say goodbye. Nearly fall down the steps from her front door because I'm not looking where I'm going.

I wish I could see Jaffa. He would listen. He might even know what to do or he might not but I'm sure that he would listen. He's not at school and he hasn't been in the park for the last two Sundays. I keep going to look. Like today, I go to the park as usual but he's still not there. Don't know what's happened to him. Can't believe how much I miss him. I hope he's coping. At least he won't be trying to commit suicide like Steve.

Jaffa's strong. Even after his Mum has died, he's strong. I don't think that anything could break Jaffa and I realise that it's his strength that makes me like him. He's sad but he won't break. Steve, on the other hand, is already breaking. I keep trying to save him but I can't. Only Mum can save him and she won't. Suzi says that nobody can save Steve except himself but that doesn't make sense. She's contradicting herself because even Suzi said that people need help sometimes. Like Miss Smith said to me over my writing.

I'm not doing my homework anymore. Just don't feel like it. I'm still typing but I'm not doing my assignments, I'm writing a diary. I like writing as long as there's nobody to judge me and give me marks out of ten. I'd get minus marks if anyone could see what I'd written. At school, they've started calling me lazy again. My spot in the sun as a good girl didn't last long but I don't care. There's nothing left to care about really, but no, that's not true. I'm still trying to find a way of helping Steve and getting him back home but no luck so far.

Living with mum in her gloomy state is driving me mad and I haven't seen Steve since his accident or talked to him on the phone. I wonder if Mum has seen him and knows things that she's not telling me. She won't give me his address and when I get through on the phone to Paul, he says he doesn't know where he is. How can he lie like that? Nothing works. I've tried begging, reasoning, shouting, but he just puts the phone down on me.

It would help if I had some cash. Mum gives me practically nothing for pocket money and then says it's plenty. The only thing I could sell is my bike, but I don't think I'd get much for it and I'm fond of it. It's useful. I'd have no transport if I sold it. Can't sell the second one either. First of all, it's for Mandy and secondly, it's not finished. I consider a bit more and have to add that thirdly, I don't suppose it's worth much. I'm in the cellar working on Mandy's bike and look around in a desperate attempt to identify anything worth selling. Anything. There's nothing. Unless, of course, I could sell the bus seat. It was once red, I think, and might be made of leather but it's shabby and dirty. It might be considered an antique. Then again, probably not. More likely, it's what it looks like. A dirty old bus seat.

Seems that I spend my whole life either down here or up in my room. I avoid the living room because that's where Mum is. The house feels empty and quiet. No Steve. No Suzi. Nobody drops in anymore. Just me and Mum avoiding each other. Can't even hear any sounds from next door and they're usually quite a noisy lot. I think I'm going to go and get a drink and take it upstairs. It's getting cold down here. The paraffin heater works well but it's nearly out of paraffin and the shop isn't open on Sundays. Mum says it smells and it does a bit, but I quite like it. At least it heats the place.

Upstairs, I sit on the bed and realise that I need some overalls. I used to have some once. Grandpa gave me some of his and I used to roll the legs up but I must have lost them somewhere. I'm thinking this as I notice a grease mark on my bedspread. Right in the middle of one of the crocheted squares, a red one, cheerful. Nice. Uncle Ted gave me this bedspread. His mother made it. I ought to call him Great Uncle Ted but I never have. He is Grandpa's friend. Not a relative at all. That's what my whole family is like. Relatives who are not relatives. My mind is wandering and I look again at the grease mark. It's come off my jeans. These are my favourites but I'd better change. I spit on my hanky and rub at the mark which gets fainter but spreads out a bit. It'll be fine.

The most important thing that I need to do right now is to find Steve and I think I've figured out how to do it. I'm going to go to the university and ask for his address. He's a student in the Russian Department so it should be easy. I wonder why I didn't think of it before. I might as well go tomorrow because I can't leave it until the weekend. It will be closed then. I'll pretend to set off for school and then come back to get my bike. I don't take my bike to school but it's not a problem to come back and get it. I've got a house key. I'll just leave as usual and then come back after Mum's gone.

When I put this into practice, it doesn't work as smoothly as I'd hoped. I come back well after 9 am but Mum is still there. I can see the Honda parked on the path so I slink past the gate ducking behind the hedge and carry on down the street. Lucky she didn't look out of the window because you can see a long way from our living room window. I get back to the house again at just gone 9.30 but the Honda is still there. Frustration builds. Why hasn't she gone yet? Isn't she going? She's been marking all weekend and muttering occasionally about 7G. (She's more interested in them than she is in me.) Then I remember that she doesn't have to start until 10 now that she's swapped her form mistress duties for the drama club, so I go for another tramp around the block and when I get back for the third time, the Honda has gone at last.

It takes only about half an hour to cycle over to the university and I'm hot by the time I get there. It was hard work pedalling because there was a strong wind blowing against me. It will be easier on the way back. I arrive at the Russian Department (on the third floor) and locate the secretary's office. Had to leave my bike outside but I've locked it up. Easy so far. I go in and tell them I'm looking for Steven Wilson. He's moved lately I say and I haven't got his new address. I'm his niece on a visit to Leeds. I've thought this through and I realise that a) the woman behind the desk didn't ask for all that information, and b) it sounds unlikely, but it was the best I could think of. Sure enough, the woman looks at me suspiciously as she takes some papers out of her filing tray.

'Steven Wilson is no longer a student here,' she says. 'He has suspended his studies.' I feel shocked but pull myself together and ask again.

'Yes, I know he's had an accident,' I say. 'Could you give me his address, please. I've come to Leeds to visit him.'

'Sorry,' she says and looks at me a little more kindly. 'We can't give out student addresses. You'll have to ask your mum and dad,' she pauses, 'or phone your uncle.' For a minute, I don't know what she's talking about but then I realise that if I'm Steve's niece, then he must be my uncle. I look at her again and I can see that she doesn't believe anything I've said. Not a word of it, but she doesn't look cross.

'Are you sure you can't give me his address?' I ask beginning to feel desperate. 'His phone is out of order and my parents haven't got his address.' Even less likely, I realise as I dig myself ever deeper but I haven't got a plan b and I do have to find him. 'If you could give it to me, I won't say where I got it from.' At this, the woman's face breaks into a smile, but she shakes her head and turns to deal with the next person. That's it. Failure.

I decide that it's not worth going back to school today. It will be just as hard this afternoon to explain why I was absent as it will be tomorrow so I cycle back and go and sit in the park. There's no sign of Jaffa of course, but I sit on our bench and, as usual, watch nobody playing tennis. At three o'clock, early enough to be on the safe side, I take my bike back and put it in the cellar, then leave again ready to arrive home at the usual time. It's all gone according to plan except for the fact that I still don't have Steve's address. And I still haven't thought of a plan b. Mum doesn't notice anything. I can't believe how easy it was although I still feel uneasy about what I'm going to say at school tomorrow.

11

Later on, it seems as though I needn't have bothered with any of my efforts because there's a knock at the door and it's Steve. He looks normal apart from his bandaged arm. I needn't have bunked off school after all.

'Hello, Ess,' he says to my mother who has opened the door. 'I'm not coming in. Just wondered if Dani might like to go for a drive. If she's not got too much homework.'

'Why didn't you ring?' Mum asks. 'Would you like to come in for a minute?'

'Steve,' I say. 'I'm so pleased to see you.' I can hardly believe it's him and he looks more or less normal. I wonder how he will be able to drive with only one hand. 'Yes, of course, I want to go for a drive and no, I haven't got any homework.'

'Great,' Steve says to me, and 'No, thanks,' in reply to Mum's invitation to come in. He smiles at her but I notice his leg is shaking. 'Come on then, Dani.'

We say hardly anything in the car because Steve looks as though he might crash into something at any minute. He rests his arm on the steering wheel (because his hand is completely bandaged up) and the steering works OK for some of the time but not always. Every so often, the car veers jerkily to one side or the other (luckily it's mainly to the left) and we hit the pavement several times. Just the edge that is. Finally, he manages to get us downtown where he drives into a large car park miles away from the town centre. It must be so that he can park without hitting anything. He's trying to make it into a joke but looks shaky. Good job Mum's not here I think to myself as we get out and set off to walk the half mile to the town centre. I'm exaggerating. It is probably only a quarter of a mile and we finally arrive at a coffee bar that serves fish and chips and meat pies. Stuff like that. It's a place with plastic tomatoes on every table and they're full of sauce that is not made by Heinz. I haven't been here before.

We sit down and he goes to order some cheeseburgers which I get up to carry for him because the tray is impossible for him to hold. While we're eating, I start to tell him that I went to the university today to try and find his address. But he already knows. That's why he's here. The woman from the Department phoned him and told him about me. His turning up was not surprising after all and not a coincidence. I ask him why he hasn't been in touch and he says that he was just waiting for his arm to heal a bit more. It would have been soon, he says. He has kept thinking about me and he would have come soon in any case.

'Why aren't you a student anymore?' I ask. 'The woman I spoke to said you weren't a student now.'

'It's true,' he says. 'But it's fine. Nothing to worry about. I've suspended my studies until the beginning of the next academic year. That will give me until September to catch up and I need the time. '

'Is it because of Mum?' I ask. 'That you're so badly behind?'

'No, it's because of all the driving jobs I've been doing.'

I don't entirely believe him but I can see that he thinks the suspension is a good idea so we don't talk about it anymore. We stop talking completely for a minute or two while we concentrate on the food. I give up on the tomato sauce (which I usually like). This stuff is watery and tastes peculiar, like vinegar but I don't say anything. I switch to the little sachets of mustard. Much better. Quite nice with the cheeseburger. Steve's having fish and chips.

'I've been worried about you, Steve,' I tell him. 'Are you better now?'

He tells me he's fine and says once again that he would have come to see me soon even if I hadn't turned up looking for his address. His face looks OK but under the table, one of his legs keeps starting to tremble. I don't mention his accident but I can't help looking at the thick bandage that stretches from his hand all the way up to the elbow.

'Lucky it was my right hand,' he says as he sees me looking. 'I've still got the left hand available for changing gear. I can rest my bad hand on the steering wheel.' He's trying to make a joke but I don't feel like laughing.'

'Yes, I saw,' I tell him. ' It looks terribly dangerous.'

'Oh, no,' he says, 'it's not dangerous. Of course, it isn't. I can manage fine like that.' He probably sees that I'm not convinced and adds, 'but better not mention it to Esme.' For the first time tonight, I smile properly.

'Understood,' I say and give him a little salute like we used to do when we joked about her in the past.

'Tell you what,' he says. 'I know a better place than this. With better coffee. Eat up and let's go.' We walk back to the deserted car park. Only one other vehicle there apart from ours and it isn't a car. It's a lorry. I'm feeling more cheerful now and am starting to enjoy the evening. It feels like an adventure until we set off again and then it goes back to being scary.

'I can manage fine like this,' he says. 'Look, it works.' We leave town and head towards Leeds 6. He's driving more slowly than before and his face looks tense but he's stopped hitting the kerb. I feel relieved when we reach Hyde Park corner and Steve manages to park. He takes me to a cafe that I haven't been to before. Seems to know his way around but I'm sure we never came to this place when we lived near here. It's still quite early but the place is already filling up. Mostly students. Instantly, I like it a lot more than the other place. I grab a table while Steve goes to the back of the cafe to order our food. He turns to look at me.

'Cheeseburger,' I mouth. I'm sure I can manage another one.

There's somebody in front of him so it takes quite a while. This place is warm so I take off my jacket and hang it on the back of the chair. I wonder yet again what he was thinking when he hurt his arm and if he did it deliberately. I know he won't tell me, but he ought to because I'm the one who understands. I know what it's like to make yourself hurt. To look for pain. I don't suppose he realises how much I understand. I've never wanted to kill myself but when you look for the pain, you always need enough. Enough to make you forget. For the first time, I realise how easy it could be to miscalculate. To do it too much. To go over the edge.

Eventually, he comes back and asks me to go and get the drinks from the counter. The cafe staff will bring the food he says. He sits down and moves the chair closer to the wall so that his arm won't get knocked when people walk past.

'How are you feeling?' I ask.

'I told you before,' he says and grins. 'I'm fine, Dani. You sound like my mother.' I feel annoyed but try to hide it. Why won't he talk to me?

'I mean how do you feel about Mum and not living with us anymore?'

'I'm fine, Dani.

'You don't look it,' I say. Just the opposite of what I meant to say. I had wanted to cheer him up and make him feel better but now he's here in front of me, I just feel angry. Feel more like hitting him than cheering him up. Can't stop myself hammering away at him. If I hammer hard enough, he'll start to talk. Won't he? Or do I want him to say he's sorry? Sorry for trying to hurt himself and making us worried.

Gradually he does start to talk. Says he was miserable to begin with but that he's all right now. Better for him and Mum to live separately he says. (What about me?) Better for him to live separately so that Mum doesn't have to pretend that she wants him there when she doesn't. It would never have worked, he says. Not fair to any of us. (At last, I'm included, but almost as an afterthought.} And so he goes on. I can hardly believe my ears. It could be Esme talking. I don't agree with any of it and I'm sure he doesn't either. It's bullshit. I can hear his thoughts. They are desperate and unhappy but at least they're real. What's coming out of his mouth is a load of lies. Then he says something that makes me listen. He tells me that at least he's got a friend he can talk to.

'Do you mean Paul?' I ask. I don't like Paul. Not since he refused to give me Steve's address and lied to me on the phone.

'No,' Steve says. 'Not Paul. I've got a new friend called Sandra. You'll like her.'

Sandra? Is she a friend or a girlfriend? I feel shocked. I try to tune in to his thoughts to find out what's going on but I can't do it anymore. It's a blur. How can Sandra have happened so quickly? He's been with Mum for years. How can he have changed so fast? But then I realise that Mum's done the same thing. She's had affairs or at least I think she has. Steve says he's got a friend and I suppose I should feel pleased but instead I find it depressing and I feel myself getting angry again.

'You'll have to meet her,' he says. 'You'll like her.'

Yes, I nod, but I won't. Can't stand the thought of meeting her and don't know how he could suggest it. I have to get back I tell him. I do have a little bit of homework. He smiles and I help him to drape his jacket over his bad arm. He doesn't believe me. We're both lying now.

He manages to drive me back and we don't hit many kerbs but he doesn't come in. We're mostly quiet in the car because he has to concentrate, but he says he'll come and collect me on Friday if I want and take me with him to stay over. He's missed me he says and is back at Paul's again. He'll bring me back on Saturday. I'm pleased that he wants to see me and when I go in, I ask Mum if it's OK. Of course, she says, it's fine.

After he's gone, she asks me how he was but there's not much I can say. Fine, I tell her. He's fine. And he's got a girlfriend. Mum glances up from her marking at this piece

78

of news and looks delighted which makes me feel more depressed than ever. I go to bed deflated. I should be pleased that Steve came and that he's getting back to normal. More or less better. That he's got a new friend. But I don't. I feel angry. And I wonder what I'll say at school tomorrow to explain where I was today.

Next day, it's surprisingly easy. I say I had to go to the dentist and Miss Smith asks me to remind Mum to send a note next time. That's it. No more said. Well, that's one problem less and Steve has promised to come and collect me on Friday night. The thought of spending time with him at the weekend is cheering me up despite the worry about Jaffa and the news about Sandra. Maybe she doesn't exist. He might have invented her to protect his pride. I expect I'll find out at the weekend. I know I shouldn't, but I'm hoping that he's invented her. I'm hoping that some miracle will happen to get him back together with Mum. But I don't think it will.

12

Week after week when I walk out of school on a Friday afternoon, I feel pleased that it's the weekend, but it often ends up being pretty crap. Especially now Jaffa isn't around. I miss him. I wish he'd come back so we could sit on the bench again and talk. This should have been a brilliant weekend because I'd worried about Steve for so long and now he's here and I've just spent Friday night with him. But instead of feeling pleased that he's better, I've switched immediately into worrying about Jaffa and feeling irritated by Paul and Sandra (don't know her but she's already irritating and unfortunately, she does exist). I'm in the car with Steve going home again now. Feeling grumpy.

I suppose it was good to spend time with Steve although I nearly always imagine it's going to be better than it turns out to be and especially this time after worrying about him so much. It was frustrating last night because we hardly got any chance to spend time alone together. Paul was there the whole time and this morning again, too. I don't like Paul and I don't think he likes me. I keep trying to avoid him but it's not easy.

It's the afternoon now and we're nearly home. Steve will bring me back later next time but he's got a driving job lined up for the evening. I half wonder if the evening's driving job is actually a meeting with Sandra but there's no way of knowing. He's told me a bit more about her and the more I hear, the less I like her. Wish he would shut up but no, he keeps on talking about her. I'm starving when I get back because we didn't have time for lunch.

'I'm back,' I shout as I walk in.

'I'm upstairs, Dani,' Mum calls to me. 'Down in a minute.' I can smell a food smell coming from the kitchen so I go to investigate. It doesn't look as though anything is cooking and I trace the smell to the bin. Gingerly I open the lid. It is full of greasy wrappers and empty cartons of food from the Chinese takeaway. There are two lots.

'Who's been here?' I ask as my mother appears in the doorway. 'Who've you had in while I've been away?'

'Don't you take that tone with me,' my mother says. She sounds just like the school teacher she is. I feel sorry for her pupils. 'Joe came round to eat with me, and then we went to the pub.'

'Joe!' I nearly explode. 'Another boyfriend! Mum, you're a whore.' Before I know what's happening, Mum has slapped me across the face and then she slaps me again.

'Don't you ever speak to me like that again.' Esme is furious and beginning to tremble. 'Now go upstairs and don't come down until I say you can.'

My face is stinging. I turn around, grab my bag and rush out.

'Not out there,' my mother yells after me. 'Upstairs.' But I'm already on my way. I run down the street. Unfortunately, Mandy is out, so I change direction and go to Suzi's.

'What's the matter, Dani?' Suzi asks when I arrive at her door. 'Come in and tell me what's wrong.' I go inside and find it hard to hold back the tears. 'What's happened to you?' Suzi asks.

'Mum hit me,' I say. 'I told her she was a whore, and she hit me.' To my amazement, Suzi starts to smile.

'You said what?' she asks.

'I told her she was a whore,' I repeat. 'She had a man in while I was over at Steve's.'

'Well, why shouldn't she?' Suzi says. 'She's a human being, Dani. She works all week. Every week. She deserves a bit of fun.' I feel myself getting angry again.

'Fun!' I say. 'They were eating together. Chinese takeaway.'

'I can think of worse things,' Suzi replies and looks at me. 'Can't you?'

'But she won't invite Steve in and eat with him,' I say. 'After all the years we've lived together. After all the things she's said about how we'd always be a family, she won't eat with Steve.'

'Now that's the real reason you're angry,' Suzi says and she puts her arms around me. 'I understand that. I understand why you're angry.' She stops speaking and moves back a little so she can look at me. 'But that doesn't make your mother a whore. And you were well out of line to say that.' I don't agree with her. Suzi is just siding with Mum. Suzi doesn't know what Mum's been doing in Chapeltown and how people are talking about her. And in any case, my mother should not have hit me.

'And what about my face?' I ask lifting my hand to feel my cheek.

'Does it hurt?' Suzi asks. 'It was a bit red when you walked in, but there's nothing there now so far as I can see.'

'She shouldn't have hit me,' I say.

'No,' Suzi agrees. 'She shouldn't have hit you, but she's human, Dani, and you'll live. She loves you, but she's not a saint.' Suzi has walked to the sink but now she walks back to where I'm sitting and bends down to give me another hug. 'Come on now, let's go back to your house. Your mum will be going frantic with worry.'

When we walk in, I watch my mother rush up to me and try and hold me close, but I feel myself going stiff. It's not all right. Nothing's all right.

'Sorry,' Esme keeps saying. 'I'm sorry I slapped you.' I turn around as I hear a noise behind me and see the door closing as Suzi slips away.

'I'm sorry, too,' I mutter. 'I shouldn't have called you a whore.'

For the rest of the evening, things feel a bit better between us, but by Sunday, everything is back to normal. My mother is nagging about the same old things and I still can't talk to her about Steve. Soon it will be too late now that Sandra is on the scene. I'm feeling depressed and things just keep getting worse. I want my dad back. But then I remember that Steve isn't my dad and then the dream comes and I want that dad back. I do and I don't. How can I? If that dad came, he might kill me, but I'm sure that he loved me. He's the one who really loved me.

13

Esme gets a piece of paper and a black felt tip pen and sits down at the table to make a list. The Saturday shopping has been done and Dani's gone to see Mandy. Due back at half five. They haven't caught the Ripper. The police still think it's somebody from Newcastle and say they're closing in on him but he's still out there, and it bothers her. If her daughter isn't at school or in the house where she can see her, Esme worries.

Maybe she shouldn't. He hasn't killed anyone as young as Dani and the police say that he targets prostitutes. But it's not true. Some of his victims were not prostitutes. Someone was killed not far from where Joe lives. (And where Darius lives. No, she won't let Darius into her thoughts.) The one who wasn't a prostitute was a mistake the police say. The Ripper made a mistake? Well, that's not reassuring. Not at all. In any case, it doesn't matter whether the woman was a prostitute or not. We're all the same. All females. All vulnerable in one way or another. Her thoughts run on.

Esme looks at the paper. It's a sheet of A4 and she turns it so that it's in landscape mode. She's going to divide the paper into three columns. The first column will be a list of the good things in her life. That's to cheer herself up. The second column will be a list of her worries. And the third column will be to write notes on what action she's going to take about each of the worries. It was on the radio while she was washing up last night. It is called 'taking control' and is supposed to be an effective way of coping with depression. Not that she's really depressed. Esme knows about that because she's been down there once or twice in her life. This is mild but she's sinking. Needs to climb out of it. First, she needs a cigarette. Still hasn't given up. She'll do it in the New Year. Not long until Christmas now.

She settles down and stares again at the paper. Still hasn't started writing. First, she'll make a cup of coffee so she gets up again. Peers out of the window. It's pouring with rain but the house is cosy. She makes the coffee and takes it to sit on the floor ready to 'take control'. Ha ha. Isn't that what she's been trying to do all her life? It's only a bit of fun she reminds herself. No need to take it seriously. Leaning against the sofa and stretching out on the hearthrug in front of the fire is one of Esme's favourite positions. It's where all her best thinking gets done. She puts the mug down on the tiled hearth next to the large glass ashtray and leans back against the sofa, rests the paper against a large book of Rembrandt's paintings.

Column one: Good Things, Well, there's Dani. If she needs to choose the very best thing in her life, it has to be her daughter. Then there's Steve. At last, things are getting a little easier with him. He has been her trusted friend for years and she hopes that he will be again. He is Dani's father figure and Esme values him more than he knows. Things are still difficult between them but it's getting better. Steve's got a new friend. Hopefully a girlfriend. That's all positive.

Esme writes Dani at the top of the Good Things column, then Steve and Suzi in quick succession. She hesitates before adding Darius. He hasn't been in touch but Esme still considers him an amazingly good thing to have happened. She's still glad that she met him. (That's two men in the Good Things section who are no longer in her life.) After a minute she adds Mum and Dad. Her parents are such a basic part of her support system that she takes them for granted, almost forgets them. When she thinks of her mother, she remembers to add Health to the first column. Her mother is always telling her that health is everything but Esme is never ill so health is another thing she takes for granted.

Now for the worries. First on the list is Dani. Then Steve and finally, Darius. These three are the top three on both lists! Hmmm. The first two parts of the task didn't take long.

It's time for the action list. She rolls another cigarette but doesn't light it. The fire is making her warm and she's feeling sleepy. Esme puts the paper down, moves the cushion and curls up with her back to the fire but it's not long before she starts to burn and has to move again. Yes, she'll get up and take the paper over the road and do this with Suzi. It's the sort of thing that should be done with a friend. They can do it together and have a laugh. She jumps up, switches off the fire and rushes out into the wind and the rain. Realises she hasn't left a note for Dani or even put a coat on so she goes back, scribbles something hasty on a piece of paper and grabs her jacket before setting off once more.

Esme seizes the lion and beats out an energetic tattoo. She's getting drenched. Bangs the door knocker as hard as she can. God, where is Suzi? Isn't she in?

'Hi, Ess, are you trying to break the door down?'

Esme smiles and steps inside scattering drops of water everywhere.

'Thought you weren't in. I was getting soaked.'

'I was upstairs. Coffee or tea?'

'Coffee, please.' Esme dumps her wet jacket, goes to sit at the table and grins. 'I've come to take control with you.'

'What?'

'It was on the radio last night. How to take control of your life. All you need is a piece of paper and a pen. I already started and then thought it would be more fun to do it with you.' Esme takes the piece of paper out of her bag and waves it at Suzi before unfolding it and smoothing it out on the table. While Suzi makes the coffee, Esme explains what you have to do. 'I'm already ahead. I've filled in the first two columns. That's the easy part. It's column three that's hard.'

'What's column three again?'

'What action you're going to take about each of your problems.'

Esme waits while Suzi goes to fetch an A4 pad from upstairs and looks at her own list. Wonders if it's normal to have identical entries in both the Good and the Problem columns. She sips the coffee. Excellent. Just what she needed. She watches as Suzi sits down opposite her, rules three columns and inserts four items into column 1.

'What have you written?'

'Pete, Parents, House and Job,' Suzi replies.

Esme notices that Suzi hasn't included her in the list of good things but doesn't say anything.

'OK, now what about column 2?'

'Not sure that I've got any worries.'

'What about Pete?'

'What about him?'

'Aren't you worried about Pete?'

'Not really,' Suzi replies but then writes down something that Esme can't see. It looks short.

'What have you written?'

'Job,' Esme sees Suzi hesitate, 'and Baby.'

'Oh, Suzi,' Esme says as a warm, happy feeling rises up in her,' that's great,' and then she, too, hesitates. 'But why is that a problem? I thought you had decided that you did want to have kids.'

'Yes,' Suzi says. 'That's the problem, Ess. I do want a baby, but I can't get pregnant.'

'Have you been to the doctor's?'

'There's no point,' Suzi says and her hand starts to shake a little.

'Why not?'

'Because Pete won't go with me. We'd both have to go.' Esme digests this information and is surprised at how upset Suzi looks. Ess had no idea and doesn't know what to say. 'He does want kids,' Suzi continues, 'but he's scared to go and be tested in case it's his fault. He doesn't want any bad news about his manhood.' Esme feels a sudden spurt of anger against Pete but realises that it won't be helpful to say anything. What Suzi needs is comfort. And a way forward.

'I'm sorry, Suze, I didn't know.' Esme draws on her roll-up so that the end glows brightly and the hit of the smoke arrives deep inside her lungs. 'Couldn't you ask for at least you to be tested? By yourself? Then if it was you, you could tell Pete and have artificial insemination or whatever they recommend. If it wasn't you, you could tell Pete and at least he would know.' She puts the cigarette down for a minute. 'Are you sure that you both have to go?' Suzi shrugs but does brighten slightly.

'Maybe it is worth a try. And what have you written? What's in your column 2?' Suzi asks.

'Dani, Steve,' Esme hesitates, 'and Darius.' She sees Suzi look up at her and pay attention.

'Darius?' Suzi asks. 'Why is Darius a problem?'

Esme puts her pencil down on the table and starts to talk. Tries to explain how important Darius is to her and says she's sure that Suzi won't understand. Won't sympathise. But she does seem to understand. And she does sympathise.

'That's how it was with me and Pete,' Suzi says and picks up the familiar, light blue, squashy pack of Gauloises from the table, shakes the packet and pulls out a fat unfiltered cigarette from one end. 'We both knew that we had to be together.'

'You mean you believe in fate?'

'I suppose so,' Suzi replies. 'I believe in fate and free will at the same time but it's hard to explain how I manage to do that.'

'The way I feel about Darius,' Esme says slowly (this is the first time she's talked to anyone about this), 'is that I'm sure we've got a connection. A powerful connection. And I'm sure he feels it, too.'

'Then what's the problem? You've asked Steve to go. You're on your own again.'

'He doesn't get in touch,' Esme admits. 'I had a date with him and we had a fantastic afternoon together. I was sure he felt the same as I did, but he hasn't been in touch since then.'

'Perhaps you've got it wrong? Perhaps there isn't a connection between you?'

'But I'm sure there is so I can't understand why he stays away.'

Esme looks at Suzi and sees the knowing look on her face and feels miserable. She shouldn't have told her. Expects her friend to tell her to forget him.

'Why don't you get in touch with him?' Suzi suggests and Esme feels herself blushing.

'I already did, ' Ess says. 'I gave Joe a note to give to him, but there's been no reply.' Suzi gets up and without asking, takes Esme's cup to the coffee machine for a top-up.

'Why do blokes usually not respond?' Suzi asks.

'Well, the main reason is that they don't feel any attraction.'

'OK,' Suzi says, 'and if it's not that?'

'They've got someone else,' Esme says.

'Is it possible?'

'I suppose it might be,' Esme concedes. 'I've seen him twice with Joe's sister, Helen. But he asked me out after that. I don't think they're together.' She pauses. 'I really don't think that they're together.' Suzi doesn't reply and looks at her with concern. They both light up. 'What shall I do?'

'You could meditate,' Suzi says and Esme frowns.

'I already tried that. Just can't seem to empty my mind as you're supposed to do. Do you meditate?'

'Sometimes,' Suzi says and gives a half-smile. Esme is surprised. Suzi continues to surprise her.

'But meditation isn't an action to solve problems, is it?' Esme says and once again Suzi surprises her by telling her a story. It's about the Buddha asking one of his disciples to fetch him some drinking water from a nearby lake. The disciple goes twice but an oxen-drawn cart has just passed through and stirred up the water. It is muddy each time. Undrinkable. The third time the disciple goes to the lake, the water has settled and it's clear. When he brings back the drinking water, the Buddha smiles and drinks. He says that all the disciple needed to do was wait and let things settle. To solve the problem of getting clean drinking water, he didn't need to do anything. No action required. Just had to wait.

Oh, Esme thinks to herself, if only life were as simple as that.

**

While sitting in the staffroom staring at 7G's exercise books, she comes to a decision. Esme will write to Darius one last time and she will go and post the letter personally. Perhaps Joe didn't deliver her note. Perhaps he doesn't want her and Darius to get together. She writes quickly. Doesn't check it, just puts it straight into an envelope and delivers it on the way home from school. Esme walks quickly up the long garden path to Joe's door and almost runs away on the way back. Stupid. She is being stupid.

When she gets back, Dani is waiting for her. The fire is on and her daughter looks cheerful.

'Hi Dani, you're home early. No library today?' Dani shakes her head.

'Do you want a cup of coffee, Mum?' Aha, Esme thinks and laughs.

'Yes, please,' she says, 'and then you can tell me what you want.'

'Yes,' Dani says as she goes into the kitchen. 'You're right. There is something I want to ask you.'

Esme is still wearing her bike clothes. She takes off the helmet and shakes her hair free which is still plastered against her head then pushes it out of her eyes as she goes over to the shelves in the corner and puts the helmet down at the bottom. Every day it's a struggle pulling off the blue plastic garments that she wears for the bike. They're ugly and they're too tight. She emerges with a sigh of relief and dumps the bike clothes in the corner. Puts her hand up to push the hair out of her eyes again. Her fringe needs cutting.

'What is it?'

'I need some wool,' Dani replies getting straight to the point. 'And some knitting needles.'

'Oh,' Esme says feeling surprised. That wasn't what she was expecting. She remembers Dani's pathetic attempts at knitting. 'What for?'

'I want to make a Christmas present for somebody.'

'Hope it's not a jumper,' Esme says and Dani's face breaks into a smile.

'No, Mum, I'm going to knit a scarf, but I haven't got enough money to buy the wool or the needles. Can you lend me some?'

'Possibly,' Esme says. 'Depends how much you want. When were you planning to go and buy the wool?'

'Now,' Dani replies. 'I need to get on with it immediately because I might be slow.' Esme laughs again and they look at each other. They both know that Dani will definitely be slow. Judging by the past at any rate.

'It's too late now,' Esme says. 'The shops will be shut.'

'Not the little one up past the police station,' Dani says. 'It might still be open if I hurry up. I can rush up there now.'

'No, Dani. That shop will be expensive. The best place to get wool is down the market. You could go tomorrow after school.' Esme watches her daughter slump. Once Dani has an idea, she can't wait. Has to do it immediately. No patience she thinks but remembers that she used to be like that. (Used to be?)

The phone rings and as usual, Dani grabs it.

'It's for you,' she says and Esme's hopes shoot sky high. 'It's Joe,' Dani says and Esme makes an effort to hide her disappointment. He asks if she'll go for a drink with him on Friday and after a short hesitation, she agrees. If Darius doesn't get in touch at least she might be able to find out what's happening.

'Are you going out with Joe again?' Dani asks as soon as Esme puts down the phone.

'Yes, Dani, but he's only a friend,' Esme tells her. 'It might be nice to go out for a drink while you're with Steve.' She looks at her daughter who doesn't look pleased but at least she's not turning hysterical like she did before.

14

By the time Friday evening arrives, Esme's hopes have sunk again. Darius hasn't responded and she thinks she might have made a mistake in agreeing to go for a drink with Joe. She will have to let Darius know that Joe is just a friend. The possibility that Darius doesn't want to see her is something she fails to consider.

It's cosy in the pub. Not the same as one they visited before. They've gone up the road this time, up past the library. It's warm inside and already lively. Esme follows Joe who heads straight into the back room and turns to ask her where she wants to sit. She gives a little shiver and leads the way to the table nearest the fire.

'Sit down, Ess. Same as last time?' Joe asks. 'Pint of lager?'

'Yes, please,' she says as she puts her jacket on the back of the chair and unwinds the long red scarf from around her neck. The log fire is blasting out heat and Joe is in good form. Tells Esme about his week of teaching practice and makes it sound like a heap of fun. Esme remembers that her own teaching practice hadn't been like that at all. It had been exhausting and stressful. She drinks quickly, starts to relax and begins telling Joe about her own experience. She'd made what seemed like hundreds of clocks none of which she could get completely round. The clocks were intended to teach the time in German she starts to explain but grinds to a halt in mid-flow. Can't concentrate on what she's saying. Almost as though she's losing interest even as she's speaking and Joe notices.

'What's wrong?' he asks.

'Nothing,' she says and manages a strained smile, 'I'm tired, Joe. It's been a long week.' She stops for a minute and glances at her empty glass. 'Are you ready for another one?' Joe nods despite the fact that his glass is still over half full. Ess doesn't spill much on the way back from the bar but her hand shakes as she puts Joe's Guinness down and it slops on to the table. 'Oh, I'm sorry,' she says. 'I must be more tired than I thought.' Joe reaches into his pocket for a tissue but Esme is faster. She pulls a whole wad of kitchen roll out of her bag and Joe laughs as she mops up the spill.

'It's fine,' Joe says as Esme apologises again. 'Calm down, Ess. It's only a drop of beer.'

'How's the Saturday School?' Esme asks. 'Have you started teaching the maths yet?' Joe shakes his head.

'No time,' he says, but Mummy won't stop nagging about it. I'll do it when I've finished my teacher training year.'

'And how's everyone else?' Esme goes on. 'Sheldine and Helen? Darius?'

'Shelley's fine,' Joe says. 'And Gerry's so busy that she doesn't get home until late. Always working long hours, day after day.' Joe stops for a drink.

'And Darius?'

'He's gone home for Christmas,' Joe says and Esme feels a huge surge of relief. So that's why he hasn't been in touch. Feels herself relax at last.

'And Helen?' she asks.

'I was going to tell you,' Joe says. 'She's gone to PNG with Darius.'

'Oh,' Esme says and feels herself starting to shake. She tries to pull herself together but fails. 'I'm sorry, Joe,' she says. 'I really am tired. I think I need to go home. I'm really sorry.'

'It's fine,' Joe says and his face turns serious with concern. 'Come on. I'll take you back.' Esme is quiet while they walk along. She hasn't fastened her coat and her scarf hangs lopsidedly, but she hardly notices. Ess looks down at the pavement and watches her feet as she walks. One step and then another. Her black leather boots need cleaning. She hadn't realised how dirty they were. There's a scuff mark on the left one and she bends down to rub at it with her gloved finger. Licks the glove and tastes the wool. Rubs her mouth and tries to spit out the hairs then reaches down again to rub at the scuff mark. She sees Joe looking at her in surprise. What is she doing? Ess grins at him and carries on.

It's not far and when they reach her house, Joe follows her up the steps to the front door. She's about to tell him that he can't come in when a wave of misery sweeps through her and she changes her mind.

'I've got a bottle of red in the kitchen' she tells him. 'Do you want some?' Joe looks surprised yet again.

'It's all right,' he says. 'I'm not putting anything on you, Ess. I've realised there must be somebody else.' He pauses. 'Is it Darius?' he asks. 'I saw the letter that you pushed through the letterbox. Was it urgent?'

'No,' she manages. 'Not urgent.'

'We haven't sent it on,' Joe says. 'The post takes ages to PNG. We put it in his room so it will be there when he gets back.'

Esme puts the fire on and takes her coat off. She had offered him wine before she even got through the door.

'Aren't you going to take your coat off?' she asks as she heads for the kitchen. 'I'm going to open the wine anyway. Are you sure you don't want a glass?'

'What's wrong, Esme?' Joe asks again. He's by the door, his jacket still on. Hasn't taken his gloves off. 'And you didn't answer my question,' he continues. 'Is it Darius? The someone?'

'Of course not,' Esme replies trying to smile. 'Don't be silly. I'm sorry, Joe. I'm just tired, that's all. There isn't anyone. No-one at all.' She can see that Joe wants to believe her but that he still isn't sure. She knows he wants her but he's sensitive. He doesn't want her if she doesn't want him. Esme opens the wine, fills two glasses and carries them to the table. She starts drinking almost immediately. Joe takes off his jacket and sits down and Esme sees him watching her drink but she doesn't care. She drinks two glasses one after the other and feels suddenly ill.

'I'm sorry,' she manages again and rushes upstairs to the bathroom. When she comes back, she's shaking again. Can't stop. Joe walks towards her and puts his arms around her but she can't help shrinking back. 'I'm sorry, Joe,' she says for the third time. 'I don't feel very well.' Joe almost laughs but speaks kindly.

'I'm not surprised after one and a half pints of lager followed by two glasses of wine,' he says. 'You need to go to bed.' Esme looks alarmed but there is no need. Joe puts his jacket on and says good night. Doesn't even try to kiss her. No wonder Esme thinks, I've just been sick. When she thinks about it later, she laughs despite herself as she imagines what she must have looked like. And smelled like. Joe has won her respect. He was good-humoured and kind to her all evening.

At last, Esme has to come to terms with the fact that Darius is not interested. It's Helen he wants. It's Helen he's taken home with him for Christmas. And she hadn't known about it. But she supposes that in some part of her mind she did know. She's seen Darius with Helen, has been aware of the intimacy between them. Then why did he ask her out? Why had their meeting in the cafe and the walk in the park been so intense? Stop it, she tells herself. Stop it. Stop it. Stop it.

***

Dani gets the wool and the knitting needles. Esme had suggested getting the variegated wool that produces patterns as you knit and that's what Dani has bought. Surprising. She usually does the opposite of anything Esme suggests. Dani started the scarf as soon as she got home. Started off attempting rib but it was clear that if she continued to struggle with knit 2, purl 2, the scarf would not be finished for several years. Esme stifled a smile and persuaded her that plain knit stitch would look fine with the variegated wool. And it does. The scarf is beginning to look good. She's been working on it night and day but won't say who it is for despite Esme's constant pestering.

'Just somebody,' she says. 'Stop asking, Mum. I'm not going to tell you.'

They buy marzipan for the Christmas cake and eat it before the cake is baked just like they do every year, so they have to buy some more. Make mince pies and do all the other Christmas things but Esme's heart feels empty. Dani chatters on almost like the old days although she is asking some odd questions. How can people be traced? Keeps on asking but won't say why she wants to know. Esme wonders, not for the first time, why her daughter is so secretive. Dani seems to alternate between looking worried and then cheerful again. Seems to be enjoying the knitting and the scarf is progressing slowly but surely in a satisfying riot of greens and blues (mainly lime green, bottle green and sky blue).

Dani's scarf is coming on fine, but Esme has nothing to look forward to. There's Christmas in Summer Lane, but that isn't very exciting. She feels guilty because she knows how much her parents look forward to spending Christmas with them and how her mother will be working on all the preparations. Esme does the Christmas shopping, buys things, wraps things, writes cards, posts them. Doesn't smile much. Doesn't sing. Even Dani notices that she is miserable.

'What's up, Mum?'

'Nothing,' Ess replies. She can see that Dani doesn't believe her, but her daughter knows better than to ask again.

***

The Christmas holidays have started and everything is packed ready to take down to Summer Lane. Steve has lent her the car for the Christmas trip. It's kind of him. She's grateful. It's Friday and they're due to drive down this afternoon. Dani's promised to be back from Mandy's by midday so they can set off in the early afternoon.

Esme checks her list to see if she's packed everything and done everything that needs to be done. She was going to get some lunch ready but changes her mind. Nothing left in the fridge anyway. They can stop on the motorway and have something there. The double whammy of it being both Friday and nearly Christmas will ensure that the motorway is jammed with traffic. No way of avoiding it but the earlier they set off the better. Esme sits at the table with a cup of coffee and watches a heap of post fly through the letterbox. Doesn't even feel the usual pleasure at receiving the Christmas cards that keep arriving. Today there look to be quite a few.

It no longer seems strange to have a door that opens straight into the living room as it had at first. Ess had never lived in a house without a hall or a porch before this one. But she had lived in a series of flats some of which had been small and shabby. She's lucky to have this house and she knows it. The mortgage doesn't cost much. It's a lot cheaper than paying rent. Her parents are to thank for the house. Without the deposit money they gave, she could never have afforded it. She remembers the thrill of moving in. Their very own house. That was when Steve was still with them. It will be the first Christmas without him. Ten years they'd been together. Wearily Esme gets up and goes to pick up the heap of cards that have landed on the mat.

Looks through them and notices something that isn't a Christmas card. It's a blue airmail letter. With a PNG postmark.

15

We've just arrived in Summer Lane. Here for Christmas and I'm in the front room looking at the big grey book of Beethoven's Sonatas which is on the piano. There's a huge picture of Beethoven on the front cover. Just his head. It's not in black and white but in lots of different greys. Grandma must have been playing and then dumped it on top of the piano as she rushed out to meet us. I pick it up and look at Ludwig's face. I've seen it lying around for years but I've never looked carefully. He doesn't look ordinary but I don't suppose any of the men of that time would look ordinary to me. I think it's the long wavy hair although that shouldn't look odd nowadays. No, it's his eyes, but he doesn't look like a real person. Not like somebody I would meet in the park or shopping in the supermarket.

On top of another pile of music, I see Mendelssohn's *Songs without Words*. Looks as though it's beginning to fall apart. The cover's coming off and a couple of pages are loose. There's a picture of Felix Mendelssohn on the cover and this time it is in black and white but he doesn't look as impressive as Ludwig. I wonder if that's because Mendelssohn's face is on thin paper that is torn compared to Ludwig's face on the thick, good quality paper. The paper does seem to make a difference. Since I talked to Jaffa about drawing, I've looked at things differently. And especially faces. I wonder where Jaffa is and how it feels to be without his mum. Wonder if Jaffa likes music. We've never talked about music. I like hearing Grandma play and a fleeting desire to learn the piano crosses my mind but I'd still rather be a drummer.

It's cold, but Grandpa's up the garden as usual. Haven't seen him yet. It would be nice if it snowed for Christmas but it never does and I don't really care. Nothing's going to make it feel right with Steve missing. Mum's started going out again. I know she's been to the pub with Joe. I hope she hasn't been out with Darius, but I think he's away for Christmas. He was going to go home for the holiday back to Papua New Guinea.

Suzi says that Mum's got a right to go out and that I'm being mean. Suzi says I'll get used to Steve not being with us and she reminded me that I do see him regularly. Well, I do. But it's not the same and I'm not getting used to it. I miss him more and more. And the weird dream keeps coming. It's funny because the dream isn't about Steve but when the missing him gets bad, I seem to have the dream about my first dad.

Nothing in my life is going well. Steve isn't here. I'm worried about Jaffa and I haven't worked at my assignments since Darius stopped the lessons. I'm getting into trouble again at school. A bit. Not too much. But I'm still practising my typing and I'm not biting my arm. I've brought the typewriter with me. A few weeks ago, I was typing a lot more, but since I decided to knit this scarf for Jaffa I've had no time for anything else. (I will never in my life knit another scarf.)

Mum's right. I'm slow at knitting and it's still not finished so it's a good job that Jaffa didn't turn up before we left to come here. I'll find him after Christmas and give it to him. It's taken hours but it has been worth it. Just this one time. I think it looks great. It's two different greens, lime green and dark green and three different blues. Light blue, sky blue and a dark navy blue. I hope he likes it.

We've done all the usual things. I went with Mum to do our Christmas shopping. Mainly down in Kirkgate Market. They've got everything there and it's all cheap, but better not go when you're hungry or you'll spend a fortune. The smells are enough to drive you crazy. I love the cheese stalls. Steve used to like eating pie and peas when we went market shopping although he didn't often go shopping with us. Still I missed him when we went downtown this year. I suppose it was the thought of not being able to share it with him, the stuff that we bought. And now we're in Summer Lane getting ready for Christmas, it feels worse. He should be here.

In the last couple of weeks, Mum did some Christmas baking (like she always does) and asked if I would help her (like she always does), but I didn't feel like it. I didn't want to join in but Mum looked miserable, so I did. We did it but not cheerfully. We made the Christmas cake together and mince pies but then we gave up and bought the Christmas puddings from the shop. I kept thinking that Steve wouldn't be eating any of it. And Mum kept forgetting what she was doing, kept staring into space and most of the time looked gloomier than me. Funny that because she's the one who wanted him gone. Mind you, when I tuned into her thoughts, it was usually Darius she was thinking about and it was making her miserable. Mum's thoughts were scary, so I stopped empathising. That's what it is when you tune in, you get drawn in to how the other person feels and I couldn't bear it. What's the point I asked her? Why bother making any cakes and puddings? To enjoy Christmas, she said. Life goes on.

Esme has been irritable and moany for weeks, but she cheered up just before we set off to come here. She even sang in the car like in the old days and today she's still cheerful. I expect she's making an effort for Grandma and Grandpa (and possibly me), so now I'm the only one who's still moping about. I wonder if Steve is missing us? Or whether Sandra is cheering him up. She's not very nice. Small and dumpy with mousey hair and she's always smiling. Very irritating.

Grandma's left the piano lid open. That's unusual. I touch one of the keys and listen to the sound, then another, then two together. I sit down and pretend I can play pressing the loud pedal to make the notes sustain. According to Steve, the loud pedal is the same as having reverb. Oh, Steve, where are you? You should be here with us I think to myself as I close the lid and prepare to go next door to talk to Grandma.

I stretch my mouth into a smile ready for acting cheerful and look in the mirror to see what I look like. I look horrorshow. (I don't like the violence in *Clockwork Orange*, but I love the language. Did you know that 'horrorshow' is Russian for 'good'?) But I don't look good. My face looks as though it's me who belongs in a horror movie. My smile looks fake. My smile *is* fake. I'll have to do better than that (but it's very hard to smile at yourself in the mirror and make it real – you should try it). I can hear Grandma talking to my mother and Grandpa has just come in from the garden. Grandma is expecting me to help her put up the Christmas decorations like last year and I don't feel like it but Mum says I've got to.

'Dani,' Grandma shouts through to me. 'Dani, it's teatime. What are you doing in there?' I move away from the mirror and go into the living room. Grandpa's sitting in his chair by the fire. He starts coughing, pulls a handkerchief out of his pocket and splutters into it. Grandma looks at him with concern, but he grins at her.

'Don't look like that,' he says. 'I'm not going just yet, you know.' ('Going' means 'going to die'. He's always talked like that.) And he turns away to cough again.

'You shouldn't spend all that time outside,' Grandma says. 'Not in this weather.' But we know she might as well save her breath. She pours the tea and we sit down to eat.

'It was kind of Steve to lend you the car for Christmas,' Grandma says. 'How is he? Do you see much of him?'

'Not anymore,' Esme says, 'I think he's got a new girlfriend. Or so Dani tells me. I haven't met her.' I notice Grandpa frown when Mum says this and Grandma glances over at me, but I look down at my plate. I was going to let it pass but change my mind.

'He says she's just a friend, not a girlfriend,' I say. I'm surprised at this thought. Steve did say that to me and I hadn't really considered it until now.

After we've eaten, I go with Mum to unload the car. We usually do it as soon as we arrive, but there's all the Christmas stuff this time. The boot and the backseat are crammed full so that's why we decided to leave it until after tea. Mum's tired. We never seem to get here early and the traffic was awful all the way down. I grab what I can and follow Mum back into the house lugging the typewriter in one hand and a couple of bags in the other.

'My word, you're loaded down, my duck,' Grandpa says. 'Put something down before you collapse.'

'I won't collapse, Grandpa,' I tell him as I put everything on the sofa so there's nowhere left to sit down. It takes nearly another half an hour to finish unloading the car.

'Whatever have you brought?' Grandma asks as bag after bag appears and then gets carted off upstairs.

'Well, it's Christmas,' Esme says.

16

Everybody tries hard, but it feels as though we're only pretending. We put up the decorations. Grandma finishes making the mince pies and we sit down together to eat the first one and to make a wish.

'It's stupid,' I say. 'It never comes true.'

'Well, you never know,' Grandma says.

'Yes, I do know,' I reply and Grandpa laughs and says that I sound just like Mum which annoys me. I go off into the front room. I was going to write my diary. but can't bring myself to get the typewriter out. (Yes, I'm still writing a diary? Who'd have thought it?) I need to finish the scarf but don't feel like doing that either. Think I need a rest from knitting for today. I'll carry on tomorrow. Decide to read but instead, I lie on the sofa and do nothing. Lie and think. I'm always trying to think things through but never manage to get anywhere. Never come to any conclusions. Actually, that's not true. I come to conclusions over and over again, but they change. Then they recycle. It's like looking into a kaleidoscope. All the same bits but never the same patterns. Not quite.

Can't seem to concentrate on anything. I will start practising my typing again soon and get back to writing my diary. What I like best is reading it through afterwards. If I practise the typing, it will help me cope with the work next term. I was doing quite well until Darius decided I didn't need any more sessions. But it's not fair to blame him. He was right. I didn't need any more lessons. It's practice that I need. Just practice (and a bit of praise - that's what I miss - I'm a wimp).

I'll get back to the typing tomorrow. For now, I look in my bag for the transistor radio that I take everywhere. Steve gave it to me. Grandpa says I'll go deaf listening to it and he means it as a joke but his jokes are irritating these days. He's gone out again now and I can hear Mum and Grandma talking next door. They're talking about Steve. Even though Esme's told them that Steve's got a girlfriend, I can see they're still hoping that he'll come back to us.

'We're not suited to each other, Mum.'

'Well, you used to be suited. What's changed?'

'Nothing's changed.' Esme sounds irritable again. She carries on talking. 'We've always liked each other and we still do, but that's not enough.'

I decide to go and join them but as I walk in, I hear the back door bang and see that Mum's gone out.

'Where's she gone?' I ask.

'Gone for a walk,' Grandma says, 'she'll be back soon. Go and make a pot of tea for us, Dani. I think I need a sit-down.' Unheard of. Grandma needing a sit-down but I look at her and she does look tired. When I come back with the tea, she's got the cake tin out and I pick out a chocolate marshmallow.

'Are you all right, my ducky?' Grandma asks, and I'm about to say 'yes, fine' when it all starts pouring out and instead of telling her about Steve I find myself telling her about the dream.

'I think I'm going mad, Grandma,' I say and try to speak lightly as though it's a joke.

'Why's that, my duck?' she asks. She's sitting on her usual chair next to the window stirring her tea. 'It's a nice cup of tea you've made,' she says. I don't reply and Grandma carries on stirring it. The sugar must be dissolved by now but she's still stirring. Slowly I start to talk.

'I really do think I'm starting to go mad,' I say and realise that I'm pulling at the tassels on the tablecloth, twisting and pulling like I used to do when I was little. 'I keep having this dream. The one I've told you about before and it won't stop.'

'Tell me again,' she says and I put the half-eaten marshmallow on the plate and start to talk. I tell her in detail but, as always, I miss out the end. She listens like she always does. With concern but without looking shocked. Grandma never looks as though the world's going to end. She makes everything seem manageable just by the look on her face. Her calm makes it possible to go on talking. When I finish, she looks very serious as though she's making a big decision.

'I don't think it's a dream, Dani,' she tells me and I start to feel afraid.

'What do you mean?' I ask.

'I think it might be a memory,' she says and then she starts to tell me about the day my father died. She tells me that nobody knows what happened after he took me from Summer Lane. But he was extremely distressed. And drunk. He and Mum had had some sort of terrible row in Leeds. Grandma is not sure what it was about, but Dad had arrived to say that he was going to teach Esme a lesson and had driven off with me (I was staying with Grandma then).

Later in the day, the police had arrived to tell them that Dad had been killed on the motorway but I wasn't with him so they had gone to Dad's house to look for me. I was there in the bedroom. Terribly upset and I'd stayed upset for ages.

'But what makes you think it might be a memory?'

'Because when you started to speak again two days after we found you, you said the same things that you're dreaming now.' Grandma stops for a minute and moves to get more comfortable. She does look tired. I wait and then she continues, 'Over and over again you said, *Daddy kill Dani, Daddy kill Dani*, but you were clearly not dead so we didn't believe you.' Grandma hesitates. 'And then there was the other thing...' She stops talking. I look at her.

'What was the other thing, Grandma?'

'You kept putting cushions and pillows over your face and you'd never done that before. You said *Daddy kill Dani* every time you pulled a cushion over your face.'

I don't say anything. I'm feeling shocked. Grandma goes on.

'The other thing you kept saying was *Daddy loves Dani*. I don't know how that fits in, but I'm beginning to think that you remembered what had happened and were trying to tell us.' Grandma looks at me but I look away and start eating the marshmallow. I need to think. 'But you were small,' she says, 'only two. We thought you didn't know what you were saying. Thought you were making it up and Esme was upset because Andreas had died. She couldn't bear to hear anything bad about him. Especially from you.'

Grandma speaks slowly and I'm managing to look at her now. 'Your mum didn't want you to think badly of your father. She wanted you to have good memories of him.' Grandma stops again, lost in thought. After what seems an eternity, she adds, 'But he might have done it, Dani. He might have tried to suffocate you. He couldn't bear to hear you crying and he was very upset. Your dream might be a memory of what happened.'

'But I told Mum,' I say, 'and she said it was just a dream.'

'That's what she's always believed,' Grandma says. 'She was telling you her truth. But there's only one person alive who knows what happened before your Dad left that house. And that's you.'

'So how can I find out?' I ask. I'm feeling very strange.

'You can't,' Grandma says. 'You can't, my ducky, but it might help to know that your dream might be a memory. It might help you to be free of it. You've had it for so long now. Since you were small.'

'Yes, and it's been getting worse. I mean it's been happening more often.' I suddenly feel that I can't bear to talk about the dream anymore. I need time to think about what Grandma has said. I'm going to look for Mum I tell her and get my coat. but I'm not going to look for her. I'm going for a walk in the field by myself.

17

Christmas Day arrives and Mum seems cheerful, but it's a subdued celebration. We exchange presents and say thank you to each other. They all watch as I open my present from Steve. It's a rucksack, a beautiful, bright red rucksack.

'Hundred percent waterproof and windproof,' I read out, 'guaranteed for five years.'

'That'll be a good un,' Grandpa comments approvingly. 'That must have cost him a bit.'

'Yes,' I say. 'Steve always buys good stuff. He says you get what you pay for.' Grandpa nods. I turn to Mum. 'What did he give you, Mum?' I ask.

'*Crow*,' she replies. 'He gave me *Crow*. It's a book of poems by Ted Hughes.'

'Do you like it?' I ask. 'And can I read it?'

'Yes, and yes,' Esme says but nothing further.

'And what did you give Steve?' I ask.

'I sent him a card,' Mum says. I almost gasp. Look at Grandma but she looks away. How could my mother treat Steve like that? After all the years we've lived together.

Grandma starts talking about the weather. The weather! Anything to change the subject.

'Yes, Frankie,' Grandpa says, as he gets up to tap the barometer. 'I think you're right. The glass is going up so it won't snow. Looks like we might have a frost.'

Uncle Ted arrives as usual at about half ten and helps prepare the vegetables. Brussel sprouts are his speciality.

Christmas dinner is perfect. Grandma's food is always brilliant and I eat more than I mean to. Can hardly move. Mum washes up while Uncle Ted and I dry the dishes. Grandpa stretches his legs and then puts them on the stool. Grandma is supposed to be having a sit-down but actually, she's clearing food away and organising it in the pantry. After that, it's the Queen's Speech. Obligatory in my grandparents' eyes. A tradition that they love. Esme disapproves of the royal family but keeps her views to herself for once. I agree with Mum. What's the point of listening to someone read out a speech that's been written for her by someone else? Grandma and Grandpa won't even argue about it. They just give you a special look that means *Be quiet. This subject is not up for discussion.*

It's gone four when Aunty Mary and Aunty Beattie drop in to wish us a happy Christmas. Aunty Mary has brought Beattie in her car. Mary doesn't talk about it, but she's proud of her car. Howard says you can tell what people are like from the cars they drive, so I wonder what conclusions he'd come to about Aunty Mary. She drives a blue Hillman Minx. Has had it forever. It's a safe, boring car, but I think that's what he means. It suits Aunty Mary. What I'd like is an E-type Jag (ha ha). Actually, I'd be happy with anything, but there's another three years to wait before I can drive on the roads (I've already had a go on a dirt track in Howard's car, but we didn't tell Mum.) Any kind of car would do for me. I'd be thrilled. Freedom!

Grandma leads the way and we follow her into the front room to sing some carols. This is what Mary and Beattie have come for. Happens every year (and I like it). Grandma gets out the book of carols and sits down to play while Mum, Aunty Mary and me stand around the piano. Grandpa sits in the armchair and Beattie perches on a chair that Mum has brought in for her. It's crowded. The front room is full of furniture and people, but we manage and everybody's jolly. Grandpa's got a rich, deep voice with a bit of vibrato but you can never hear Grandma because she sings so quietly. Has to concentrate on the playing she says. The person you always hear most is Aunty Beattie who has a huge, wobbly voice that she's very proud of, especially on the high notes that are usually not quite high enough. She strains hard and Mum shoots me a stern look that means *do not giggle.*

But I do like it, the carol singing, and despite Aunty Beattie, we don't sound too bad. Almost like a choir. After a while, Mum takes over from Grandma on the piano and the two Aunties say goodbye. Grandma goes out with them and after that, there's only me, Mum and Grandpa left and we go on for hours. Uncle Ted listens from the living room. He always stays there. Says he likes it but can't sing. Grandma says we shouldn't nag at him to come in because his father died singing carols.

'Died?' I ask, not believing her. How can you die from singing?

'Yes,' she says. 'Uncle Ted's father was still young when he went ('went' means died). He had a wonderful voice and sang with the Moira Male Voice Choir. He collapsed and died one Christmas in the middle of a rehearsal.'

'How young?' I ask.

'In his sixties,' Grandma says in a hushed voice. 'He was only in his sixties.' Well, I think and suppress a smile wondering what age you need to be for Grandma to consider you old. Can't imagine ever getting to that age. I'll probably die before I'm 30. I think about it and work out that Grandpa must be in his sixties. And he is definitely old. He's been old for as long as I can remember.

It's a normal Christmas Day and we carry on eating. I sneak down the pantry steps and help myself to bits of chicken. It's where Grandma always puts it. On the stone thrawl at the bottom of the steps, on a serving plate covered in foil. I prefer it in a sandwich with tomato sauce but that can wait until tomorrow. Loose bits will do for today. Tastes yummy. In the evening Grandma and Grandpa go to Chapel for the service. Uncle Ted left about half an hour ago, so there's only Mum and me left in the house. Aunty Mary and Aunty Beattie will be at Chapel, too, but they won't come back here. They'll go home afterwards.

Mum is drinking wine and asks me if I'd like a glass.

'Yes, please,' I say and she pours me some. Maybe if I get drunk, it will help me speed up with the knitting. I've got it out again because I have to get it finished but I'm getting sick of it. I sip and try not to pull a face. It's red wine again, the kind she usually drinks.

'Have some nuts with it,' she says pushing a bowl towards me, 'then the alcohol won't make you sick.' And then she adds, 'On second thoughts, you won't need the nuts because your stomach must be full to bursting,' and finally, 'but do have some, Dani. You can't be too careful.' I look at the minute amount she's poured into my glass and think that it would have to be a hundred percent proof and then some for that drop to make me ill. I sigh. Don't suppose she'll change, but still, I help myself to the nuts and sip at the wine. It tastes every bit as bad as last time, possibly worse, but I persevere.

'Do you like this wine?' I ask her.

'Yes, it's a good one. Tastes smooth. Mellow,' Mum says swishing the wine around in her glass and sipping some more. 'It's a Merlot. You can get poor quality wine that tastes awful.' I sip again and decide to take her word for it. Try not to pull a face a second time or she might not give me any more and I wouldn't mind getting drunk. Just to see what it's like. 'I've got something to tell you,' she carries on, sounding cheerful. My spirits rise. Perhaps she's going to tell me why she seems so much happier lately. I still have a faint hope that it might be good news about Steve, but whatever it is, she is looking pleased so it will be good news about something.

'I'm going to start seeing Darius,' she tells me. Oh, no. My spirits sink. I thought we were safe from Darius. Was sure that he didn't like her. 'I like him a lot,' she says, 'and I know you do, too.' Mum looks at me as she says this and can surely see how wrong she is. At least, I do like him but only as long as he doesn't go near my mother. 'He's gone to PNG for Christmas but when he comes back, he's going to start dropping in.'

I look at her and decide to say nothing. As Suzi says, Mum's got a right to have friends and go out. Even if I don't like the thought of it, but just as I finish thinking these sensible thoughts, I think of Steve's face and his smile.

'No,' I shout at her. 'No way, Mum. If Darius comes to our house, I'm leaving,' With difficulty, I manage not to smash my glass on the table as I remember in the nick of time that it's Grandma's house. Instead, I pick up the wine bottle, fill my glass and calmly leave the room. I'm going to be the ice queen. I take my wine and my knitting and go into the front room. Then I barricade the door. Quietly and methodically. I'm not letting her anywhere near me. And I'm not letting her put anyone in Steve's place. NOT ANYONE.

18

Esme heaves a sigh as she watches Dani's face flush red and then turn pale as she controls her anger. Watches her pick up the wine bottle and fill her glass before walking off into the front room with her knitting. No banging and slamming but there are noises of furniture being stacked against the door. Why can't her daughter be reasonable? Only five minutes ago they were having a pleasant time together eating nuts, drinking wine and chatting. Is it Dani's age or is it just Dani? Esme feels like shaking some sense into her but knows it's impossible.

All that Esme has said is that she's going to start seeing Darius after Christmas. And Dani always said that she liked him. She was disappointed when Darius stopped the writing sessions. Esme doesn't expect her daughter to stop loving Steve or to stop seeing him. Dani is not being offered a replacement for Steve, but she behaves as though she is. She is being completely unreasonable.

Ess decides that the best thing to do is to ignore her. She won't let Dani stop her inviting Darius for dinner when he gets back from PNG. Dani is turning into the family dictator and it's time it stopped. But she's not looking forward to the confrontation. Esme hates it when her daughter is upset and perhaps Dani is right. Ess had decided it was over with Darius and now she is rushing to see him again.

There is still no explanation for his rude behaviour. She hardly knows the man she is so anxious to invite into their house. Into their life. She doesn't know him, but she is convinced that he is important. If it works out between them, then Dani is right. Darius will become Steve's replacement, Dani's third father. Darius, the man from Papua New Guinea. The man Esme hardly knows.

Esme is leaping into the future. Leaping much too soon. How can she be considering Darius as a possible father for Dani before she knows him? She reminds herself that she has seen Darius only four times and only once was she alone with him. On the strength of a letter that says practically nothing, she is considering a permanent relationship.

Yes, she is mad. And stupid. But she has to be clear about what might happen if she starts to see Darius because whatever she does will affect Dani. Esme is determined to walk into this relationship with her eyes open. If she walks into it at all. Dani is already distressed because Steve has gone. If she brings another man into the family, it will have consequences. For Dani's sake, she ought to go back to Steve. But she can't. For Dani's sake, she should at least be aware of what she is doing so Esme is doing her best to manage at least that.

Ess pours out the rest of the bottle. Only half a glass left. She should have stopped Dani helping herself. Thirteen! Too young. In her head she can hear Dani saying things like *In France, even children drink wine* and *I'm not a child, Esme.* Yes, Dani will soon be fourteen. Not a child, but not yet an adult. Esme sips at her drink. Very nice. She looks at the bottle. Hungarian. Pity there's no-one to share it with and for a minute she allows herself to dream of sharing it with Darius. She has felt happy since she got the letter from him. So happy that she's conveniently forgotten to worry about Helen. Esme pushes the thought away. She will ask Darius about Helen when she sees him. Until then, she will try not to speculate. Surely Dani's attitude towards Darius will soften. In any case, having Darius come to dinner might not lead to anything.

Darius has behaved strangely ever since she first met him and Esme can't stop trying to work him out. Does he want her or doesn't he? At the Zephaniah concert, he asked to speak to her alone, but when they were together with the others he paid Helen more attention than he did to her. It's she, Esme, who has done nearly all the running. Not Darius. She blushes to remember the notes that she's written to him that Joe and presumably the rest of Joe's family will know about. Ess has made a fool of herself.

She thinks of how critical she's been of Suzi's blindness to Pete's behaviour and finally realises that she, Esme has been a hundred times worse. She shudders as she imagines Joe's family discussing her as they sit at the dinner table. And does Darius join in and laugh about her like so many men do? She doesn't think so but there she goes again thinking the best of him. She's got to change. She's got to stop trusting him. She's got to be careful.

The wine's all gone but there are still some nuts and Esme eats them automatically. Nuts are moreish. She's glad that they're already shelled. How lazy of me she thinks. But Esme is not lazy, she is hard-working and determined. In fact, she's more like her first husband, Andreas, than she ever cares to concede. They were different from each other in so many ways but they were both stubborn and determined. Determined to fight for whatever they wanted for as long as it took and at whatever the cost. *God help Dani* flashes through Esme's mind. God help Dani if she's inherited that stubborn streak from both her mother and her father. But even as Esme decides that character traits are not heritable, she knows she is wrong. Dani *is* stubborn. Such single-mindedness can make you blind to reality.

Esme glances at the clock. Her parents will be back soon. She ought to start getting the supper ready but she doesn't move. Starts thinking about the afternoon she spent with Darius in the park. They had walked and talked. She remembers kicking up the leaves. It was months ago in the early autumn. She remembers the copper beeches and the last rose. Just one. Darius had hummed and sung that Bonzo Dog Doodah song all afternoon. He had kept singing the same few lines:

I'm the urban spaceman, baby.

I've got speed.

I've got everything I need.

But he'd missed the last line and it had been nagging at her ever since. Suddenly she remembers what it is:

I'm the urban spaceman, baby – here comes the twist.

I don't exist.

Esme gets up and goes into the pantry to get another bottle of wine but changes her mind. Instead, she helps herself to her father's whisky. Darius is rude and baffling. Rude because he didn't reply to the notes she sent. Baffling because after that wonderful afternoon, he didn't ask her out again. And then finally, there is this letter. She had waited so long to hear from him that when the letter had dropped through the letterbox, it was more a shock than a surprise. At first, she'd been thrilled, but since then Esme has alternated between pleasure at hearing from him and anger that he has not been in touch sooner.

Ever since it came, Esme has carried the letter around with her, but she's annoyed with herself for doing that. Darius should have explained himself long ago. She takes it out of her bag and has another look. By this time, the letter is so creased that the writing is barely legible and there wasn't much writing in the first place. It's brief. He apologises for his silence and promises that he will explain things when he sees her after Christmas. He gives the date of his return and asks if they can get together for a meal when he gets back. Including Dani, he says. All three of them.

Esme has spent a long time trying to work out whether his suggestion to include Dani is a good sign or a bad one. But from Dani's furious response, it doesn't look as though a meal with the three of them is going to happen. Esme sighs again and looks up as she hears her mother and father walking up the path. They are back from Chapel. All smiles. Full of Christmas cheer. Frances puts the kettle on as soon as she gets into the kitchen.

'Hello, Ess,' she calls through. 'We're gasping. Do you want some tea? What about Dani?'

'Dani's in the front room,' Ess replies, getting up. 'I'll make it. Come and sit down.'

'You missed a treat,' Frances says, 'didn't she, George? The singing was lovely. The choir's changed completely since Mr Causer's taken over.'

'Not bad,' George agrees.

'You'd have loved it,' Frances goes on. 'The music was marvellous.' George takes his coat off and goes to hang it up. He sits down and, with difficulty, bends to put his slippers on then sighs with satisfaction as he settles himself into his armchair and reaches for his pipe.

'That's better,' he says as he lights up and makes himself comfortable. 'I'll have to start taking a cushion with me.'

'Where's Dani?' Frances asks.

'In the front room,' Ess says again, gesturing towards the curtain leading past the coats into the front room. 'She wanted to be by herself for a bit.'

'It's her age,' George says. 'Coming up to fourteen, it's a difficult age. It'll pass.'

Esme imagines her daughter listening next door and pulling faces at Grandpa's remarks. But there might be some truth in what he says. He certainly doesn't seem to worry about Dani's moods like she does. But then he's not her mother. She is. And he's not the guilty one. She is. It's her fault that Steve has gone. Esme makes the tea, stirs the pot to make it brew more quickly and brings it through from the kitchen. Damn it, she thinks, Dani can't have everything her own way. She sees Steve regularly enough. Sees him more than some daughters see fathers who are living at home. But Esme won't have Steve back and that's that. Esme, too, has a right to her life.

'The *Sound of Music*'s on in a few minutes,' Frances tells her. 'Do you fancy watching it, Ess? Shall I put it on?'

'Yes,' Esme says and decides to fetch another bottle of wine from the pantry. She sees her mother look at the wine bottle and decide to let it pass.

'I'm off to bed,' George says, looking unimpressed with the viewing decision but pleased to have an excuse to go and lie down. 'It's been a good Christmas. Night night, Ess.'

'Night night, Dad.'

Esme is surprised. It seems to her that both she and Dani have been grumpy and difficult, but her Dad thinks it's been a lovely Christmas. She feels pleased and settles down with the wine and some more nuts. Her mother fetches the box of Milk Tray that she opened earlier. They've just put their feet up and switched on when the front room door opens and Dani comes out.

'Hello, my ducky,' Frances says. 'Have you come to join us? Come and sit next to me.'

'I've come for some wine,' Dani says.

'Well, a little drop won't hurt you,' Frances says. 'and it is Christmas. What do you think, Ess?' Esme fetches another glass and pours a little for her daughter.

'I haven't changed my mind,' Dani says looking at Esme.

'What's that about, ducky?' Grandma asks.

'Mum knows,' Dani replies.

19

Back in Leeds, I go straight round to Mandy's and ask her to cut my hair. It's time I changed my image. I've been the good little girl for too long. I already got rid of my bunches when somebody said it made me look young. Mandy had said that bunches made me look like a sweet German Heidi girl. It was easy to change my hair style, I just tied my hair back into a ponytail. It's time for more drastic action now.

'What's wrong, Dani?' Mandy asks. 'You've come back in a terrible mood. What's happened?'

'I'm fine,' I tell her. 'Everything's fine. I just want my hair chopped off.'

'But I can't cut it,' Mandy says. 'I'm not a hairdresser. It will look awful if I do it.'

'I can't afford a hairdresser,' I tell her, 'and I don't care if it looks awful.' That's not quite true. What I mean is that I don't care if it looks untidy. What I want is a spiky look, so I explain that.

'You definitely need a hairdresser for a spiky look,' she says. 'That's hard to do.'

'Karen's done it,' I say.

'Yes,' Mandy says. 'Karen had it done in town. It cost a lot.' Frustrated I take the pair of scissors out of my bag that I've brought with me and wave them at her.

'If you won't do it, I'll chop it myself.' I turn and move the stuff off the stool in front of the dressing table in her attic room. The mirror's dusty, but a quick swipe with my hand clears most of it off to leave an uneven oval shape in the middle. I can see well enough to manage what I'm doing.

'Ok,' she says. 'Do it yourself then.' And I do. I undo the ponytail clip and shake my hair loose. Pause. Holding the scissors at an angle, I hack at my long blonde hair until it's short all over with chopped uneven lengths. It looks awful.

'What do you think?'

'It's awful,' Mandy says. 'You need a hairdresser.' I look at myself in her dusty mirror and wave my hands around to admire the Devil's Blood nail varnish I've got on (it's not new, but it's my favourite). My hands look good, but she's right, my hair looks awful. I do need a hairdresser. I'm seeing Jaffa on Sunday (he's back) and school starts on Monday. I'll have to do something before then.

'Oh my God,' my mother says when I walk in. 'What have you done to yourself.'

'Cut my hair, 'I say. 'Obviously.'

'It looks awful, Dani. Whatever possessed you?'

'I want a new image. I want a spiky look.'

'Well, I'll just have to have a go at it then,' my mother says, 'and help you out.' But I back off.

'No way,' I tell her. 'I need a hairdresser.' She looks at me, sighs and surprisingly, she agrees, so we set off downtown. It's a good job that it's winter. Cold enough to wear a hat on the way there. She takes me to Maxine's and once again, I'm surprised because it's expensive, but I'm pleased and when I get back, I look good. Even my mother agrees that my new style looks fine although she says that Grandma and Grandpa will be shocked.

'Let's see what Darius thinks of you,' she says. 'He got back last night and he's coming round for dinner.' I hesitate as I contemplate locking myself upstairs or going out so I don't have to see him but decide that it might be better to stay in and check out what's going on between them. In any case, I'm hungry. I remind myself that I don't have to like him. They've betrayed me. Betrayed Steve. I will certainly not trust either my mother or Darius in future but there's a certain happy feeling rising within me that I can't quite ignore.

I go upstairs into my mother's bedroom so I can use the mirror. I only have a small mirror in my room and I need something full length. I inspect my denims with the holes that are beginning to fray nicely and wave my shiny black nails in front of my face. Satisfactory, I think. I've got three nail varnishes in the Blood range - Dragon's Blood (green), Mouse Blood (grey) and Devil's Blood (dark red, nearly black). Devil's Blood is my favourite, so my hands look good and I like my hair. I don't look like me at all. Mum's cooking curry and the smell is wafting up the stairs. Perhaps I'll get a glass of wine with it.

I hear the front door open and the sound of happy welcome in my mother's voice. She's been much more cheerful lately and there he is, sitting at the table when I come down. I haven't seen Darius since that last writing session.

'Dani,' he says when I come into the room. 'Look at you.' As usual, he pays attention to me, looks at me long and hard, a bit like Jaffa does. Maybe Darius draws, too. I'll have to ask him. 'I like the haircut.'

'Thanks,' I say and find it hard to remember to be angry because I'm feeling so pleased that he likes my hair. He looks at me admiringly and it feels good.

It's the kind of evening where we all talk a lot, even me (back to my old ways I can see Esme thinking as I chatter on), but I can't remember much about what anybody said afterwards. Pleasant. Darius tells us how hot it was in Port Moresby and all about the Christmas he's just spent with his family and we tell him about Summer Lane. I do get a glass of wine. Two actually although my mother has found a special small glass that she thinks is suitable for me. A bit like a thimble. Darius says that curry should have beer with it, not wine but my mother says that's tough because wine is what she's got and they smile at each other. Practically everything they say makes them smile and I'm enjoying it, too. Mainly because I keep thinking about my hair and how nice it looks. My neck feels cold even inside. I'm not used to having no hair around it so I keep being reminded that this is a different me.

Darius doesn't stay late. Soon after the meal is finished, he goes and I suspect that they've arranged this in advance to get me used to him coming round, but Mum says no, Darius has got jet lag. I still think I'm right. Transparent behaviour on their part. They think I'm a kid but I realise that they do care what I feel or they wouldn't have gone to the trouble. Unless it's true what Mum says and Darius went early because he really did have jet lag.

After he's gone, I follow Mum into the kitchen and pick up the tea towel to dry the dishes. There are too many to fit on the draining board all at once so some have to be dried and put away as she washes up. I have a momentary pang of annoyance at Darius who hasn't offered to stay and wash up. Steve always did lots in the kitchen. Darius didn't even clear anything away.

'What do you think?' Mum asks me and I see her eyes are shining.

'What about?' I say. I'm not going to make things that easy for her. She's not home and dry just because I'm in a good mood tonight, but I'm half-joking because I'm pleased that she's happy. I remember a time when she was almost always cheerful and we used to talk a lot and enjoy each other's company. I remember looking forward to her coming home from school so we could sit and chat. Steve would stay upstairs when she came in so that the two of us could sit at the table and chat about the day, have some private time together. Seems so long ago. Oh, Steve, I do miss you.

'About this evening,' she replies. 'About Darius,' but before I can reply she adds, 'I do like him, Dani. I can't help it. It happened by itself almost. You do like him, don't you?'

'He's all right,' I reply, 'but I still love Steve. I miss him. I don't want Darius instead of Steve.'

'I know that, Dani. Nobody can ever replace another person. I know you love Steve.'

'I always will,' I say.

'I didn't mean it to happen and I don't understand why we like each other or where it will lead,' Mum says as she balances the salad bowl precariously on top of the heaped draining board that I'm not clearing quickly enough. I don't know what to reply to that and think that if I'd said that to her as an explanation for something that I'd done, she wouldn't have been impressed. I tell her what I'm thinking and she considers what I've said.

'You're right,' she says. 'And I've thought about that, too. The feeling that something is so powerful that it happened without my will. But then, it didn't. My will was part of it. I wanted it to happen. The mystery is why it happened. Steve's a good man and he didn't really change. It was me. It was my fault. I've thought of many reasons and they all sound credible but in the end, I don't know why I don't want to be with Steve anymore. That feeling started before I met Darius.'

'And where do I fit in?'

'You always fit in,' Mum replies. 'You fit in because you have to. Because you're my daughter. My family. It's a hard question to answer honestly because I know you want Steve and that it makes you miserable that he's gone. I did try to make it work especially after you damaged your arm, but having Steve back for the second time only made me more sure that I was right the first time. Steve wouldn't have been happy knowing that I didn't love him like I used to do and you would have had to live with parents who were never properly happy.'

'I wouldn't have minded,' I tell her, the words out before I've had time to think them through, 'but I didn't have any choice.'

'No,' she concedes. 'You didn't.'

We could have gone on, but we'd both said enough and the pleasant feeling from after dinner was morphing into a seriousness that we didn't want. We wanted to laugh and be happy and to stop thinking about things. At least I did.

'Let's watch the news,' she suggests, 'and have another piece of cheesecake.'

'Good plan,' I reply thinking that the cheesecake sounded better than the news, but Mum likes News at Ten (or news at any time actually), so she switches it on. We sit together on the sofa and even though we're full, we both manage to eat quite a large piece of cake. Then I turn around and lean against the end and put my feet on her lap. It's comfortable and I haven't done that for a long time.

20

Esme turns over in bed and pushes the hair out of her eyes. Her fringe is too long. She should have got her own hair cut when she took Dani down to Maxine's. She'll have to make an appointment. Can't sleep. Because she's too happy, too wound up. She reflects that the Buddhists (according to what Suzi says) and Grandma have got a lot in common although they don't know it. Both agree that the ideal life is one of moderation. Esme needs to aim for some calm state of being in between ecstatic and depressed. Right now she is heading towards ecstatic.

Darius came and Dani was happy. Darius came and Dani was happy. These two phrases ring like bells that chime in harmony and form rainbow images that chase each other backwards and forwards in ever more amazing arcs of joy. Glorious. Esme tries to calm down. The three of them had a marvellous evening. They ate together. They talked. It was easy. And when Darius left, Dani stayed downstairs to talk to her. They chatted together and had fun. Just as they used to do. Calm down she tells herself, it wasn't that much of a miracle. And it might change. Esme knows that it might change but doesn't think that it will. Both Dani and Darius were relaxed together. Why should that change?

However, she thinks and as her thoughts run on, she remembers how often Steve used to say that word. However. Dani had teased him about it. However, Esme continues with her internal monologue, Darius didn't do any explaining. In the letter, the very brief letter that she'd received from him, he said that he would explain when he saw her after Christmas. Explain his lack of contact. His absence. But he hadn't explained anything. They'd just sat together, eaten and chatted as though there were no urgent questions hanging between them. Nothing hanging in the air to be opened up and explained. She supposes that it might have been difficult to talk about things with Dani there and it's true that she had been there for just about the whole visit. Maybe Darius can be excused. Then Esme remembers that Darius had asked for Dani to be there. Was that to protect himself? To avoid any questions? The other thing that sinks in after the joyful feelings have settled is that fact that once again, she doesn't know when she's going to see him again. She expects that he'll phone or drop in and silences that small voice in her head that reminds her that he didn't last time.

By the time she gets to the next day, Ess is beginning to feel slightly depressed. Her bad dreams about Steve have returned to plague her, but she doesn't know why. He seems fully recovered from his 'accident' and Dani reports that his girlfriend is definitely real. Her name is Sandra and Dani says that she does seem more like a girlfriend than a friend. Steve seems mostly back to normal, but Esme can't help noticing the look in his eyes when he glances at her. Every time when he comes to pick up Dani, that look is there and it's those little signs that won't allow her to let go of the guilt. *Dumped him just like that. After ten years together.* She's heard Jenny whispering about her at work.

It's Sunday morning and Dani's already up. Esme can hear her banging about in the cellar. Apparently, the second bike is proving more difficult than the first. Howard could probably help but she hasn't seen him lately. He seems to have temporarily disappeared. Woman trouble, she supposes. He likes women and has an on-off relationship with someone she doesn't know called Sheena. It's been going on for years, but it never seems to go anywhere. She doesn't think Howard will ever commit. Esme can hardly believe that once upon a time she had fancied Howard herself and had dreamed of a permanent relationship with him. It's odd. She can't imagine how she could ever have felt that way about him, but she does like him and she trusts him. He will always be a friend.

It's time to get up. How quickly the Christmas holidays have whizzed past. It's school again tomorrow for both her and Dani. Thank God Darius diagnosed Dani's writing problem and offered help. That, at least, does seem akin to a miracle.

'Are you awake, Mum?' she hears bellowed up the stairs.

'I am now.'

'Soz,' Dani answers. 'Just wanted to let you know that I'm off to Mandy's.'

'Thought Mandy had her Buddhist meeting on a Sunday.'

'She does, but it's cancelled this week. Can't remember why. And they've invited me for lunch. I told you yesterday. Remember?'

'OK. Make sure you're back here by half five. Or sooner. They'll have had enough of you by then.' Esme hears Dani make a sort of harrumphing sound.

'Bye, Mum.'

'Bye.'

Esme turns over and decides that if Dani's going out, she'll have a bit longer in bed. It's warm and comfortable and she feels herself drifting off. When she comes to, she wakes with a jolt. What was she dreaming? It's gone but it wasn't good. It was something to do with Steve again and her heart is thumping.

It's nearly midday and she wonders how she could have slept for so long. Darius might have rung she thinks and jumps out of bed to rush downstairs to see if he's left a message, but there isn't one. No messages at all and the house is freezing. She switches the fire on and the room is soon warm. Wonders what to do with herself this afternoon. She could go and see Suzi she thinks as she goes to have a look for something to eat. She could have muesli and there's a yoghurt in the fridge. She pours some orange juice and puts the kettle on for coffee. Notices that Dani has washed up her breakfast dishes.

What about ringing Darius? There's no Dani this afternoon. They could have some time together. No, she's being too hasty Esme tells herself as she carries the bowl of muesli to the table. She's running after him again. That won't do. She'll go to Suzi's instead. But it's a terrible shame to waste a Dani-free afternoon. By the end of the second bowl of muesli, she's changed her mind three times and is still not sure what to do.

She needs music and looks through the LPs stashed on the special shelf that Steve made. Beethoven's 7th. That's what she needs. Esme puts it on and sits with her coffee and tobacco tin on the hearthrug in front of the fire. The room is warm now. Too warm so she turns the fire down. Listening to music must be like meditating. Her thoughts disappear while she listens, but a knock at the door cuts through the orchestral sound. Her heart leaps. She jumps up and rushes to open it.

'Hello, Esme,' John says. 'How are you?'

Oh no. She had made it quite clear last year that she wasn't interested in him. She wonders if he's back with his wife but supposes not or he wouldn't be standing on her doorstep.

'I'm fine. How are you?' she says casting around desperately for an excuse so that she doesn't have to invite him in. 'I'm sorry, John, I'm going out this afternoon. I'm just getting ready.' Esme hasn't seen John since the terrible dinner party last September when he'd let the cat out of the bag about her goings-on in Chapeltown. By the look in his eye, he still seems to have a crush on her.

'Oh,' he says looking disappointed. 'Just wanted to wish you a happy New Year and give you this.' He hands over a small parcel wrapped in gold paper.

'Thank you,' she says, flustered and waits for him to leave.

'I hear that Steve's left,' John says, not moving from the step and continuing to gaze at her.

'Yes,' Esme says. 'That's right. Steve has left but I'm busy. I'm going out this afternoon.' John still doesn't leave and Esme wonders whether she could close the door in his face.

'Will you come dancing with me again?' he finally asks.

'No, John' Esme says and manages, at last, to start closing the door. 'I'm sorry,' she says as she pushes it closed. 'Take care.' She stands inside shaking slightly while trying to look through the kitchen window to check that he's gone. What would Darius think if they had turned up at the same time? She shouldn't care, of course, but she does.

The music is still playing but she takes it off. Can't listen anymore. Decision made. She'll phone Darius and see if he's free. Esme dials the number and waits. Heart still hammering from the encounter with John but there's no reply. She tries again with the same result. Where are they all? Surely, they can't all be out? She forces herself to wait five minutes and tries again. This time she gets a result. It's Joe.

'Hi Joe,' Esme says. 'Can I speak to Darius?'

'Hi Ess,' Joe replies and she can hear the welcome in his voice. Joe always sounds pleased to hear from her. 'I'm sorry but he's out. Are you in need of company? Will I do?'

'No, it wasn't that,' Esme says trying to think of what to say next. 'It was just something that I wanted to ask him.'

'Can I take a message?' he asks.

'No, thanks,' Esme replies. 'It's not urgent.'

'Ok. I'll get him to call you back,'

'No,' she says. 'No, don't bother. It really wasn't urgent. And I'm sorry I'm not free this afternoon. School starts tomorrow and I've got a friend coming round.' Relief. She's managed to think of a plausible excuse for being busy although school starting and a friend coming round don't fit together. Never mind, she thinks. It was better than nothing. But where the hell is Darius?'

21

I'm looking forward to seeing Jaffa. When I got back from Summer Lane, there was a note in the Christmas card that he'd pushed through our letterbox. It was just a note on a separate piece of paper inside the card. *Meet me in the park. Sunday.* That was all it said. Not even a signature. I inspected the Christmas card to see what it said inside. *Happy Christmas from Jaffa.* That was all. Disappointing. No special message. Think that it might at least have said 'love from Jaffa', but it didn't.

I've got a card for him but I still don't know where he lives so I haven't given it to him yet. I've written 'With love from Dani' in mine and I wonder whether to erase the 'love' or find another card. The 'love' is quite big because I can't write small. I decide to leave it because I kept the best card for him. It's got a picture of a dove in a tree and the colours and the patterns are lovely. Blues and greens like the scarf but totally different. The colours on the card are pastel and peaceful but the colours in the scarf are bright and shouty. I think he'll like it. The card that is. If I cross out the 'love' it will spoil the whole thing.

And I've got his present finished at last. Jaffa's scarf. It has nearly killed me knitting this and I'm never going to knit another one. The plain knit stitch that my mother recommended looks good. There are occasional knobbly lumps but I agree with Mum that they give it a nice individual look. She was right. If I'd gone for the rib with knit two purl two, I would never have finished it. Mum still doesn't know who's getting it and she never will. Only Jaffa will know. It's got lots of colours in it but the predominant colour is green. Lime green. There is more green than blue. That variegated wool was another good idea of Mum's. Much easier than using two colours and making stripes which was what I had originally intended. And more exciting. The colours are fantastic. He'll like it. Well, I hope he will.

He's there already when I get to the park. Sitting on the bench. It seems ages since I've seen him because he wasn't in school for weeks.

'Hello, Jaffa,' I say and park my bike against the usual bush. My bush that's next to his bush.

'Hello, Dani,' he says and gives me a long, intent look. Then smiles. 'How are things? How was your Christmas?'

'Not too bad,' I say. 'What about yours?' I remember that it's his first Christmas ever without his mum.

'Empty,' he replies. 'It was empty.'

'Where were you?'

'With Annie and Granville,' he says. 'I'm still living up here but Dad's disappeared again. He's not stopped drinking since Mum died. He can't bear life anymore.' He looks at me. 'He didn't mean to hurt her.'

'No.'

'But it was Dad who pushed her. I saw him.' And then he's said enough. He asks me what I did at Christmas and how things are at home. I sit on the bench and tell him everything. About going to the university to track down Steve. About Steve's new friend, probably a girlfriend, and finally that Mum is getting together with Darius. I hesitate before telling him this and try to explain how I felt at first and how my feelings are changing even though I don't know why. I suddenly remember my hair.

'Do you like my hair?' I ask him.

'Of course,' he replies.

'Why, of course?'

'You're beautiful with any hair,' he says and stares at me so hard I feel myself starting to blush. Can't control it. 'You'd be beautiful with no hair,' he tells me. 'It's your bones.' I don't know where to put myself or what to reply but Jaffa has said it all so matter of factly that it's almost believable. He means it and it's almost not a compliment. I reach into my bag and get out the present that I've made for him and the card. I watch him unwrap the present and take it out. He's pleased. I can see how pleased he is and I feel a rush of relief and pleasure.

'Do you like it?' I ask, but I don't need to. He puts it on and wraps it around and around. It's long. I've made it very long.

'Long,' he says. 'The best scarves are long. And brilliant colours. This is the best scarf, Dani. The very best scarf.' And then he says that he's got a present for me. He's spent the last few weeks making drawings of his mother and one of them is for me.

'Would you like it?' he asks. 'You never met her, but I wish you had. You would have liked her. And she would have liked you.'

'Yes, please, Jaffa,' I say. We sit together and look at the picture of his mother and he says that he'll tell me more about her one day. Not now. In the picture, I see a beautiful young black woman sitting in an armchair with a book on her lap. I'm surprised to see that she looks so young and that her clothes look expensive. The dress is blue and soft looking, like cashmere (I've got a cashmere jumper - it was a Christmas present). His mother's dress fits closely and it's long and elegant. It's got thin straps over the shoulders almost like a ball gown but she's sitting there with her hand on the book as though she's just looked up from reading it so she can't have been going to a ball. I had expected his mother to look old. Don't know why because Esme doesn't look old. But I say nothing and he changes the subject.

Jaffa turns to me and says, 'Show me your arm, Dani. Pull your sleeve up and show me your arm.' I take off my jacket and pull up the sleeve of my jumper. He doesn't know that I nearly started biting again after my mother told me about Darius. But I didn't and my arm looks OK. I see Jaffa looking at it and smiling.

'Well done,' he says. He's really pleased about my arm.

'Something must have worked,' I say and this time I blush hot and long. I hadn't meant to say it but he just looks at me and grins.

'See you next week,' he says.

***

School isn't too bad and it's getting easier to type because I do so much of it. That's why my typing is improving. Darius was right. It's practice that makes the difference. Thousands of hours of practice. Miss Smith is still kind, but she's started to be stricter in the way she marks my work. I don't mind that. In fact, I prefer it. I know that when I get a good mark that I've deserved it. I don't have to report to her anymore and I missed it at first just like I missed my writing sessions with Darius. But it's better like this. I'm just the same as everyone else now. Or nearly. I still submit my work on typed sheets and I've got a small tape recorder for classwork so that I can type it up later. I can't have the typewriter with me in class because it's too noisy (and too big).

Sometimes I do well with my assignments and every so often I actually enjoy doing them especially some of the English homework. So I'm doing OK, but the problem is that Steve isn't. Steve is getting so depressed that he can't work. He can hardly talk anymore. And Mum still won't have him back so that we can look after him. Don't know what's happened to Sandra but she doesn't seem to be doing him any good at all.

Mum and I are on our own almost all the time these days. Suzi drops in occasionally, but Darius hasn't been back to see us since that dinner just after Christmas. But Mum still won't let Steve back in. Won't budge. I'm beginning to hate her again.

'Are you coming round tonight, Dani?' It's Mandy poking me in the back to get my attention. She's sitting behind me this term. They said we talked too much when we sat next to each other so we had to move. I turn around and nod.

'Usual time?'

'Usual time.' I turn back quickly. Miss Smith is looking at us. She's kind but she's not stupid so I shut up. I don't like sitting this close to the front. We girls never manage to get the seats at the back. They're the best seats and the boys always get them but I've never had to sit this far forward before. Maybe my new spiky image has worked and I'm getting a reputation as one of the bad girls. But I don't think so. It's mainly the talking that gets me into trouble. I always seem to talk too much.

Miss Smith carries on. It's a history lesson. She's talking about the industrial revolution and I look around the room. Jaffa's at the back. I saw him earlier but we don't talk to each other in school. I look into the corner where he sits and catch his eye but look away again fast. I miss sitting next to Mandy. The desks used to be doubles but they changed them and we've all got singles now. It's like being in an exam room but I do like this classroom because the sun shines in through the big high windows. Just after lunchtime, it shines straight on to my left shoulder. Like it is doing now, making my arm warm and making me feel sleepy.

Our classroom is in the main building which is Victorian. The classrooms for the infants are outside. They're separate prefabricated buildings on breeze blocks in their own separate yard and the parents keep complaining because they were supposed to be temporary years ago. Never got replaced. They're not too bad, but the classrooms in the main building are much nicer. Light and airy. Maps all over the walls. We should at least know our geography I think as I stare at the map of the world on one side of the board and the British Isles on the other. But it doesn't work. Doesn't actually teach us anything because we never look at them except from a distance. At least, I don't go and look at them and I've never seen anybody else having a look either.

'Daniela?' I hear Miss Smith's voice but I didn't hear the question.

'Could you repeat the question, please?' I ask.

'Can you tell us what 'urban drift' is and why it happened?' I hesitate. Haven't been listening and haven't got a clue. 'I thought not,' Miss Smith continues as I remain silent. 'Stop dreaming, Daniela and pay attention.'

'Yes. miss.'

***

I get back before Mum so I do what I always do. Ring Steve, but tonight there is no reply. I'm not going round to Mandy's until after I've had my dinner and tell Mum it's to do homework together but it isn't. I type mine and my typewriter's here. Mum doesn't mind me going to Mandy's but she insists on coming to collect me because I stay until half-past nine and she doesn't think it's safe for me to walk back alone. It's the Ripper she's still worried about. Stupid because it's only two streets away but there's nothing I can do about it. I sigh. There are so many things that I can't do anything about. Worst is Steve but I try to push thoughts of Steve to the back of my mind.

It's already dark but the street is well lit. Good enough to spot stones that need kicking although I kick less now. It's because I'm always thinking about other things. Mainly Steve. When I get to Mandy's the door opens even before I knock.

'Hi Mand,' I say and follow her upstairs. 'How's your mum?' I ask.

'She's fine,' Mandy says as she sinks into the blue bean bag where she always sits. 'She's still on three-monthly check-ups but after the next one, it will change to six-monthly. She's doing fine.' That's what I'd thought but it's nice to hear her say it.

'And what about you?' she asks. 'How's Steve?' I shrug. Not much to say really.

'No change,' I say, 'if anything, he's worse.' I look at her and turn away. What can I do I ask her while I stare at the dusty bookshelf next to where I'm sitting? When she's kind it makes me feel like crying.

'Nothing,' she says. 'There's nothing you can do, Dani. You can't look after Steve, you're too young.' She's probably right, but it doesn't help. 'Tell me about you and Jaff. How's that going? Did you see him on Sunday?'

'What do you mean?' I ask.

'I mean how are you and Jaff getting on?' she repeats.

'We're just friends,' I mumble and it's true actually. All we do is talk but I think that I might be in love with him. I've thought about this a lot but I would never tell anybody. Not Mandy. Not anybody. I look at her and see that she's grinning at me.

'What about David Williams?' I ask getting my own back.

'It's over,' Mandy tells me.

'How come?' I pause. 'Don't tell me you went for a walk with him and he kissed you like Breally?'

'Not quite,' Mandy says and starts laughing.

'Well, what happened?'

'We went for a walk and I kissed him.'

'What?'

'I kissed him,' Mandy repeated. 'Girl power.'

'And then what happened?'

'He ran away,' Mandy says, 'and he hasn't spoken to me since. I keep trying to smile at him in class to let him know it's all right and that I'm not going to tell anybody, but he's avoiding me.'

'You've just told me,' I remind her.

'Well you don't count,' Mandy says and chucks me a bag of crisps.

22

The blue plastic cagoule doesn't keep her warm. Esme shivers as she gets off the bike and pushes it on to the path. It's already dark and she's only just got home from school. The drama group was exhausting.

'Dani,' she shouts as she opens the door. 'Are you in?' There is no reply so Esme walks in and looks on the table. The usual note is there. Typed. Dani always uses the same one. For speed, she says. It is kept in the kitchen drawer when not in use. Gone to see M. And underneath it says D blob. It used to say Dx then the x had been tippexed out, got written in again but has now disappeared once more under a thick, white blob that stands out more than the D.

Esme switches on the gas fire, takes off the helmet, gloves, plastic trousers and cagoule and dumps the heap of outdoor gear at the end of the kitchen. Considerably lighter now (so what would it be like if she'd been wearing leathers...but oh, if only...), she sits down as close to the fire as she can get. Holds out her hands towards the glowing heat and feels the relief of the warmth seep into her body. Last of all, she pulls off her boots. Her fingers are warming up. She couldn't get the boots off when she first came in because her hands were numb. Now they're pink. Rosy with warmth like normal fingers again.

She pulls on a pair of thick, woolly socks, blue and grey flecked. Nice. Her favourites. She's only got one pair like this. A present from her mum. Better than slippers she thinks (and that's why her mother bought them for her –

she'd got fed up with seeing Esme walk about the house with nothing on her feet). Time for a cup of tea and a ciggie. Time to relax and practise banishing Darius from her thoughts. She's getting better at it but it's harder when she's tired.

She is weary. Bad dreams about Steve disturb her sleep. She sees him when he comes to collect Dani. He's looking increasingly gaunt and getting shaky. Before Christmas, he had seemed to recover. Had found a new girlfriend. Or a girl who was a friend. More important than a girlfriend Esme thinks. What has happened to Sandra? Esme had held out high hopes when she first heard about the new friend, but now Steve looks haunted and there is a growing emptiness in his face. The emptiness is the worst thing.

When she goes to sleep, Esme dreams that she sees a bundle sticking out from underneath the bed. Gets up and pulls it out. It's a soft, flaky package of newspapers. Falling apart. Not very clean. She can't bear to touch it but she needs to see what's inside, so she gets the long-handled brush from next to the wardrobe (there is a real one next to the real wardrobe). Turns it around and gently pokes one end of the package with the end of the pole. Newspapers fall off and she sees a foot. No shoe. A foot in a green sock with a white stripe around the ankle. She knows the sock. It's Steve's. A present but he always complained about the white stripe. Preferred his socks to be plain. It's a dead foot and Esme uses the brush handle to push the bundle back under the bed. Out of sight. From the corner of her eye, she can still see it as she settles back in the bed.

Each time she wakes up covered in sweat remembering every detail. Gathers her courage and leans over the side to look under the bed. Nothing there. Gets out of bed and goes to the brush which is propped in its usual place next to the wardrobe. Inspects the end of the handle to see if there are any pieces of newspaper sticking to it. Looks to see if any have dropped on the floor. Nothing. Stupid. It was only a dream.

Then there is another one. Another dream. Bright sunshine this time and Esme is getting the washing out of the washing machine. The sunshine doesn't lift her spirits because she knows that she's killed somebody and has hidden the body. The problem is that she can't remember where she's hidden it. It takes ages to get the wet clothes out of the machine because they're all tangled up but eventually, she manages it and lifts the cane wash-basket which is now heavy with wet clothes to carry it outside. The basket is wearing out she thinks. Some of the canes are broken and one of the pillowcases is catching on a broken piece that is sticking out.

The sunshine is glorious as she steps outside and she manoeuvres her way around the Honda. But the line isn't empty. Hanging at the street end next to the gate, there is a body pegged up by the shoulders, head hanging forwards towards the path. It's half wrapped in newspapers and when she looks down, she sees that a foot has fallen off on to the path. The foot is still wearing the green sock with the white stripe but the stripe has a dirty mark on it. Looks like grease or oil from the bike.

The dreams are proliferating. At first, there was only one, but now the dreams have different endings. She has killed somebody and hidden the body but the body won't stay hidden. That part is always the same, but now the corpse turns up all over the house and sometimes outside. Always wrapped in newspaper but she never knows where she will see it next.

Esme wakes with a jolt and realises that she's fallen asleep in front of the fire. She goes upstairs to the bathroom to wash her face and wake up. She smells the faint scent from the Pears soap and starts to feel better but her legs feel shaky. A cup of coffee will help. Ess sits at the table and stares out of the window trying to pull her mind away from Steve. Suzi says she shouldn't worry. Steve will soon be fine. It takes time, she says. Esme hardly sees him now. He picks Dani up from school on Friday afternoons and brings her back on Saturday evening. Ess relies on reports from Dani and her daughter no longer says much, but still the dreams come.

'How's Steve?' Ess asks her when she gets back. Dani used to tell her in detail, but it always ended with desperate pleas to get him back which would then turn into arguments, door slammings, stormings off. Just lately, Dani's face has turned stony and she hardly replies.

'Ask him yourself why don't you.' Not a question. All one word.

Ess goes into the kitchen to start the food and then returns to sit at the table. Once more she sinks into a pool of dismal thoughts but the pan boils over and she goes to turn the gas down. She's cooking potatoes in their jackets to go with fish fingers and peas. It will be late when they eat tonight. Dani ought to be full already from the sandwiches Ess left for her but Dani is never full. She'll be able to eat a dinner on top of anything she's eaten earlier.

It's only eight o'clock so Ess decides to leave the dinner for a while. She's not going to fetch Dani until 9.30. She turns off the gas and writes a note. Gone to see Suzi. Come and get me. Mum x. The note shouldn't be necessary because Dani is not supposed to come back from Mandy's by herself. But just in case.

'Hi Ess, you don't usually come round on a Thursday,' Suzi says. 'Dani at Mandy's?' Esme nods and goes to stretch out on the sofa (not lumpy and uncomfortable like theirs). She watches as Suzi fetches cake as well as coffee. Smells good.

'I shan't want any dinner if I eat that.' It's homemade fruitcake, dark, rich and moist.

'You don't want any then?'

'What do you think?'

'How do you find the time?'

'I like baking. There's always time for the things you like.'

'What am I going to do about Dani?' Esme says without preamble. Suzi says nothing and the question hangs in the air. 'Dani says that Steve's getting more and more depressed, but she hardly tells me anything these days. She barely speaks to me.'

'She hasn't forgiven you for throwing him out,' Suzi says as she gets up to rinse her hands. 'And she blames you for his suicide attempt.'

'I blame myself,' Esme says

'Well, you shouldn't,' Suzi picks up her pack of cigarettes and offers one to Ess who shakes her head and reaches for the tobacco tin.

'Why not?' Esme asks feeling surprised. 'If I hadn't thrown him out, he wouldn't have tried to kill himself.'

'Of course, he would,' Suzi replies.

'How do you work that out?'

'Steve was obviously unbalanced in the first place. Nothing to do with you.' Suzi pauses, pushes away her plate and lights up. 'Would you have tried to kill yourself if Steve had left you?'

'No, of course not,' Esme says, 'but it's different. I'm not in love with him.' She pauses. 'And I've got Dani to look after.'

'And if you were in love with him?' Suzi persists.

'Don't suppose so,' Esme replies. 'But it's still true that he did it because I didn't want him anymore.'

'If this hadn't happened, it would have been something else,' Suzi says. 'There comes a time in all our lives when we're miserable. When we hit rock bottom.' She draws on the cigarette, and Esme breathes in the familiar aroma of the Gauloise. Acrid. Comforting. Much stronger than the smell of the Golden Virginia that she smokes in her roll-ups. 'But we don't all attempt suicide,' Suzi finishes. Esme considers what Suzi has said. It isn't the first time they have talked about Esme's guilt over Steve's accident, but this time Suzi's words start to sink in. Esme can't have listened before. Funny how you can listen but not hear.

'Perhaps you're right,' she concedes. 'But that still doesn't help me know what to do about Dani.'

'There's nothing you can do,' Suzi says. 'She's nearly fourteen. It's an awkward age. Give her time.'

After that, they talk about Pete for a while, but there is nothing new. Esme daren't mention anything to do with baby news. She thanks Suzi for the cake and looks at her watch.

'I'm picking her up at half nine,' Esme says and hastily puts on her shoes and jacket. Hurries off to Mandy's. But Dani has already left. Esme smiles at Marsha while cursing under her breath and sets off back home. When Ess walks in, she finds her daughter lying on the sofa watching tv.

'Why didn't you wait for me to come and pick you up?' Esme says as soon as she's through the door. 'You promised.' But Dani just shrugs and carries on watching tv. 'And why didn't you fetch me from Suzi's?' Still no answer. 'It's not safe, Dani. The Ripper is still out there looking for young girls.'

'Not usually young girls,' Dani mutters while continuing to watch tv.

'How was school today?' Esme asks but her daughter doesn't reply so Esme gives up and goes into the kitchen to finish getting the dinner ready.

23

Esme lies in bed. It was a long day but good to see Suzi. Has tried to read herself to sleep, but it doesn't seem to work these days. Sleep won't come. Her thoughts start to wander. School? Not too bad. Her pupils are doing well on the whole and she's getting fond of them. Steve? Well, she's spent all evening worrying about Steve but she has to admit that she feels slightly better after talking to Suzi. Dani? Oh, Dani. No change there. Things between them are as bad as ever. Is Suzi right that there's nothing she can do? And finally, despite all resolutions to the contrary, her thoughts reach the place where they go no matter how hard she tries to stop them. To Darius. The bastard. The shit. How can he be such a shit?

Ess didn't discuss Darius with Suzi. Not this time. Because she knows exactly what Suzi would say. Forget him. And she will. That's what she has to do, but Darius won't disappear from her mind. She can't get him out. If they had argued. If the dinner had gone badly. If Darius had provided some explanation for his behaviour so she could understand why he had stayed away and why he would stay away again. If, if, if. But he hadn't. So that's it. It's over.

The mere thought of him makes her clench her fists. He owes her an explanation. She will write him one last letter and tell him what she thinks of him. Tell him that he owes her an apology but that she doesn't expect to get one. One last letter to put him in his place. To – finally - lay the whole thing to rest.

Having made the decision, she can't wait. She gets out of bed and pulls on her dressing gown. It's freezing. Fetches her writing pad. It's an A4 pad, lined, used for school, not intended for writing letters but it will do. She sits up in bed and starts to write but can't get comfortable. She gets up and goes to sit at the small desk she uses when she works in the bedroom. It's her childhood desk brought up from Summer Lane. The wooden top slopes. It had been specially made for her out of a music stand the choirmaster used at Chapel. It's nice for writing on, although she rarely uses it because it's warmer downstairs. And for the school work, she needs more space. For letter-writing the desk is perfect. Here we go again, she thinks, but this time her note will not be an entreaty. Esme is angry. She writes as fast as she can, doesn't read it through, puts it in an envelope and seals it. Goes back to bed.

She thinks about what she's written. It is the final paragraph that bothers her. Is that really how she wants it to end? In anger with no possibility of friendship? No, she thinks. She'll soften it slightly. Darius has worked a miracle with Dani's writing. Maybe they can still be friends. She switches on the light, gets up, rips open the envelope and writes out the letter again. What a waste of an envelope. Esme takes another one out of the pack, addresses and seals it yet again. Her stamp box is nearly empty. Just two second-class stamps. Second class will have to do. She will post it tomorrow. Sorted.

Esme gets back into bed but as soon as she lies back on the pillow with the light out, waiting once more for sleep, she knows that she will have to change it back. Will have to put back the part about no ongoing relationship of any kind. No softening. This is the end of the road, Darius. It's over.

***

On Friday evening, Joe rings. Esme has just got home from school with the prospect of a bleak weekend stretching before her. Dani is with Steve.

'Hi Esme, happy New Year,' Joe's cheerful voice rings in her ear.

'It's a bit late for that,' she replies, 'it's already the end of January. But OK, happy New Year.'

'I called because there's a letter for Darius. Is it from you?'

'Yes,' Esme says and waits. Second-class post is picking up. She only posted it yesterday.

'I just wanted to tell you that he's not back yet. He had to go to London for some sort of Embassy do. I could ring him if it's urgent, but he won't be back until the middle of next week.'

'No,' Esme replies. 'Not urgent.'

'Oh good, I thought it might be something to do with Dani. I'm sure it's Wednesday they're due back but I can check for you if you like? Gerry will know.'

'They?' Esme asks.

'Yes,' Joe said. 'He's coming back with Helen. She's going to travel back with him so she can have a long weekend back home before she gets properly stuck in.' Joe doesn't seem to notice Esme's sudden silence and he carries on talking. 'She's absolutely broke now. After the PNG trip, you know, and she wasn't going to have come back at all this term. But Darius persuaded her. Said he'd lend her the money. Helen says she'll pay him back.' Joe laughs. 'He'll be lucky! My baby sister is so deep in debt that it will be years before she manages to pay anybody back. She owes Gerry for the PNG trip and she owes Mummy for paying her accommodation fees for this term. And I'm sure that's not all. Who knows who else she's done a little begging and borrowing from.'

Joe rattles on while Esme tries to compose herself. She's relieved that this conversation is happening on the phone. 'Helen says she's going to get a job in the holidays but I don't believe it. She's always promising to get a job but she doesn't do it. In the end, she puts the studying first and Mummy encourages her.' Joe is still talking. 'Gerry and Mummy will grow old waiting for their money and Darius will be the same. They won't get their money. At least not for a long time.' Joe laughs again. 'Not for years.'

'So how are things with you?' Esme rushes in, having had time to recover herself a little and saying whatever comes into her head in an attempt to disguise her agitation. And why should she be feeling agitated when she's just written a letter to Darius telling him there can be no further relationship between them? She is angry with herself. 'How are you getting on? How's your course?'

'Fine, fine,' he replies. 'But why don't I come round later on and take you out tonight. We can catch up. We could make a night of it. I could come round early and we could have some fish and chips?' He hesitates slightly. 'Or are you feeling sick again?'

'No,' she replies. 'Not sick, but I'm not sure.' Esme feels flustered, furiously trying to gather her thoughts together, then, 'yes, why not.' She pulls herself together. Much nicer to go to the pub with Joe than to sit here alone. 'I've only just got in, Joe. Give me an hour or so and come about eight. We can fetch fish and chips and bring them back here. After we've eaten, we can go to the pub.'

'Great,' Joe says, 'I'll call for you at eight.'

'OK. See you later.'

24

How stupid was that! Agreeing to go out with Joe when she's exhausted. Esme doesn't want to go anywhere. She is worn out. Weary in bone and brain. Can't think straight. Despite everything, her mind can't accept the news that Darius is with Helen. Despite the fact that she has come to the same conclusion several times before and despite the fact that she has already made a decision that she would never consider dating him again, she can't believe it. It can't be true but it is. Time to move on she tells herself. It's time to move on.

She runs a bath and soaks trying to put Darius out of her mind. The anger against him is gone. She's feeling sad and empty. Stupid. Get a grip she tells herself. He's just a pathetic rat. To feel better she needs her anger but she's tired. Instead, her thoughts turn to Steve and Dani and she wonders what they are doing. Dani no longer tells her anything when she gets back. Oh for the time when Dani would chatter endlessly, pouring out all her thoughts. The water gets cold as she lies thinking. Esme turns on the hot tap again. That's better, but it's time to get out and get ready. She can't shake the weariness and knows that she should have said no. She would rather go to bed.

Joe is nice. She likes him but she isn't attracted to him. Well, only very slightly. She's watched women react to him and she has to agree that he's good looking, interesting and intelligent. Sexy, too. But he seems young. Not in years. She's sure that he's about the same age as she is. Must remember to ask him. But he feels young in other ways. She thinks his life has been sheltered. He's still living at home, isn't he? In any case, nothing can compare with the experience of bringing up a child. It ages you someone said and she agrees. Ess hopes that she hasn't sent the wrong message to Joe. She doesn't want to get into any more complicated messes. Best to keep clear of romantic relationships. Perhaps she should tell him that she lied before. That there is someone else.

Joe arrives at five past eight and apologises for being late. It's fine, she tells him, and they set off together to the Chinese chippy. Esme notices that he orders sweet and sour pork which she personally finds sickly and unpleasant. What does she want he asks? Esme decides on chicken fried rice and then argues with him because he insists on paying for everything. He's the one who invited her out he says, so this time she has to let him pay. Esme resolves once again to put their relationship on a clearer footing so that Joe understands that it's friendship and nothing more. That should take care of the arguments about who is paying for what. But he *is* tall and good looking. Yes, and sexy...

After ordering, they sit down on the long bench that runs down one side of the big bare space in the middle of the room. There are several chairs on the opposite side where a lone woman is sitting, obviously waiting for her order. She looks impatient. Every so often she glances over at them but doesn't smile. Looks bad-tempered and miserable. As though a smile might crack her face. Probably had a bad day Esme thinks trying to be charitable. Apart from the three of them, the place is empty. Perhaps it gets busy later on.

She and Joe sit in silence. It's somehow impossible to talk to each other with the woman listening. And whispering would be even odder. Esme wonders if it would be easier to talk in here if she and Joe knew each other better but thinks not. If they talk, the woman will hear and it will feel as though they are saying things they want her to hear. Impossible to talk normally but at bus stops, it doesn't feel rude to talk to the person you're with and exclude everyone else. Is that because it's outside? The time stretches. No food appears and the silence in the room begins to feel uncomfortable.

Joe looks at his watch.

'How long have we been here?' Esme asks him.

'About ten minutes,' he whispers back and grins. It's cheering. Joe's grin.

'I've been here for nearly twenty,' the woman opposite joins in. 'I'm not coming here again. Bloody Chinks.' Esme squirms in embarrassment and looks away. Is it worth starting an argument? Joe looks uncomfortable and as Ess is deciding what she should say, someone appears from the kitchen, comes to the counter and smiles at all three of them, sweeping round the room.

'Not long,' he says. 'Nearly ready.' It sounds like 'nearly leddy'. The 'r' sound must be difficult for Chinese people to pronounce. Esme wonders how difficult it would be to learn to speak Chinese. Cantonese, for instance, that is spoken in Hong Kong. She knows that it's a tonal language. It matters whether your voice rises or falls on a word. Changes the meaning.

While she's musing about tonal languages, another customer comes in. An old man who looks even less friendly than the woman. He's wearing a dilapidated leather jacket with studs and dirty jeans that are falling down. Not suitable clothes for an old man Esme thinks, but who cares. It's his face that is really off-putting. Looks as though he's ready to punch anyone who looks at him. And he looks as though he might be able to do it despite his age. He glances across at them and scowls then stumbles slightly as he walks to the counter. He's drunk. He reaches the bar and hangs on to it while ordering fish and chips which are served immediately. He turns to the woman sitting opposite and nods towards Joe and Esme.

'Disgusting,' he says loudly. 'Shouldn't be allowed,' and the woman nods her agreement. 'Disgusting,' he mutters again as he pays, picks up the package containing his food and heads for the door. He is about to go out but changes his mind. Stops, turns around and stares at Joe and Esme. Then he moves closer, addressing Joe directly. 'Go back to where you came from,' he says. 'Bloody darkie,' Esme watches transfixed and thinks he is going to spit, but he doesn't. 'And leave our girls alone,' he splutters as he heads back towards the street. Esme watches as though hypnotised. When the man gets to the door, he pulls it open, and stands there unsteadily, hanging on to the doorframe.

'And you,' he shouts at Esme. 'Should be ashamed of yourself, you cheap bitch.'

Esme stands up and is about to go after him, but Joe shakes his head and catches her arm. 'Leave him be,' he says. 'He's not worth it.' He takes a deep breath. 'Just an ignorant old man.' Ess turns and looks at Joe. 'Let him go,' Joe repeats." By this time, the man has left so she sinks back onto the chair. The woman opposite stares and says nothing. And the man who is serving is equally silent but has managed to smile throughout the exchange. Esme resolves never to come here again.

As they walk back with their packages of food, Joe seems strangely unbothered by the whole affair, but Esme feels shaky and angry with herself. How could she have sat there and not said anything? First, there was the woman spewing out racist remarks about the Chinese. And then it was their turn to be sworn at. They had said nothing. And what about the owner of the place? The man behind the counter? Why didn't he tell the man to shut up? Why didn't he ban the man from the shop? Refuse to serve the woman? He had stood and smiled throughout. Joe had sat, his face impassive and had said nothing. As for herself... shame floods her brain. Why didn't she say anything? Esme looks up at Joe as they turn into Potter Terrace. She knows they won't talk about it. Without a word, Joe has closed off the incident and put it out of bounds.

After the food, they decide to go to the *Shoulder of Mutton*, the same pub they visited the first time, but by the time they get there, it is getting late and the place is full. They head for the more comfortable back room where they went the first time and are lucky to find one of the cubicles unoccupied. The atmosphere is warm and comforting after the cold wind outside. You can feel the cheer of a Friday night. Esme likes the *Shoulder*.

Joe is good company and entertains her with stories of student life. He manages to sit with his arm across the seat behind her and his leg touches hers from time to time. Esme can't figure out whether this is accidental on account of his long legs, or whether he is chatting her up but she's pretty sure it's the latter. She remembers that she had decided to invent a lover to keep Joe off but she doesn't get round to it.

By the end of the evening, Joe's intentions are clear but Esme still hasn't breathed a word about the someone else. Partly because although Joe's intentions are clear, she's not sure what her own are. She's mellow with the warmth and the drink. Doesn't think she has any intentions but she might have. Joe walks her home and waits while she opens the door. Before she steps in, he kisses her. She feels herself pull back, but he holds her and she feels his strength as he slowly finishes the kiss. It feels good. Surprisingly good.

'I like you, Esme,' he says as he bids her goodnight. 'Till next time.'

'Goodnight,' she replies.

25

I arrive back home at five o'clock on Saturday. I usually come back later in the evening, but Steve has a driving job tonight so he's brought me back early.

'I'm back,' I shout as I walk in.

'Upstairs,' Esme shouts back. 'I'm upstairs. Down in a minute.'

I slump on the sofa. Am exhausted. When is Steve going to get a place of his own? I asked him again this weekend but he just shrugged. I think he's still hoping to come back here but we don't talk about it. Even I've given up hoping that Mum will change her mind, but Steve hasn't. Surely, he can't stay at Paul's forever. There's not enough room for one thing. Not for Steve and even less so when I'm there. I have to sleep on Paul's couch and it's uncomfortable and stressful. It's in the living room so I can't go to sleep until Paul and Steve are ready to go to bed and I have to get up early so that I'm not still lying there when they want to come in for their breakfast. The living room is where everybody eats. It adjoins the kitchen so there is no way out of this dilemma. Even without the added stress, I am not sleeping well. My bad dream that Grandma thought might disappear comes more regularly than ever.

'What's wrong?' Esme asks as she comes down the stairs into the living room. 'You're back early. Is everything OK?'

'Fine,' I reply. 'Steve's got a job tonight.'

'And are you all right?'

'I'm fine. Just tired.' I'm sitting on the sofa in my coat and boots. Too tired to take them off. Feel worn out.

'Take your things off,' Esme says, 'then you'll feel better.'

'No, I won't,' I say but I'm too weary to launch into an argument. My words hardly make it out of my mouth. I am barely alive.

'Didn't you sleep well?' Esme asks and I sigh. Here we go again.

'Oh, Mum, I've told you before. I have to sleep on Paul's couch in the living room and it's uncomfortable. I go to bed late and have to get up early. Why can't you let Steve come home? Then I wouldn't be tired.' I see that Mum isn't going to reply to this. She's learned better. Instead, she comes to sit down next to me. There's not enough space but she manages to put her arm around me coat and all.

'I'm sorry,' she says. 'I'm sorry, Dani.' Then adds, 'Are you all right apart from that? How's school?'

'Fine, ' I say (apart from that)!

'How's your writing?'

'Fine,' I say.

'But you've been tired all week. Not just today. What's wrong?' I hesitate. I want to tell her, but I'm not sure. I've tried before. It's as though everything is always all right and she's super loving towards me until I hit on one of her sore spots. One of these is Steve coming back. No point in mentioning it anymore. Another much older sore spot is Andreas, my German father. Once again, I can talk about him all I like but if ever a word of criticism passes my lips, she says No. Not correct. Clams up then shuts down entirely. Conversation over. According to Mum, Andreas was a paragon without compare. Impossible, I always think but Andreas is like the Queen's Speech with Grandma and Grandpa. Not up for discussion.

'My dream keeps bothering me,' I say. She knows which dream I mean. There is only one. I turn around on the sofa so I can look at her. Mum looks concerned.

'Is it still the same?'

'Yes,' I tell her. 'Always the same. It never changes' I decide to carry on. 'I talked to Grandma about it at Christmas.'

'And what did Grandma say?'

'She said it might be real.'

'Well, I'm sure it is real,' Esme says. 'I just wish it would stop coming so you could be free of it.'

'No, Mum. Grandma said it might not be just a dream.' Mum reaches for her tobacco tin and I see her hand tremble.

'What do you mean?'

'Grandma said that my dream might be a memory. It might be true that Dad tried to kill me.' There I've managed to say it. I watch Mum roll a ciggie and light it. I expect her, as usual, to deny that my dream could bear any resemblance to reality. But she doesn't.

'I've started to think the same,' she says slowly. 'The not knowing what happened bothers me like it bothers you.' No, it doesn't, I think to myself. How would Mum feel if she had a recurring dream about her father trying to kill her? A dream that wouldn't go away. She has no idea what it's like to have a dream that tortures her. But I wonder why she's changed her mind.

'You always said it was just a dream.'

'Yes, because that's what I believed.' She draws on the cigarette and I watch the end glow red. 'But maybe it's what I wanted to believe.'

'That's what Grandma said,' I tell her. 'Grandma said that you couldn't bear to think that Andreas had done anything bad.'

'Yes,' she says. 'That's right. But there was a personal reason why I couldn't bear it.'

'Yes, I know,' I tell her. 'You'd had a row with Dad and he had rushed off to get me. He was going to teach you a lesson.'

'It was more than a row,' Mum says, and I wait. 'He found me in bed with another man. He couldn't bear it.'

'Who was it?' I ask, but she shakes her head.

'That's not important,' she says, 'but for a long time, I thought that it was me who had killed him. It was me who drove your father to his death.'

I try not to react. Don't know how to react. Don't know what I feel. She's never said any of this before.

'If it hadn't been for me,' Mum goes on, 'the accident on the motorway would never have happened.' She stops for a minute - she's finding this hard. 'And whatever happened between you and your Dad that upset you so much. That would never have happened.'

She looks at me but I say nothing. I get up.

'Are you going somewhere?' she asks.

'I'm going to make a drink,' I say. 'Do you want some coffee?' She nods.

In the kitchen, I notice that my hand has started to shake. I'm trying to take it in. Did Grandma know what

Mum has just told me? I'm sure she did, but it was Mum who had to say it. It's taken her nearly twelve years.

I put the kettle on, get the mugs and spoon the coffee in.

'What are we having for dinner?' I ask her.

'Fish and chips,' she replies.

***

'It's nearly the end of February and I'm still trapped. I need to get away.'

Once again, I'm sitting with Mandy in her attic bedroom. I like being with Mandy. Things don't seem as bad when I'm with her. She makes even the most awful things seem OK. Like Grandma, I suppose, although in a different way. And we can have a laugh. It's like that with Jaffa, too. Only even better I think as I feel a rush of pleasure at the thought of seeing him tomorrow.

'Well, you're thirteen' Mandy says. 'People don't leave home at the age of thirteen.'

'I'm almost fourteen,' I reply. 'In some countries, girls get married at twelve.'

'And they're trapped even more than we are,' Mandy replies. 'In that type of country, you are owned by your husband.'

'I'll never be owned,' I tell her, 'but I can't wait until I'm seventeen.'

'Why seventeen?' Mandy asks.

'Because that's the age you can legally leave home. They can't bring you back once you're seventeen.'

'I don't think so,' Mandy says. 'I think you have to be older than that. Eighteen, I think. Or twenty-one.'

'No,' I tell her. 'It's seventeen. I went to the library to look it up.' I open my bag, take out two packets of crisps and toss one to Mandy. 'I could do it before then and could probably manage not to get caught, but I'd need money. That's the biggest problem.'

'Well, you've got the bike to sell,' Mandy reminds me.

'What do you mean?' I ask. 'Are you trying to get rid of me?'

''Course not, but you just said you wanted to go. I might want to come with you.'

'You wouldn't,' I say. 'You need to stay here so you can keep an eye on your mum.' Mandy looks at me with a mouth full of crisps. She eats crisps faster than any human being on earth. I've told her she ought to apply to get put into the Guinness Book of Records. She nods and manages to speak with her mouth still full.

'You're right,' she says. 'And I bet you wouldn't really want to go either.'

'I might,' I say. 'But the original problem still stands. I haven't got any money. And I can't sell the bike. It's not finished and it wouldn't bring in enough money.' I hold the packet of crisps in my hand but don't start eating. 'In any case, I would need an income and I can't make an income from building bikes.'

'Why not?'

'It's too slow. Look how long it takes me to build just one.' Mandy nods. 'And how much would I be able to sell it for?'

'Don't know.'

'No more than £30. That's what Howard said when I asked him.'

'He might be wrong.'

'Yes, he might be, but he knows a lot about bikes.'

'I don't want you to run away,' Mandy says. 'I would miss you.' I grin. That's what I wanted to hear.

'Thanks,' I say. 'I'd miss you, too.' I start to eat. 'And I don't think that I can. As I said, I'd need money to live on. Where would I keep getting money from if I was too young to work.' I pause and think again. Mandy doesn't answer because it isn't really a question. 'But it would be good to save up some money,' I say. 'In case I did need to leave in a hurry. Or in case Steve needed some.'

'What about your mum?' Mandy asks. 'She might need some.'

'It's Mum that I would need to get away from,' I tell her. 'I'd get money for her if she did need some, but she's got a job so it's unlikely that she'd need help from me. She gets lots of money.'

'I like your mum,' Mandy says

'You don't know her,' I reply but I'm only joking and Mandy knows that. I do love my mum. More than anyone in the world actually. I'd die for my mum. But she'll never know because I shall never tell her. She thinks it's Grandma who I love best but it's not. It's her. I start talking to Mandy again. 'You're right. Running away is not a good plan. It's not just Mum who I'd miss. If I ran away, I wouldn't be able to see Steve. Or Grandma. Or you,' I add after quite a long pause. 'It's not a good idea. But it was worth talking it through.'

'Oh good,' Mandy says. 'I'm glad you've come to your senses.' I glance up from the crisps but she's laughing. She almost sounded like Mum for a minute.

'Well, I haven't absolutely decided,' I say. 'You never know what you might need to do in the future. Best to be ready.'

'Like the girl guides,' Mandy says. 'Or is it the scouts? Be prepared.' I shrug.

'I still wish I could get some money.'

'How?'

'I could steal some,' I say and laugh.

'Stealing is wrong,' Mandy says. She doesn't believe that I would steal. And normally, I wouldn't. Not unless I needed it urgently and there was no other way to get it. But then I might. I know that for me stealing is a possibility. Because for me everything is a possibility. I might do anything in the world. Given the right circumstances. It would depend.

26

I wake up on Sundays feeling joyful. It's because of Jaffa but nobody knows. I see Mum looking at me sometimes when I start to sing. Or smile to myself and I see how pleased she looks. But she doesn't know the reason. It's not far to the park but I always take my bike so that we can go for a ride if we feel like it. Sometimes we do. Mostly we don't. Mostly we spend the whole time sitting on the bench watching nobody play tennis. Talking. Or sometimes not talking. It's never long enough. But through the week, the happiness starts to fade. I fear each time that it's too good to be true. That this might be the last time. But on the other hand, I'm hopeful. I vary, but mainly I'm an optimist.

I'm early today but I want to be early. Don't want to waste one minute of our time together because I've decided to tell Jaffa about my dream. I still don't know if I'll be able to tell him but I think I will. I pedal gently and ride into the park. I'm early, but he's earlier. Already there. Wearing his scarf. Whoopee.

'Hi Jaffa,' I throw my bike against the bush. Not so worried about it these days but still clean it quite a lot. He looks at me and grins.

'Hi, Dani girl.' He's never called me that before. I like it. Don't comment.

'How are things?' He smiles at me but he doesn't look happy. He hasn't looked happy since his Mum died.

'Not bad,' he says. 'Not too bad.'

'How's Granville?'

'Seems OK.'

'Is he going to school now?'

'Sometimes,' he says. 'What about you, Dani? How's your Mum? How's Steve?'

'Mum's all right. She's not happy because Darius hasn't come back, but she's OK. Sometimes she goes out with Joe!'

'And what's Joe like?' he asks. I suppose I haven't given much thought to Joe. Hardly know him.

'All right,' I reply. 'Nice enough.'

'And Steve?'

'Steve's depressed. Doesn't talk much now.'

'Did you go this week?'

'Yes, I still go and he tries to pretend that he's fine. We go to play pool with Paul. But we don't play chess. And he doesn't talk.' It's as though Steve is disappearing I try to explain and ask Jaffa what I can do, but he just shrugs. There is nothing I can do.

'And you, Dani. How are you?' I look at him and move a bit closer. 'I keep having this dream.'

'Tell me,' he says. 'What's your dream?' And then I don't say anything and neither does he.

'Will you promise never to tell?' I ask. He nods and I believe him but I still can't talk.

'Do you want to smoke?' he asks unexpectedly.

'No,' I say. 'Mum smokes and it's horrible. Grandma says it kills people.'

'Your grandma's right,' he says, 'but I still like to smoke sometimes. I smoke dope.' I am surprised. Jaffa gets a packet of tobacco out of his pocket. It looks a bit like my mother's tin. Inside there's a joint. I know what a joint is.

Everybody does. 'Do you mind if I smoke, Dani?' he asks. I shake my head and he lights the joint. Inhales. Offers it to me but I shake my head. 'Do you want to tell me about your dream?' he asks.

'Yes,' I say, 'but I can't.' He nods, smokes and then he starts to talk.

'I've done some more pictures,' he tells me. 'One good one.'

'What of?' I ask.

'My mother,' he says. 'When she was dead. I sat with her when she was dead and I drew her.' He looks at me to see what I'm going to say but I don't say anything. 'I want to show you, Dani,' he says. 'It's my mum, but it isn't her. My mum's gone, Dani, but it's my mum.' I'm not sure what he means.

'Can I see?' I ask.

'I'll bring it next time,' he says. And I start feeling lighter. All we've talked about is death. His mother. And my dream (although he doesn't know that my dream is about death) and I didn't manage to talk about it anyway. But I will next time and I'm starting to feel better. We start talking about Johnny Pike in class last week and suddenly we can't stop laughing. After that, everything we say makes us laugh but he looks at his watch.

'I've got to go,' he tells me.

'Fifteen love,' I say as he gets on his bike and he rides off laughing.

'Fifteen all,' he shouts back.

***

I go home to have my dinner and do my homework. Yes, I can do it these days and sometimes I even enjoy it!

'Hello,' Mum says as I come up from the cellar after putting my bike away. 'You look cheerful.'

'I'm looking forward to an evening of homework,' I tell her and start to laugh.

'Are you all right?' she asks. 'Have you been taking something? Drinking?' I shake my head and giggle again. I didn't have any of the smoke.

'I'm hungry,' I tell her. 'What's for dinner? Do you want some help?'

'Are you sure you're all right?' she asks again. 'Has something happened?' I shake my head again and she gives up. 'It's cheesy pasta,' she says. 'You can come and chop the onions.' Well, I think, serves me right. I did ask. But I don't really mind because I'm good at chopping onions and they don't make my eyes water because I know how to hold my hands under the cold tap. Grandma taught me that and it works. I love cheesy pasta.

Later on, it only takes me three-quarters of an hour to do my homework assignments. Two of them. I can type quite fast now. After that, I get on to my diary and start writing. I need to get my thoughts straight.

Sunday 25th February 1979

I wanted to tell Jaffa about my dream but I couldn't get the words out. I'll try again next time.

Both Grandma and now Mum think that my dream might be a memory. They think Dad might really have tried to kill me so now I keep thinking that I might have a dad who was a murderer. Or nearly a murderer. But

Mum is a normal, loving human being. How could Mum have married a man who could become a murderer? But if it did happen, I've got 2 big qs.

Q1 Why did Dad try to kill me?

Q2 Was it because Dad was angry with Mum and I reminded him of her? That would make the bit where he said he loved me more understandable. Or would it? He definitely said it was me he loved. I love you, Dani, he said. I love you, Dani. And I believed him. In the dream, I believe him. I rack my brains but try as I might, I can't make sense of it.

In the dream, I want him to come back? Why is that? He might put the pillow over my face again. If he tried to kill me, why would I want him to come back? That's what frightens me. I'm ashamed of wanting him to come back. I can't tell anybody.

It was a good day today because I saw Jaff. He called me Dani girl and I liked it but I didn't let him know. I play it cool. He was wearing my scarf and he looked gorgeous. His bounce is not back but he's missing his mum so it's understandable. He smoked today. Didn't know that he smoked dope but I don't mind. We laughed a lot about nothing. Couldn't stop. When we stood up, he was taller than I remember and he stood close. I almost decided to tune into his thoughts, but I didn't because I wanted him to kiss me. Didn't want to know why not. I willed him to kiss me, but he didn't.

Worst thing this week was yesterday. Steve is getting worse. It's as though he's fading away. I thought of asking Paul about him but I don't like Paul anymore and he doesn't like me. He doesn't like me staying there either.

Doesn't actually say anything but it's obvious. Fading away is a good description of Steve. He's got no energy. Doesn't want to go out. Doesn't want to watch tv, play chess. Doesn't want to do anything. Just sits. He's becoming a zombie. I wanted to shake him but I didn't. Doesn't seem to be anything I can do. I can only watch.

I didn't tell Mandy the details about Steve but I asked her about depression. Mandy knows everything about everything. Or seems to. Sometimes it's helpful. Mostly it's irritating. Anyhow, Mandy says that it passes. Depression passes. How do you get it to pass I asked her but she didn't know that. Not much use then.

I'm stuck with the bike building. Need Howard to come round but he hasn't been for ages. Hope he comes soon.

I'd better stop now or Mum might get suspicious about the amount of typing I'm doing. She's asked me before about my typing but I just say that I'm practising and she's pleased. I've got a spot coming on my chin. Hope it's gone soon. Don't want Jaffa seeing me with an ugly spot. He'll still like me, I'm sure but I don't like to look ugly. He said I was beautiful but I can't see any beauty in me and with a spot, all hope is gone. My hair still looks OK but it could do with another cut so I'll have to beg Mum to fork out the money for another visit to Maxine's. Time I stopped. It's addictive. Writing. Keep thinking of more things to say. Must stop. Have got to get the Devil's Blood off my nails. Pity.

27

It's Dani's birthday on Saturday and Ess has spent all week preparing for it. Grandma is coming for the weekend, but not Grandpa because he is recovering from the flu. On Sunday, Steve is coming to take Dani and Grandma out so that Dani will have two birthday celebrations. She doesn't want two, she says. Just one with everyone there. Not possible, Esme has replied. And not fair to Steve. For that remark, Dani gave her a vicious look. Esme sighs.

Since she went to the pub with Joe and he kissed her long and hard on the doorstep, he has rung several times but she has said no. To be honest, Esme is no longer sure about her feelings for Joe. When he's not there, she doesn't think about him (which is a relief), but when she's with him, she does enjoy his company. She had been sure that she only wanted friendship until that kiss. Now she's only about ninety-five percent sure.

Joe is good fun. Tall, good looking, full of good humour and often entertaining, but images of Darius still intrude. Even though Esme knows that there is no hope and that he is with Helen, she can't quite keep him out completely. She wonders what Darius thought of the letter she'd sent telling him what she thought of him. He hasn't written back, but Esme didn't expect him to. It's easier now to cut contact but she's glad she sent it. He deserved to be told. She sighs. Knows that she'll forget him eventually. It just seems to be taking a long time. Joe seems like a boy in comparison, but that's not fair. Esme hasn't given Joe a chance. She doesn't know him. She must ask him to tell her about himself and what he was doing before he came back to Leeds to do the teaching qualification.

It's mid=March and Dani's birthday morning dawns cold and windy but full of sunshine, a lovely spring day. Grandma is arriving on the eleven o'clock train and Esme sets off with her daughter up to the shopping parade to catch the bus into town. There is plenty of time and it's not far to the bus stop. Esme notices that a few boys, who are standing in a group in front of the betting shop, keep staring at Dani.

'Do you know them?' Esme asks her daughter in a low voice gesturing towards the lads, but Dani looks irritated and doesn't reply. Looks instead at her watch and says that the bus is late. They don't have to wait long and Esme watches Dani ignore the boys as they get on glancing towards her and then clattering loudly up the stairs. Dani is obviously going for the cool approach. Esme smiles to herself. She's growing up. Ess wonders if her daughter is really not interested in boys. She never mentions anyone. Too young, she thinks and feels relieved. Plenty of time for that later. They get off next to the markets and Esme looks to see if there is time to nip in and buy some of the Stilton that her father likes but decides against it. In any case, it might not travel well.

'What do you think she'll say?' Dani asks as she tries to cross over without waiting for the lights to change and nearly gets run over by a large blue van. Esme reaches to grab hold of her arm and misses.

'Dani! Are you trying to die?'

'Soz,' she replies. 'But what do you think? What do you think Grandma will say?'

'What about?' Esme asks her.

'My hair, Mum. She hasn't seen my hair.' Esme realises that she had forgotten that Grandma hadn't seen Dani's haircut.

'Don't know. It's your birthday so you're in with a chance. She'll get used to it.'

'Do *you* like it, Mum?' Dani asks while racing along the pavement pushing past mothers with pushchairs and people walking along arm-in-arm.

'Slow down, Dani. We've got plenty of time.' Esme is struggling to keep up and Boar Lane is packed with people all rushing to somewhere. Shopping, she supposes. 'Do I like what?'

'My hair,' Dani replies in exasperation. 'My hair, Mum. Do you like it?'

'Yes, I do actually. I've told you before. But you need to get it cut again, it's getting a bit long at the back.' Esme sees Dani disappearing into the distance once again. She won't have heard a word of what she just said. She catches up with her when she reaches the station. Dani is standing at the entrance, grinning.

'You're getting old,' she says, and Esme throws her a mock punch, glad that Dani's so cheerful today. It is her birthday, but you can never be sure whether or not her daughter is going to be up or down.

They have arrived in good time Esme thinks as they look for a place to wait near the ticket barriers. All the benches are full with people laden down with bags and cases, a few rucksacks and one or two hefty-looking suitcases. Since there is nowhere to sit, the two of them position themselves at the edge of the crowd. Esme prepares to wait and then remembers that she hasn't got a Saturday paper. She could read it while standing here perhaps. She asks Dani to go and get a newspaper from Smith's.

'I'll save your space,' she says. 'Go on, Dani. We've still got another five minutes.' Dani sighs, holds out her hand for the cash and disappears. It's not possible, actually, to save a space in a crowd but Dani squashes back in. The train still hasn't arrived and Esme has a go at reading the paper standing up, but it's too awkward. Big and unwieldy. Impossible to fold over so she gives up and puts it in her bag. Watches Dani moving backwards and forwards jogging from one foot to the other while waving her hands about presumably to give maximum visibility to the black nails she's so proud of.

After a few more minutes, they judge that Grandma's train will have arrived and they edge closer to the ticket barrier. Esme would have been content to stay further back but Dani pulls her forward so that they are standing as close as it's possible to get, straining their eyes for sight of Grandma in the approaching crowds. There's another long wait and Esme begins to wonder if Grandma has missed the train, but suddenly she's there, walking towards them carrying what looks like a very heavy bag. She is beginning to look old, a tall, thin, fragile lady peering through thick glasses, beginning to smile. Dressed in her Sunday best with the same blue furry hat she wears for Chapel. She walks slowly because her feet are painful. Esme has seen her mother's feet and wonders how she can manage to walk at all. Finally, Grandma is through the barrier. 'Mum,' Esme hurries towards her. 'How lovely to see you. How are you? How was the journey?'

'It was fine,' Grandma says. She puts her bag on the ground and smiles as she turns and holds out her arms to Dani, who rushes into them. 'Happy Birthday, my ducky,' she says. 'Whatever have you done to your hair?'

'Had it cut spiky,' Dani replies. 'Do you like it, Grandma?' Grandma takes a deep breath before she replies with a big smile.

'It's lovely, my duck,' she says. 'You look,' and she hesitates, searching for a suitable word, 'dramatic. Very dramatic.' Esme is relieved. She had warned her mother on the phone about Dani's hair when she first had it done. Ess knows how important it is for Dani that Grandma thinks she looks all right. Esme looks at her daughter whose face is glowing, basking in the compliment of being described as dramatic. Her mother couldn't have chosen a better word. 'How does it feel to be fourteen?' Grandma asks as she hugs Dani again.

'Good,' Dani tells her. 'I like getting older.' Grandma bends down to pick up the shopping bag, but Esme takes it from her and leads the way to the taxi rank. The bag weighs a ton.

'How on earth did you manage to carry this?' Esme asks. 'What have you got in it?'

'Nothing much,' Grandma replies, and soon they are sitting in a taxi on the way home.

'We're going to do things your way today,' Dani informs her grandmother. 'We're going to have dinner now, then tea later for my birthday celebration.'

'That's nice,' Grandma says, looking happily at Dani, and when they reach the house, as soon as she's taken her coat off, the first thing she does it to start unloading the things out of her bag which include a cooked chicken, a cake, cheese scones, shortbreads and homemade jam. No wonder it was so heavy Esme thinks.

'You shouldn't have,' she says to her mother who merely smiles.

'And now it's time for Dani's present,' Grandma says. 'Just let me sit down and catch my breath.' Esme goes into the kitchen to make a pot of tea and start the lunch. She prepared everything last night so she only has to turn on the oven and set everything going. Dani stayed at home last night so that she could be here for her birthday. They have changed her time with Steve to tomorrow. Surprisingly, her daughter was both helpful and cheerful while helping with the preparations. Had even hummed and sung some of the time. Like she used to do. What a change from her recent behaviour. Esme hardly dares to hope that things might be getting better.

While the food is cooking, Esme and Dani sit at the table watching Grandma drink her tea. They are waiting to find out what the birthday present is. Grandma and Grandpa always choose something special.

'It's something old,' Grandma says as she takes a small package out of her handbag. She turns to Dani. 'We were going to wait until you were twenty-one,' she says, 'but Grandpa thought you were old enough to have it now. We know you'll look after it.' Grandma hands the package to Dani, and Esme watches as her daughter carefully removes the ribbon, and then the pretty blue wrapping paper.

Inside, there is a black leather box with a little push button catch. Dani presses the tiny button and opens the box. It's a watch. A silver watch with an old-fashioned face. The middle of the face underneath the hands is cream but in a circle around the outside, there is a ring of delicate sky-blue dotted with sprigs of pink roses. The strap is a silver expander bracelet.

'We took it to the jewellers to get the expander adjusted,' Grandma says to Dani, 'but you'll have to try it on. It might need further adjustment. The spare bracelet links are in the little compartment in the middle. You'll probably need those when you're older.' Dani picks it up and puts it on. Her wrist looks delicate against the silver expander. Even at this time of year just after winter, Dani's arms are still full of freckles. The bracelet fits perfectly. 'Is it too tight?' Grandma asks.

'It's perfect,' Dani says, and Ess can see that her daughter loves it. Her parents had asked her some years ago if she would mind them giving the family heirloom to Dani, and she'd said of course not. The watch had once belonged to Esme's grandmother. Dani puts her arms around Grandma and hugs her hard.

'Goodness,' Grandma smiles and says what she always says. 'You'll squash the life out of me, Dani,' but Ess can see that she's pleased. Dani rushes off upstairs to have a look at herself in the mirror. Ess thinks that Dani's shiny black nails look a bit odd with the delicate watch but she can see that her daughter likes the combination.

'She's growing up,' Grandma says, and Esme realises that it's true.

After lunch, they have a gentle afternoon. There is not much left to do. Esme has been preparing food all week and the birthday tea is ready. There is far too much for Dani, Mandy, Grandma and herself. Just the four of them today because Pete and Suzi are away but Dani is planning to take birthday food to share with Steve and Paul tomorrow so it will all get eaten. Not today though. When Grandma's contributions are added, you can't get it all on the table.

They have just sat down ready to start eating when there is a knock at the door. Esme wonders who it can be. She doesn't think that Steve would gate-crash the party since he has made his own arrangements for Dani's birthday for tomorrow. Things seem to be getting a little easier with him now but he's not stable. Dani still worries about him. Pray God, it isn't John she thinks as she goes to open the door.

28

'Darius!' she says in amazement and feels herself tremble as she steps backwards and holds the door open for him (every resolution never to forgive him forgotten in an instant). 'Come in.' He looks bigger, taller, darker than she remembers.

'I hope I'm not intruding,' he says. 'I can't stay. Just wanted to wish Dani a happy birthday.'

'Darius,' Dani shouts from inside. 'Come in and meet my Grandma.' She jumps up and rushes to the door to greet him. 'And my friend, Mandy.'

'Hello,' Darius says and puts down the enormous bag (more like a sack) that he is carrying before he goes to shake hands around the table. 'Pleased to meet you,' he says then turns to Grandma. 'I'm delighted to meet you. Mrs Gardiner, isn't it?' Grandma nods and smiles. 'Your granddaughter often talked about you.'

'I'm pleased to meet you, too,' Grandma says. 'I wanted to thank you for helping Dani with her writing. She's a changed girl.'

'We're all changed, Mrs Gardiner,' Darius says. 'I learned from her, too.' (Typical Darius comment, Esme finds herself thinking and feeling pleased as she tries to stop the heat rising to her cheeks.) Dani keeps pressing Darius to sit down and eat with them, but he apologises and insists that he has to go. Says he is working. Before he leaves, he reaches into the bag and takes out an enormous box for Dani and a very small package for Esme. 'It's something I promised you long ago,' he says to Esme looking into her eyes just as he always has done. 'I'm truly sorry that it has taken so long.' Then he smiles, says goodbye and leaves.

Esme picks up her package and slips upstairs with it. She wants to open it later when she is alone. She is annoyed to feel herself blushing and shaking, but in the general birthday merriment, nobody seems to notice. Grandma and Mandy are urging Dani to open the box.

'We can't wait until after we've eaten,' Mandy says. 'We want to know what it is. Come on, Dani.'

Dani looks around. 'It's heavy,' she announces as she lifts the box with difficulty on to the sofa.

'Do you know what it is?' Grandma asks.

'Haven't got a clue,' Dani replies. 'I haven't seen Darius since he came to dinner with us just after Christmas. We talked about my birthday in one of the early writing sessions, but I can't believe that he remembered.' Dani manages to open the top of the box and gasps.

'What is it?' Esme asks.

'It's a typewriter!'

Esme goes to help Dani get it out of the box. It's an Olivetti. A much better model than the one her daughter has on loan. Unbelievable. There is a card inside wishing her a happy birthday and exhorting her to keep on writing forever.

'Forever,' Grandma says as Dani reads out the message. 'That's a long time, Dani.' And she laughs with pleasure to see her granddaughter looking so joyful. Esme, too, has not felt so happy in a long time. She ought to hate him. He's treated her badly, but she can't manage it. Even though he's with Helen, she was still pleased to see him. What a wimp I am, she thinks but doesn't care. He's been good to Dani, so he's worth forgiving. It's good to feel happy and she can't wait to open her own small parcel.

'What about your present?' Dani asks, remembering that her mother has also received a package.

'I took it upstairs out of the way,' Esme replies. 'It's just a book he promised to lend me a long time ago.'

Esme's ad lib response to Dani turns out to be correct. When she's finally alone at the end of the day, she opens the package and finds a book of poetry, Darius's first published volume. What a marvellous present, she thinks as she picks up the little book. He couldn't have given her anything nicer. As she flips through the pages something falls out. She bends down and picks it up off the carpet. It's a letter. She wonders if it's a reply to the letter she sent telling him what she thought of him. Esme hardly dares to open it.

March 15th 1979

Dear Esme

I hope you'll forgive me. I did receive the letters you wrote. All of them. But I hesitated. We were together twice. Once in the park and it was a time I shall always remember. Onee at your house for dinner with you and Dani. Oh, Esme, I was happy to be with you. But I hesitated again.

I hesitated because I knew that if we got together, it would be serious. I could manage a casual relationship with most women, but not with you. And there were problems. There still are problems.

191

First of all, I come from Papua New Guinea and I shall return to my country in September. If we have a serious relationship, I would want you to come back with me, but I have to tell you that although my family would welcome you as a visitor, they would not be able to accept you as one of us. You are white and not of my people. My country is very different from England. It would be difficult both for me and for you.

And then there is Dani. We like each other, but at the last two writing sessions, she begged me to persuade you to go back to Steve. She misses him. These reasons should have been enough to keep me safe from you. But I can't get you out of my mind.

Will you meet me next Saturday where we met before? Same time? Same place? I'll be there but will understand if you decide not to come.

Darius

On the night of Dani's birthday, Esme lies on the mattress on the floor of Steve's old workroom. Her mother is in Esme's bedroom on the floor below and her daughter is asleep in the bedroom next door. She will remember this day. Once again, Esme can't sleep but this time it's because she is happy. She keeps switching on the light to read the letter again.

He doesn't mention Helen. She reads the letter again to double-check. No, there is no mention of Helen. Perhaps he is not with her. She will find out next week, but she dares to hope. As she scrutinises the letter one more time, she almost laughs out loud. I'll wear it out if I keep on reading it like this. I'm a fool, she thinks, and I know I'm a fool. But how do I stop?

Eventually, Esme falls asleep, and the week passes slowly. She is in a state of excitement that she can neither subdue nor contain. She can't wait for the weekend. Can't believe that she will see Darius again. Esme wonders constantly about Helen. Surely, it must have been some kind of misunderstanding. She will ask him on Saturday. Be careful, she tells herself and don't hope for anything. Don't hope. But she does.

29

It's going to be a good weekend because I'm going with Steve to Summer Lane. It was arranged last Sunday when Grandma came to Leeds for my birthday. Hallelujah. That's what Aunty Beattie used to say all the time and Grandpa used to laugh, but it's catching. I use it myself. Hallelujah. I won't have to see Paul and sleep on his horrible sofa. Hallelujah. And I will be able to see Grandma and Grandpa even though it won't be for long. Steve is taking me back first thing Sunday morning but that's good because I'll be able to see Jaffa. Another hallelujah.

Steve picks me up from school so that we can go down on Friday night. He seems happier than usual but doesn't say much on the way down. It feels like polite chat. It never used to feel like this but at least I'm glad that he seems happier. Less depressed.

'How was school?' Steve asks.

'Good,' I reply.

'How's Mrs Richards?'

'That was last year, Steve,' I remind him. 'It's Miss Smith now.'

'Oh yes,' he says. 'Of course, it is.' And he asks me to choose a tape so I choose the usual. A Jimi Hendrix but change my mind and look for something else. Can't see anything good in his collection so I go back to the Jimi Hendrix and we listen to swooping guitar solos the rest of the way.

'Hello, my ducky,' Grandpa says when I walk in. 'Happy Birthday.'

'Thanks, Grandpa,' I say. I know that he wanted to come with Grandma last week, but she said that he wasn't well enough. He doesn't look too bad. 'How are you?'

'Not bad,' he says. 'Fair to middling.' He turns away to cough and I think that he's never going to stop, but he does. Turns back to look at me. 'Getting better,' he says.

'Do you like my hair, Grandpa?' I ask him. I think we'd better get it out of the way right at the beginning. I haven't sat down yet and Steve's still unloading the car.

'Hmmm,' he says and then smiles at me. 'Not too bad,' and I heave a sigh of relief. Grandma must have warned him. It's even shorter now because Mum took me to Maxine's this week. It looks good. My hair looks good. My new watch looks good, and I've brought it with me so Grandpa can see what the watch looks like on my arm. I'm not going to wear it for school in case it gets damaged, but I've got it on now. I put it on in the car. Actually, it looks really good with my black nails but Mum thought that the hair would be enough for Grandpa to cope with for this weekend. One thing at a time, she said so my nails are bare like I have to have them for school.

'Look at my watch,' I say and hold out my arm so he can see. 'Thank you so much, Grandpa.'

'Let's have a look,' he says. 'Does the expander fit? We had it altered for you. Do you like it?' he asks.

'I love it,' I tell him and it's true. The watch is beautiful. And it's old. It's special. I hear the back door and see that Steve is coming through the porch. He walks in covered in red geranium petals. They're growing huge those geraniums. Grandpa says they need cutting back, but Grandma stops him. They've got a nice smell, she says and she likes the plants big and bushy. They're straggly, Grandpa says, not bushy, but he's leaving them for the time being.

'Hello, Steve,' Grandpa says. 'It's nice to see you.'

'Where's Grandma?' I ask, surprised that she hasn't appeared yet. Perhaps she's in the bathroom.

'Back in a minute,' Grandpa says. 'She's just nipped round to Mrs Sutton's to take her the paper. Thought you wouldn't be here until later.' As he speaks, I hear the sound of footsteps coming up the path. Grandma walks in and I hug her. It's good to be here.

Next morning, I wake up early. I'm upstairs in Esme's old bedroom and Steve's downstairs in the front room. I can hear Grandma and Grandpa talking in the living room speaking to Steve. They stairs door must be open. It doesn't shut properly sometimes so I can hear much better than I usually can from up here. I hear Steve say that he's going for a walk. That's a surprise. Don't remember him ever going for a walk before. He's changing. I don't want to get up yet. It's still early and it's nice and warm in bed. I turn over and stretch out, but I'm completely awake. I look at my watch. Not even eight o clock. I'm still considering whether or not to get up when I hear Grandma talking downstairs.

'She's on a path to misery,' Grandma says. Who's that? I wonder and then I hear a pouring sound. Grandma's pouring a cup of tea. After that, there's a stirring sound and I know that she's stirring the sugar into Grandpa's cup. He always has two sugars and Grandma always puts them into his cup and stirs it before she hands it to him. Grandpa didn't look too bad last night but his cough didn't sound good. He's coughing again now. It goes on and on. The 'flu must have turned into bronchitis.

'Have you stirred it?' Grandpa asks. He must have seen her stirring it but he always seems to ask. It's a habit. I expect Grandma's nodding because I can't hear her saying anything but then she speaks again.

'I wish you'd go to the doctor's, George,' and then silence before she sighs and says she might as well not waste her breath. 'You're not better,' she says. 'Look at you. You can hardly lift the cup.'

'Dunna fret,' he says. 'I'm all right,' and then he starts coughing again. When he stops, he asks her, 'What do you mean she's on a path to misery?'

'I wasn't going to say anything,' Grandma says, 'but I can't stop thinking about it.' There's another pause. Surely they don't mean me? Why would I be on a path to misery?

'I just wish I'd had time to talk to her before Steve came to pick us up on Sunday morning,' Grandma goes on.

Oh no. She's talking about Mum. I sit up in bed so I can hear better.

'I saw her at breakfast but Dani was there, and then Steve arrived. No chance to have a word with her.'

'Get a move on, Frankie,' Grandpa says. 'I've no idea what you're talking about. What's Esme doing now that's got you in such a state?'

'Well, I don't know for certain,' Grandma says and then it goes quiet again.

'Spit it out,' Grandpa says after a long gap and starts coughing again.

'Have a drink,' Grandma tells him. 'I'm going to make an appointment for you on Monday. Whether you want one or not.' Grandpa doesn't reply but I can imagine his face. And Grandma will know that Grandpa won't go to the doctor's until he decides to go. If he ever does. She's nagging at him but it won't work. I wish Grandma would carry on talking. What on earth is Mum doing? I haven't noticed anything.

'Well, I'm not completely sure,' Grandma's speaking again, 'but I know the signs. I do know my daughter. She's happy now but she doesn't know what's coming.'

'Well, go on then. Tell me what's wrong with her.' (It is Mum they're talking about and now I can hear Grandpa poking the fire.)

'It's Darius,' Grandma says. 'Esme's besotted with him. As soon as he arrived, she blushed and trembled. I couldn't believe my eyes.' (I think back to last week. I was so pleased that Darius had remembered my birthday that I didn't think about Mum. Perhaps Grandma is right. Mum has certainly been happy all week.)

Be careful, I hear her say. You'll set the house on fire if you're not careful. Aha, Grandpa must be lighting his pipe. He's got a new lighter. I saw it last night. It's a petrol lighter and the flame is huge. Grandma's right. It does look dangerous but he seems to like it. Then I hear my name.

'Dani didn't seem to notice,' Grandma goes on. 'She was so excited about her birthday. And she likes Darius. Was pleased to see him.' Another pause. (She's right. I was.) 'Dani talked to me about Darius when we were at Steve's.' (Yes, I did.) 'She said that she'd asked Darius to persuade her mother to have Steve back, but he'd told her that he couldn't. That it wasn't his business.' (Grandma had listened well. That was more or less exactly what I did say. And as I think this, I imagine Steve's voice saying that you can't say 'more or less exactly'. But more or less exactly is what I mean.)

'What did Esme say to him when he turned up?' Grandpa asks. 'Have they been seeing each other?'

'I don't think so. Dani said it was the first time she'd seen him since just after Christmas. And it was clear that Esme wasn't expecting him either.' Grandma stops again. Wish she'd hurry up and say it all. Steve might come back at any minute. 'But she was thrilled that he came. He handed her a little present, but she shot upstairs with it. Didn't show it to us at all.'

'Doesn't sound good,' Grandpa says. 'If she finds somebody else, there'll be no chance of her getting back together with Steve. What does he do? Darius?'

'He's at the university doing a master's degree of some sort,' Grandma says. 'He's the one who helped Dani with her writing. He's a writing specialist I think.'

'And where's he from?' Grandpa asks.

'Papua New Guinea.'

'Never heard of it,' Grandpa says. 'Is it in Africa?'

'No,' Grandma replies. 'Dani told me it was next to Australia somewhere. I'm sure that's what she said.'

'Let's hope it goes no further then,' Grandpa says. 'Between her and Darius. She couldn't go much further away than that.'

'And there's Dani,' Grandma says. 'She would go with them.'

I can't believe all this. I'm sure Mum hasn't been seeing Darius. He's not visited since the dinner just after Christmas. It's almost funny. They sound so serious. I nearly go downstairs so I can tell them not to worry. Then I hear Grandpa speak again.

'What about Steve?' he asks Grandma. 'How is he getting on without them?'

'Much better,' she says. 'He seems fine. He's still doing driving jobs to supplement his grant. Said the research was going well.' Hmmm, I think. He hasn't told Grandma then about suspending his studies.

'When does he finish?' Grandpa asks, but at this point, I hear the back door open. Steve's back and I'm getting up.

30

When I get downstairs, Steve's eating bacon and eggs, Grandma's sitting at the table with him drinking tea and Grandpa's in his chair by the fire. He's coughing again. Grandma's right. Grandpa does sound poorly. Grandma gets up and goes to get him some water. I've been hoping to get Grandma on her own so that I can talk to her about my dream being a memory. I want to tell her what Esme said about it but I'll have to wait. Steve's talking to them. Actually, he's talking to Grandpa. About plants! He is definitely changing. Can't ever remember Steve being interested in plants.

After breakfast, I go back upstairs to read for a bit. And to keep an ear out for what's going on downstairs so that I can go down when Grandma is on her own. From the sound of it, I might have to wait quite a while. I have a sudden urge to try Grandma's Lily of the Valley. I never used to like perfumes but I think I'm changing my mind. I like Mum's lavender. On her that is. I wouldn't want it on me. But I might like Grandma's Lily of the Valley. The bottle is there on her dressing table so I open it and have a sniff. Don't like it. It smells nice on Grandma, but I don't like the smell that's coming out of the bottle. Put the top back on and go into the back bedroom where I'm sleeping.

I haven't actually brought anything with me to read so I go to the wardrobe to see if I can find some of the old books that I left here. Grandma will have put them away and she might have put them in the wardrobe with my old toys. There's nothing in the wardrobe drawer except clothes. Nicely folded although not quite the same after I've rummaged about. I'll try inside the wardrobe at the bottom. I've put stuff in there before and it gets covered in jumpers. I dig down and find all sorts of things. Jigsaw puzzles. My old doll called Julia. And a pile of books. Hurrah. Books. I pull them out and put them on the bed. There's a box in between the books. A wooden one. Don't remember seeing that before. I open it up and see that it's full of letters. Wads of letters, some in rubber bands, others tied up with string. Some tied with ribbon. I see Esme's handwriting on some of the piles. On top, there are several loose envelopes with addresses written in a handwriting I don't know and a Basildon Bond pad that I do know. Grandma always uses it when she writes letters. It's got a lined sheet inside that you put underneath the blank page to keep your writing straight. I used to try it myself but couldn't write small enough.

I open the pad and a couple of pages fall out. Must be a letter Grandma is writing. You're not supposed to read other people's letters and for what seems like ages I stand there between the wardrobe and the bed, holding the letter and hesitating, but the pages have sort of jumped into my hand. I'm curious. Just a quick look, I decide. I won't sit down. Nobody will know.

March 22nd 1979

Dear Nellie

I was sorry to hear about Fred. You must be at your wit's end what with looking after him and worrying about Barbara. I feel the same about George. He's out there now, coughing away. Can't get him to go to the doctors. Can't get him to come in and rest. All the same, aren't they? Just thought I'd drop you a line to let you know how I got on in Leeds. Well, I felt a bit worried about leaving George, but he wanted me to go.

Dani was fourteen this birthday. How the time flies. It doesn't seem long since she didn't even reach to the top of the table. Do you remember that day when we tried to measure her and she wouldn't stand still? She hasn't changed much. Still talks a lot and rushes about everywhere. She's growing up. Looks pretty in spite of her dreadful haircut. You wouldn't recognise her, Nellie. She looks like a boy! No hair left hardly and what there is - all uneven. Don't know what Esme was thinking of but you can't tell them anything these days.

(Who's Nellie I wonder and then I remember Auntie Nellie, Grandma's friend in Swadlincote. Haven't seen her for years. I am surprised to read this. Almost shocked. Not because Grandma didn't like my hair but because she pretended to like it. I didn't think Grandma would lie to me. Didn't think that she would lie to anyone.)

But I'm not worried about Dani anymore. (Anymore?) *She seems fine. And Steve is better than he sounded on the phone. A lovely young man. I'm sure that if Esme wanted to she could still get him back. But she won't and it's Esme that I'm worried about. You won't believe it, Nellie, but she's running around with a black man!*

(I let the letter fall and sit down on the bed. Surely, this can't be Grandma writing this. Not my grandma. Darius isn't *a black man*. He's Darius. A man like any other. No, not like any other. He helped me with my writing. He's special and he's nice.)

He comes from Papua New Guinea. You won't have heard of it, but it's on the other side of the world near Australia. I went to look it up in the library and it's worse than I thought. They've got girls in grass skirts with bare breasts. I've seen pictures. And cannibals, Nellie. They've got Cannibals!

After this, there are three lines of writing that are crossed out so heavily they're impossible to read. I put down the loose pages and open the pad. I see that Grandma has started the same letter again. The date is the same.

March 22nd 1979

Dear Nellie
How are you and how's Fred? And is there any news about Barbara? I remember you all in my prayers every night.
Just wanted to let you know what happened when I went to Leeds for Dani's birthday. It was a nice day and Steve seems much better now, but I'm worried about Esme. She's fallen for a black man, Nellie, and I don't know what to do about it.
You know that I think everybody's equal in the eyes of the Lord. Equal but different. Black people are not the

same as we are, Nellie, so I'm worried. He comes from a country on the other side of the world. Papua New Guinea.

I went to the library to look it up. It's independent now but only since 1975. Before that, they were ruled by the Australians, but it's not that. They're cannibals, Nellie! Well maybe not anymore, but they were cannibals until recently. I didn't have time to read it all because I had to get the bus.

I haven't told George but whatever shall I do if Esme takes Dani and goes over there with him? And they might have children.

This is where the writing stops. Grandma hasn't finished this letter either. Hurriedly, I put the letters back in the box and push it back into the wardrobe. I cover them with jumpers. As many as I can find.

***

It's Sunday now. We've just got back and my mind is whirling. Don't know how I got through the rest of the time in Summer Lane. I tried to behave as normal and nobody seemed to notice anything odd about me. I feel as though the ground has disappeared from under me. Grandma was the foundation. If she doesn't like the thought of Darius, I think to myself, what would she think about Jaffa? It's Sunday afternoon and I'm seeing him in a few minutes time.

I get to the park and the first thing I notice is that he's not wearing my scarf. Why is that I wonder? Is it because the weather has turned warmer. Or is it because he doesn't like me anymore? That's stupid. What's wrong with me? I can't think straight because my head is full of the things Grandma has said about Esme and Darius. Her thoughts about black people. I had thought of talking about it to Steve but I couldn't. Steve is almost impossible to reach these days. It's as though he's there and not there. Appears to be present but really he's somewhere else. He's nice and he smiles at me but he's almost like a robot. Lost somewhere inside his head. Was surprised that Grandma thought that Steve seemed OK. And I can't tell Esme. It would make her hate Grandma and I can't do that.

'Hi, Jaff,' I say, flinging my bike against the bush. I had dismounted as soon as I got into the park, walking slowly, pushing it, needing extra time to calm down. Thoughts flying everywhere. I'm going up and down like a yo-yo.

'Hi,' he replies. No 'Dani girl' this week. I ask if he's all right and he shrugs his shoulders which means not really but he doesn't explain. I was going to tell him about what Grandma said about Mum and Darius but find that I can't. Instead, I start telling him about my dream. I tell him everything. Every detail. When I finish telling him, I expect him to look shocked, but he doesn't. He looks sympathetic but not shocked. Not even terribly interested. Mostly, he looks tired. Don't think I've ever seen Jaff look so weary before.

'So how can I find out?' I ask him. Jaffa shrugs again.

'Don't know, Dani. Don't suppose you can.' He doesn't seem to understand how important it is for me to find out what happened with my father.

'Don't you understand,' I stand up and go to the wire between us and the tennis court. Kick hard. It hurts but I kick again. Turn back to him. 'Jaffa. I've got to. I've got to find out,' I'm almost yelling. If I'm sad or worried, he usually makes me feel better. But not today. He doesn't say any more about my dream.

'Do you want to see the picture I told you about last week?' he asks.

'The one of your mother?' I ask. 'After she died?'

'Yes,' he says. I nod and he gets his bag from the back of his bike and takes out a large stiff folder and opens it up. I look. Say nothing. I keep looking and start to feel weird. The woman in the picture looks nothing like the other picture he showed me. This woman looks old, ugly, lifeless. Dead! She looks dead. And frightening. Like a cardboard cut-out. No, that's not a good description. The picture shows a three-dimensional image but the woman is old and lifeless. Out of shape. Distorted but limp and weary-looking. Why did Jaffa draw his mother like this? It's horrible. It makes Jaffa's mum look horrible.

'Do you like it?' he asks me, and I hesitate.

'No,' I say and he gets up, grabs his bike and rides off before I can say another word. I'm just getting my bike ready to go home when he comes back and shouts something at me before riding off again. I hear it after he's gone.

'You're like all the rest, Dani,' he says. 'We're finished.'

31

Esme rides home from work feeling fit and full of energy. It's Friday, the end of the week and the little Honda feels as though it's an extension of her body moving and turning like a bird as she rides around the Ring Road heading for home. Yes, she thinks. Like a bird. A seagull perhaps. Esme has sat for hours on Scarborough beach watching the birds wheel and turn, gliding and swooping before the wings start to flap once more. It's the good weather that makes riding so good. Esme would never have believed how much she would enjoy riding the bike. Had bought it because it was cheap, but she loves it. When the weather is good that is.

As she gets off and parks the bike on the path, she can hear the phone ringing but by the time she gets inside, it has stopped. Never mind. Whoever it was will ring back. What a change, she realises. For so long, she had been almost desperate every time she heard the phone ring. She knows what has changed. It's Darius. She is no longer waiting for Darius to ring. She'll see him tomorrow and Dani has gone with Steve to Summer Lane for the weekend. Back on Sunday. Perfect. She's just settling down with a cup of coffee when the phone rings again.

'469 452,' Esme says cheerfully.

'It's me,' her mother says. 'Wondered how you were.'

'I'm fine, Mum,' Esme says. 'Glad that it's the end of the week. How's Dad?'

'Well, he's still coughing and wheezing, but he's out in the garden every day again. Rain or shine. Tells me not to fuss.'

'That sounds like Dad,' Ess says. 'Is he there?'

'Gone to have a bath,' her mother tells her. 'You sound remarkably cheerful, Ess. Has something nice happened?'

Esme starts to feel wary. Her mother has got something to say to her. She's sure of it.

'Not particularly,' she replies. 'I'm looking forward to a quiet night in. It's been a long week. Steve and Dani should be with you in a couple of hours or so.'

'Yes, we're not expecting them yet. The motorway is always busy on a Friday. That's why I'm ringing you now. While we've got the chance to talk privately.' Here it comes she thinks. But what? A feeling of anxiety starts to rise. It's rare for her mother to ring for a private chat. Her mother gives a little cough and then another. She's feeling nervous. But what about?

'How is Dani now?' her mother asks.

'She's fine,' Esme says. 'You saw her yourself last week. What did you think?'

'Yes, she seems fine, but I wondered if she still talks about Steve? Does she still ask you to take him back?'

'From time to time,' Esme says, 'but not nearly as often as she used to do.' She pauses, sips her coffee and looks around for her tobacco tin. 'I think Dani's beginning to feel better because she's worrying about Steve less than she did. He's getting over it.' The tin is in her bag and she gets it out and wonders, as usual, how she's going to roll a cigarette and hold the receiver at the same time.

'Are you still there?' her mother asks. 'You've gone quiet.'

'Yes, still here,' Ess replies wedging the receiver between an ashtray and a vase while she opens the tin and hurriedly starts to make a ciggie.

'You're very faint,' her mother says. 'Have you moved the receiver?'

'Only for a minute,' Esme says looking for the lighter and lighting up. She picks up the receiver once more. Success. 'There. Is that better?'

'Yes, that's fine again now.' And her mother continues. 'I think Steve would still have you back, Esme. I didn't say anything to him last Sunday but from one or two things he said, I think he'd still have you back if you made a move.' Exasperation rises.

'I don't want him back, Mum. It isn't going to happen.'

'All right,' her mother says and Esme hears the placatory tone. 'Calm down, Ess, but I've been thinking. Do you remember when we talked about German people?'

'German people?' Esme asks, caught off guard. 'Do you mean years ago when I was with Andy?'

'Yes,' her mother said. 'We talked about the differences between German people and us. Food and jokes and things. You said that there were some things Andy would never understand because he was German.'

'I'm sure I never said that,' Esme says. 'I would never have said such a thing. You must be misremembering, Mum.'

'No,' her mother says. 'I'm sure I'm not. But it's true, isn't it? Different peoples have different customs.'

'I suppose so,' Esme concedes warily. Where is this conversation going?

'I was asking about Dani because I don't like to ask her directly. About how she's missing Steve, that is. How is she getting on at school?' This is safer territory, and Esme replies happily.

'She's getting on extremely well. Her marks for homework assignments have been eight and nine out of ten for the last few weeks.' Esme can't keep the pride out of her voice. 'It's thanks to Darius, you know. His work with Dani has changed her life,' Esme hesitates. 'What did you think of him?'

'He seems very nice,' Frances replies but Esme can hear a reservation under the pleasant words. 'It's wonderful the way he's helped Dani with her writing.'

'Yes,' Esme says, 'it is.' But she doesn't say any more. As though she has a sixth sense for where Frances might be heading. She hears her mother take a deep breath.

'You seem very fond of him,' she says

'Yes, I am,' Esme replies. 'I admire him.'

'Is that all?' Frances asks. Her mother has jumped deep into it now, no going back. 'I wondered if you were falling for him, Esme?' How dare she interfere like this and ask such a personal question.

'Where did you get that from?' Esme replies sharply. 'And what if I am?'

'Well, I just don't want you to get hurt,' her mother says. 'His country is a long way away and he's only here for one year you said. I expect he'll be going back.'

'Don't worry about me, Mum,' Esme tries to keep the sharp edge out of her tone. 'I know you mean it nicely, but

211

I'd rather not talk about Darius.' There is a brief pause and her mother gives the hard, dry cough that signals that she's feeling nervous.

'I've been reading about Papua New Guinea,' her mother says. 'Do you know about the country?'

'What do you mean? Do I know about the country? Know what about the country?' Esme tries to calm down but feels herself under attack.

'Well, it's very different from ours,' Frances goes on. 'And if you were to get together with Darius, there would be the possibility of children.'

'Mum!' Esme says feeling her temper beginning to rise. 'What on earth do you mean?' There is a pause at the other end. Her mother is coughing a lot now, hard little coughs. Esme can hear the anxiety in her mother's voice.

'I mean if you and Darius were to have children,' her mother manages to say.

'Well, what about it?'

'They'd be mixed-race,' her mother says. 'They wouldn't belong anywhere.'

'Oh, Mum,' Esme is appalled. 'How can you say such a thing?' She stops to search for words but can't find any. 'How can you?'

'It's because I'm worried about you.'

'Well, don't be,' Ess replies sharply. 'I think mixed-race kids are the most beautiful children in the world, and if I get the chance, I'll have as many as possible.' She can hear the silence on the end of the line. Her mother is upset. 'And I've got to go now,' Esme lies. 'Suzi's coming to have dinner with me. I need to cook.'

'Don't forget Dani,' her mother says and adds, 'Bye then.'

'Bye, Mum,' Esme says and hears the click as the receiver is replaced and the line goes dead.

Don't forget Dani. Don't forget Dani. The words echo in her mind as her thoughts boil over. How could she ever forget Dani? Esme gets up and pounds around the room. How could her mother have spoken like that? She realises that Frances must feel strongly because her mother doesn't usually interfere. Or even comment. She never has done before. Her mother's voice had trembled with the stress of what she felt that she had to say.

How depressing that she doesn't seem to like Darius. Or is it just because he's black? That's an almost unbelievable thought in connection with her mother. Throughout Esme's life, her mother and father have always insisted that all people should be treated with equal respect. So what is it that has suddenly changed? She goes into the kitchen and opens the bottle of wine she had been saving to share with Darius. Pours herself a glass and rolls a cigarette.

She is shocked and angry. Sits down and gets up again. The calm, happy feeling she had when she arrived home less than an hour ago is completely gone. She needs to talk to somebody but there's no-one she can tell. Not Dani. Not Suzi. Not Darius. She can't tell anyone because she doesn't want them to judge her mother whom she loves more than she can say.

Oh Mum, her mind wails in misery. She cannot believe that her parents, and especially her mother, would not be happy to have another grandchild. Esme had thought that her parents would be pleased if she got together with Darius (and thrilled if she had another child). Darius is an educated man with a good career. She was sure they would like him. Especially after the way he has helped Dani.

The shock waves keep bouncing around in her head making it impossible to think clearly. Esme supposes that her parents would find the possibility of her taking Dani to live at the other side of the world upsetting but she pushes that to one side as she tries to makes sense of her mother's words about mixed race children. That they don't belong anywhere. It is almost as though she were saying that mixed-race children shouldn't be born. Esme draws hard on her cigarette and forces herself to face the fact that this is exactly what her mother did mean. It is unbelievable. And unbearable.

32

The next day Esme sets off for the cafe just as she did all those months ago. It feels both long ago and very recent. As she approaches the place, she peers down the road looking to see if he's coming. Last time they had arrived together, but this time there is no Darius in sight. She feels a vague apprehension but decides that he is probably inside. Esme goes in and looks around. No. He isn't here and her heart sinks. It is already two o'clock and there is no sign of him. Was the letter a joke?

As Esme sits down and orders a coffee, she reminds herself that she is going to be careful. The coffee arrives and, like last time, it doesn't taste good. She gets a book out of her bag and begins to read. A book is a comforting thing in times of trouble. She doesn't think she can concentrate, but it still feels reassuring to have the book in front of her, propped up against her tobacco tin (which, unfortunately, keeps moving slightly so she has to keep readjustiing it). It's *The Idiot* by Dostoevsky. She suppresses a hollow chuckle when she thinks of the title. At least it's a fairly fat book. Reassuringly thick to place between herself and the vaguely threatening world of the cafe with its one or two occupants who keep glancing in her direction. The book will keep her safe, so she stares at it and readjusts its position every so often. Surely he hasn't changed his mind. Esme picks up the book and finds the bookmark she left inside. It's a bus ticket. She wedges the book open and stares harder. No meaning reaches her brain. From time to time she picks up the coffee and takes a sip.

'Esme,' she hears from behind her and she turns, breathes out. There he is. Darius is standing there, tall, substantial, a broad smile on his dark face. Light brown leather jacket. Immaculate jeans. As she remembered. Same clothes as last time except for his shirt perhaps. She doesn't recognise the blue denim shirt. A wave of something passes through her. How can she describe it? It's physical. He looks at her intently. 'I'm sorry I'm late. There was a phone call just as I was leaving.'

'It's fine,' Esme returns his smile. 'I had time to order a coffee.'

'So I see,' he replies and walks over to the counter to order a coffee for himself then comes to sit opposite her. 'I won't sit next to you,' he says. 'I want to look at you. Feast my eyes.' He laughs as though his words are half a joke, but he sits down and stares at her with something like a wicked glint in his eye. Esme blushes. Doesn't know what to say and while she is putting away her book and moving the tin, a plate of homemade apple pie arrives. Like last time.

'It's been a long time,' he says. 'Hope you still like apple pie.' Esme nods. She, too, wants to look at Darius. She thought she knew his face. She has thought of him often enough. Too often. Much too often. But he is not as she remembered him. His face is stronger, more mischievous. Darker.

'You're not as I remember,' he says surprising her by saying exactly what she was thinking about him.

'How do you remember me?'

'As a ghost. A white ghost with large black eyes,' he replies.

'Oh, that was ages ago,' she says. 'At the party,' and he nods. 'But I was wearing make-up then. I don't usually.' She wonders why he liked her more when she was painted. Esme doesn't like wearing make-up.

'I liked it,' he says. 'You were my opposite.' Then he laughs. 'Now we're both brown.'

'Yes, although I'm more blotched' she says referring to the freckles that stretch as far up her arm as is visible. 'And I'm not quite as brown as you are.' Esme holds out her arm to place it next to his. To compare. This is not easy while they are sitting opposite each other. She has to twist and their arms touch.

'Not quite,' he says, then asks, 'Did you like my poems, Esme? Any of them?'

'I liked the one about the politician arriving with the crates of beer,' she said. 'That made me laugh, but it was serious, wasn't it?' Darius nods. 'And I liked the one about the moon sliding about on the black water,' she sees that he's listening carefully. 'I seem to remember it was rocking gently but still holding its shape...' Darius laughs, pleased.

'Can you quote from all of them?'

'Not quite,' Ess grins at him.

'I'm sorry I didn't answer your letters,' he says. 'Do you understand now?'

'A little,' Esme replies, 'I partly understand but tell me more.' Darius reaches towards her and picks up her hand.

'What dainty hands you have,' he says. 'but strong'. He takes her hand in both of his, and they both stare at it. Esme's hand looks pale and tiny. 'Are you strong, Esme?'

he asks, and she nods. Gently he lets go of her and starts to speak. 'The first time I saw you,' he says and then stops, 'you were dancing. I didn't see your face until you came to sit with us.' Esme feels his eyes on her. 'You looked so pale. As though you weren't there. Like a dream and I couldn't stop looking at you.' Esme doesn't know what to say. 'And you noticed me, too.' He looks at her. 'Didn't you?'

'Yes,' she replies.

'I knew even then that I had to avoid you. That's why I didn't come to dinner with Joe.'

'Why did you have to avoid me?' Esme asks with some of the old anger and frustration at Darius's behaviour rising up in her.

'Because we were being pulled towards each other. For your sake, we needed to stay apart.'

'That's bullshit,' she says. 'What do you mean? For my sake?' Esme can hear the impatience in her voice. The months of waiting to hear from him bring back her anger but when she looks at him, it starts to subside. She tries to hold on to it. He has to see that there are two of them involved here. He can't just make decisions and present them as being for her own good and she says so.

'If we get together,' Darius goes on. 'You will have to come back with me to my country. Things are different there, Esme. It would be hard for you to fit in. But if you were with me, you would have to try. You would have to succeed.'

'I'm very adaptable,' Ess tries to smile. Darius sounds terribly serious.

'You have no idea,' he says quietly, 'about what is involved. You can't imagine. And then there's Dani.'

'Yes,' Esme agrees. 'Dani likes you, but she still loves Steve.'

'I know,' he says. 'She told me. She tried to enlist my help in getting you back together with him.' Darius stops for a minute and then grins and starts to lighten up. 'But that was a step too far. It was more than I could do.' He drains his cup. 'Shall we have another one?' he asks. 'Could you cope with a second cup?'

'I think so,' Esme says.

'I miss the coffee from home,' he says. 'It grows there. In the Highlands.'

'I know,' she says. 'I think you told me before. But you said that most people preferred instant.'

'What a good memory you've got,' he says. Suddenly Esme remembers that he took Helen back to PNG with him.

'I thought you'd got together with Helen,' she says.

'Why was that?' he asks.

'Because you took her home with you for Christmas.'

'Helen wanted to come,' he says. 'So I took her with me.'

'So there's nothing between you?' Esme asks, and she watches as Darius slowly smiles.

'Nothing serious,' he says. 'But I do like her.' He pauses again. 'I have to be free, Esme. You need to know that I have to be free.' He looks hard at her. 'Do you understand what I mean?' She nods uncertainly, but if he means what she thinks he means then she doesn't like it. 'I'm not easy, Esme. I need space. I'm an artist.' Esme tries to laugh and make a joke of it but changes her mind.

'You're not the first man who thought that being an artist gave him an excuse to behave selfishly and treat women badly,' she manages to say. She feels contemptuous and irritated by the lame excuse about being an artist that she's heard plenty of times before. Always from men. She doesn't quite know how to cope with Darius. One minute he is talking as though he wants to marry her. The next he is telling her that he has to be free. Suddenly he stands up and holds out his hand towards her.

'You're right,' he says, considering. 'I'm often selfish so I'm guilty on the first count. But I don't think that I treat women badly.' Esme looks at him and remembers his long silences and lack of contact with no explanation. But she says nothing. 'We've talked enough,' he says. 'Let's go for a walk.'

So they do. Off to the park where they went before. Esme almost skips. Darius laughs and catches her hand. For a minute, she thinks he is going to try and walk hand in hand with her and she remembers John. Wonders what has happened to him and hopes that he's back with Barbara. But no, she sees that Darius doesn't want to walk hand in hand. Instead, he leads her off the path on to the grass and pulls her back and forth in a mock jive while half laughing half singing to her at the same time. She is getting dizzy and laughs when she lands in his arms. He kisses her. Gently at first, then harder. And holds her. They become quiet after that and walk on in silence.

Esme looks at her watch. 'I have to go,' she says. 'I'm going to a concert with my friend tonight. We arranged it a long time ago.'

'And where is Dani?' he asks. 'Doesn't Steve usually bring her back on a Saturday afternoon?'

'Well remembered,' she says. 'But Dani's not back until tomorrow. Steve has taken her down to Summer Lane this weekend.'

'Come on then,' he says. 'I'll take you back. Can't have you missing the concert.' Esme hopes that he will suggest coming around later after she gets back. She will be alone in the house because Dani's away, but he doesn't suggest anything like that. And when they arrive at the house, it's like last time. He won't come in.

'Next week?' he asks. 'Same time same place?'

'Yes,' Esme replies. 'Yes, Darius. I'll be there.' And like the last time, he turns and is gone.

***

Next morning Esme wakes with her mind full of questions. How are they going to go forward from here? And if they are going to get together, how can he suggest that the next meeting should be in a week's time? A whole week. The best thing to do would be to ask him to move in. Then they would be able to get to know each other. Esme looks at the clock on the bedside cabinet. It's time she got up. It's late and Dani will be back soon. Steve told her that they would be back from Summer Lane by midday.

Downstairs Ess sits at the table drinking coffee and staring out of the window. She'll see when they arrive. Hopes that Dani has had a good weekend. Esme must have fallen into a daydream because she doesn't notice when the car finally arrives and only realises they're here when she hears the car door slam.

'Hi, Mum,' her daughter says as she comes in but there's no bounce.

'Are you all right?' Esme asks. 'How was Grandpa? Did he like your hair?' To her surprise, Dani pulls a face and mutters something unintelligible. 'Didn't he like it?' Esme persists, sure that her father had been going to say something nice to Dani about her hair. She'd already primed him.

'He said he liked it,' Dani says, 'but he didn't really.'

'I'm sorry,' Ess says. 'I'm sorry, Schatzi.' She pauses. It's a long time since she's called her daughter by the pet name from her childhood. Little treasure. 'I like your hair, you know.'

'I know you do, Mum,' Dani says and Esme watches Dani look at her wrist to check the time. 'I don't want any lunch,' she says. 'I ate at Grandma's before we left. I'm off for a bike ride? I need some fresh air.'

'Fresh air?' murmurs Esme bemused. 'All right, but be back by half five. I'll have dinner ready by then, and there's still your homework.'

'OK,' Dani says and is out of the house before Esme has time to make a proper decision about whether her daughter should go out or not. And about whether or not she should have made her stay to eat some lunch.

Esme forces herself to do some marking and lesson preparation while Dani is out but it is hard to concentrate. She keeps turning over in her mind the things that Darius has said. The contradictory things. And Dani didn't seem happy so why was that?

When her daughter comes back for her dinner, she looks grim. Dani had looked miserable when she arrived back from Summer Lane but now she looks a hundred times worse. She looks as though the world has landed on her shoulders and is too heavy to carry.

'Don't want any dinner, Mum,' she says but by this time Esme has gathered herself together.

'Oh yes, you do, Dani. What is the matter with you? I'm making macaroni cheese.'

While they are eating, Esme tries talking about Darius but it doesn't go well. Her daughter's face turns from grim to stony.

'Have you seen him?' Dani asks, her voice starting to rise. 'Is that who you've been with this afternoon?'

'No,' Esme tells her. 'I saw Darius yesterday afternoon. What's the matter with you, Dani?'

'Did you have him here?'

'No, Dani, I didn't. But I might have done. What's wrong with you?'

'Nothing,' she says and turns back to her food. Esme plucks up her courage a second time.

'I like him, Dani. You know I like him. I'd like to ask him to come and live with us. See how it works out.' Dani doesn't answer. Doesn't wait for Esme to finish speaking. Her daughter jumps up from the table, flinging the fork down on to her plate. She crashes through the room and disappears upstairs.

33

My life is falling apart. I've lost Grandma. I can't talk to Grandma anymore. And I've lost Jaffa. *We're finished,* he said. *Finished.* What shall I do? What can I do? I've lost Jaffa. I like Jaffa more than anybody else in the world but I was stupid. How could I have been so stupid? It was his mother we were talking about. But the picture of his dead mother was horrible. The other picture he did of her was much nicer. She looked nice in the other picture. The picture of his mother in the chair with the book on her lap. I liked that. In the second picture of her when he said she was dead, Jaffa's Mum looked completely different. She looked empty and ugly and old. But I shouldn't have said that I didn't like the picture. It was Jaffa's mother. Oh, Jaffa. I'm sorry. So very very sorry. I wish, wish, wish I could undo it. Undo my word, my one word, No, but it's passed between us. That *no* can never be undone and he'll think it means that I don't like his mother. Not true, Jaffa, not true, not true, not true, but how can I tell you. And what did he mean when he said I was just like everyone else? What did he mean by that?

Grandma's words about Darius being black can't be undone either. Actually, Darius is not black, he's brown but I know what she means. The problem is that she meant it in a bad way. Grandma seems to think that being dark-skinned makes Darius different. How can Grandma talk like that? Being Darius is what makes Darius different. But she was right about Mum falling for him.

What a terrible weekend. Ending with Mum saying she wants Darius to move in. To move in!!!! She's only seen him four or five times and she wants him to move in. I won't let it happen. I won't let any man come and take Steve's place. If Steve can't be here then his place has to stay empty. I bet she would have let Darius use Steve's workroom. And I gradually realise that she was planning to let Darius take Steve's place in her bed. Yuck.

I'm tired. It shouldn't be tiring to sit in a car and drive down the motorway and back but it was and I *am* tired. I still haven't done my homework. Don't feel like it. I'm tired and I'm lonely. Don't think I've felt quite like this before. I want somebody to talk to but there isn't anybody. Not anybody.

I could write my diary. That's what I've been doing since my birthday when Darius gave me the typewriter, I've written every day. Just odds and ends. It's a brilliant machine. It's lighter than the other one and there aren't any twisted letters. It's like a racehorse compared to a cart horse. I like the old cart horse because it was what I started with, but the new machine is a dream. I ought to do my homework and I want to read but I'm too tired. I'll set the alarm clock and get up early tomorrow morning, say five, and do my homework then. As for now, I'm giving up. Can't cope with any more today.

'I'm going to bed,' I yell down to my mother. I'm shouting down to her because I feel sorry for the way I left the living room earlier. I should have stayed to tell her what I thought. Calmly. It wasn't a good idea to storm off. I'll try again tomorrow.

'It's early. Are you all right?' She's always asking if I'm all right.

'I'm tired,' I tell her.

'OK,' she says. 'Good night, Dani.'

So there's a sort of peace with my mother but I feel terrible about falling out with Jaffa. I'll see him in class tomorrow, but I won't be able to talk to him. It's been a terrible day. Finding out that Grandma thinks black people are different from white people (not that anybody is black or white) and losing Jaffa all in one day is too much. And that's not counting the Mum and Darius problem.

I wake up just before the alarm goes off and press the button to stop it ringing. The button's big. Easy to jam your hand on to switch it off. Not like my last alarm clock that used to ring and ring because I could never find the switch at the back. Too small and fiddly. Impossible to turn off when you're half asleep. I conveniently broke the little one and this one's much better. But now I've got a decent clock, I hardly seem to need it. Always wake up anyway.

It's cold. Still dark. I get up, get dressed and start doing my homework. Hope I don't wake Mum with the typing noise. It sounds like a machine gun. But no, there's no sound from Mum's room. She must be sleeping through it all. It's a general science assignment. Writing up an experiment on soap. I've got notes on tape but I don't need them. I can remember all of it. I'm pleased because the typing is so easy now that I don't have to think about it. I can concentrate on the things I want to say and my fingers move by themselves. It seems so long ago that I was going mad about not being able to write.

I finish my homework and it's not even six o'clock. For a minute or two, I feel pleased with myself but then I remember the row with Jaffa and the black cloud drops. I'm hoping that I can find a way to talk to him and make things all right again. And then there's Grandma. What am I going to do about Grandma? I suppose I'm going to have to talk to her. I'll have to confess that I read her letters. That won't be easy and she's so far away.

I never knew that Grandma wrote to Aunty Nellie. I suppose Aunty Nellie doesn't have a phone. I wonder why Grandma hid the letters. Presumably, it was to make sure that Grandpa didn't see them. She knows he wouldn't go rummaging about in the back bedroom. Grandma is a surprising person, but I wish I hadn't found them. She didn't sound like my grandma at all. I wonder if I'm the same. Would Grandma feel shocked if she overheard me talking to Mandy? Would she think that I was a different person? I might sound a bit different, but my opinions would still be the same. At least, I think they would.

I've started to enjoy writing. But I don't write letters. Why bother with letters when you can use the phone? No, as I said before, what I'm writing is a diary, but the only diary I've ever read is Anne Frank's diary and I loved reading that. I wonder if she meant it to be secret forever. I wonder what she would think if she knew that millions of people had read what she wrote. People like me who were not even born when she wrote it. She was dead long before I was born, but in her writing, she feels so alive. I don't think she wanted it to stay secret. That's why she invented the friend, Kitty. She wanted to tell someone how she felt. Me, too. I want to tell someone how I feel although sometimes it feels as though I'm telling myself how I feel because before I start to write it down, I don't know.

I'm hungry. I'm going to get some breakfast. I put the fire on and while I sit and eat cornflakes (would prefer Weetabix but there's none left) I think about Anne's diary. It seemed to be mostly about things that were bothering her. Is that why people write? I'm starving. Not surprising really. I missed lunch and half my dinner yesterday. My own stubborn fault. (I shake the cornflakes packet and it seems quite full. That's a relief.) Is diary writing like newspapers? All about bad stuff? Is the good stuff not interesting enough to write about?

Mum's reading *The Idiot* and I asked her why anybody would want to write a book about an idiot. She told me that it wasn't about an idiot. It was about a man who was a really good person, but when Dostoevsky first tried to write the story, he had found it impossible to make a good man into a hero. Nobody was interested because good equals boring. At least that's what Mum said. I'll have to think about that. The only way, she said, that Dostoevsky could have a good person as the hero was to make people think he was an idiot. Did it work I asked her but she didn't know because she hadn't finished it yet.

I've just finished my second bowl of cornflakes and I'm still hungry. I think I'll have just one more. That should do it. And I need a cup of tea. It's getting nice and warm in here with the fire on and I'm beginning to feel sleepy again.

What makes a story interesting? Anne Frank's story is interesting because she was in a dangerous situation, but my own life is just ordinary so it might not be interesting for people to read about. But no, I don't think that I am ordinary. I pour myself some more tea and realise that nobody thinks they are ordinary. There is not a single ordinary person in the world. Ha ha. We can all write diaries about our lives.

I don't feel too bad this morning. Not quite as bad as I thought I was going to feel. The worst thing is the row with Jaffa but I'm going to apologise so I'm hoping that we can make it up. I feel better because I didn't dream. At least I don't remember dreaming and when the weird dream comes, I always do remember it. I wake up feeling afraid. It's awful. I'm terrified to go back to sleep again so I end up tired. I was going to talk to Grandma about it again, but as it turned out, that wasn't possible. I wish I had Steve back. The old Steve.

I'm not doing very well for dads. The first one's dead and gone, and maybe he tried to kill me. The second one's nearly gone. Hopefully, there's no third one coming. I won't accept a third one whatever happens. Whoever Esme chooses next, he won't be my dad. Perhaps I'm glad that my first dad died because otherwise, I wouldn't have had Steve. And my first dad wouldn't have been as nice as Steve. Certainly, he couldn't have been nicer. Steve has spent more time with me than any other father I know. More than any of the 'real' fathers that Mandy talks about. My second dad is the best one of all.

What does 'real' mean anyway? I've asked this question a thousand times but I still can't answer it. I know that Mandy doesn't even think that Grandma is my real grandmother because Esme was adopted, so we have no blood connection. For Mandy only blood counts but she doesn't understand. Esme always says that Grandma and

Grandpa are her real parents. In that case, why can't Steve be my real father? If 'real' is anything to do with loving and caring, then Steve definitely is my real father. Must stop. I'm tying myself in knots. I'm going to put some music on. That will wake her up. I'm sure it's time that Mum got up. She's going to be late for work if she doesn't get up soon.

Still no sound from upstairs. Should I go and jump on her bed like I did when I was little? I'm getting bored sitting down here waiting for the day to start. I think I'll go back up and write my diary.

'Is that you, Dani?' I hear as I clatter past Mum's bedroom.

'No,' I shout back. 'It's a burglar.'

I put a fresh sheet of paper in the typewriter and think about my writing. Learning to type is one of the best things that has happened to me in this last year. Actually, it is the very best thing ever. The absolute most brilliant best. I never thought that I would be able to write and be like everybody else. Not stupid anymore. And I never ever thought that I would enjoy it. Hallelujah! Climb a tree. Hallelujah you and me. Oh dear, I'm getting silly now. Be serious, I tell myself.

I stare at the paper in the typewriter. I'm feeling ambitious. Maybe I'll write a story instead of the diary and get it published. Become famous. Schoolgirl. Fourteen. Writes brilliant book. I can see it already. I'll make something up. That's a good idea. I look hard at the blank piece of paper waiting for some words to land on it and can't think of a single thing. The blank page stares back at me like a face with no eyes. I realise then that what I want to write about is real stuff. My life and how I feel about it.

Not a story. I want to write my own story so I'm back to the diary again. I'll write a made-up story another day after I've finished writing my own story. Ha ha. That means when I'm dead I suppose. That's when my story will finish. Unless you believe in reincarnation of course...

I can hear Mum getting up now. She's in the bathroom banging about. Water gushing. Loo flushing. Suddenly, even the diary seems difficult. Can't think of anything to say. Maybe it's the thought of somebody else reading it. Anne Frank wanted someone to read hers, but whenever I try to imagine a friend that I could write to, I think of Mandy and I would never want her to read my diary. In fact, I wouldn't want anyone to read what I wrote. It has to be private and it is. I am always careful to hide it, especially from Mum. My mother is always snooping around, tidying things up and moving my stuff.

It is, in fact, essential that nobody should read what I write or I wouldn't be able to write my real thoughts. Sometimes my real thoughts are shocking. Even to myself. I'll think more about the diary later. I've already got a hiding place. Not much to hide yet (except the picture that Jaffa gave me and the few pages I've already written) but there will be.

'Dani,' I hear from downstairs.

'Coming,' I reply.

34

I go to school feeling hopeful. I don't believe Jaffa meant it. We can't be finished. I'll find a way to send him a message. In fact, I've already written it. Typed a note to tell him I'm sorry but when I get to school, he isn't there. Bugger and shit. Where is he? I spend all day looking round to see if he's back. Maybe he had to go to the dentist? But his seat stays empty. I can't believe how long the day lasts. I can't concentrate and keep getting told off for daydreaming. Makes a change from being told off for talking.

It's Monday but I decide not to go to the library. Don't feel like it. Could go to Mandy's but I never go to Mandy's on a Monday. I'm sure she wouldn't mind but I don't feel like seeing her. It's Jaffa I want to see. Hope he's there tomorrow. I've almost forgotten my worries about Mum wanting Darius to move in and Grandma's terrible letter in the distress over Jaffa, but I remember when I walk in just as Mum is putting the phone down.

'Who was that?' I ask.

'Nobody,' she says. 'Just somebody from work.' I don't believe her. People from work never ring. Feel too miserable to sit and talk to Mum so I go upstairs.

'What's wrong?' she shouts after me. There she goes again. Asking me how I'm feeling. Like shit, I think, but don't say it.

I lie down on my bed (which doesn't bounce - it's a futon mattress - one of those healthy things that are slightly lumpy) and think about my diary. At least I can talk in that. What I need to do, however (oh Steve, I think of you when I say *however*) is to clean my hiding place because I need more space. The clean part is minute and there is gradually more and more to hide.

We never have a fire in my bedroom so the fireplace is ideal (or it would be if I could get it clean). If you put your hand up the chimney, there is a little shelf. I discovered it years ago. The shelf will be big enough for several folders, but the inside of the chimney will have to be cleaned first. At the moment, there's only enough clean space to keep the first exercise book. I put my hand inside and feel around. It comes out covered in soot. Some goes on my skirt and several lumps drop down on to the small concrete hearth. I look at my watch (the old one that I wear for school). It's gone five. Mum will start cooking soon. Better do it later. I won't be able to get the cleaning stuff from the kitchen while she's cooking.

I go down to watch tv and Mum asks me about my day, but I can't talk about it. After a few attempts, she gives up and goes back into the kitchen. Mum doesn't look very cheerful. Maybe Darius doesn't want her if he can't move in and they've had a row. Maybe that was him on the phone. But I know that's stupid. I often think that Darius is strange, but he wouldn't want us for money or a place to live. I mean he wouldn't want Mum for those things.

I wash up after we've eaten. Mum made some sponge pudding with stewed apple and custard. Very nice but our long faces didn't shift much. I haven't got any homework tonight and I keep thinking of going upstairs to clean out the hiding place so I can carry on with my writing, but I don't do it. Instead, I watch tv all night and so does Mum.

Finally, we go to bed but it's only just gone ten so I decide to start on the cleaning. Go back down to see what cleaning equipment we've got but when I reach the living room, I'm surprised to see Mum sitting at the table marking. Or staring into space.

'Thought you'd gone to bed,' I say.

'I thought you had, too,' she says. 'What are you doing down here again?'

'Nothing,' I say as I bang about looking for buckets and cloths. 'Looking for some Flash. I'm going to clean my room.' I hear my mother make a funny noise which must be her version of an astonished gasp. I don't clean my room very often. More or less never.

'At this time of night?' Mum says trying to keep the surprise out of her voice.

'Yes,' I say. 'Grandma says 'there's no time like the present'.' Mum makes no further comment, and I set off up the stairs carrying a bucket of soapy water, a scrubbing brush and several Jeye cloths. Not easy. Have to go back down to fetch a brush and dustpan. Think I've got enough to make a start.

I work hard. I brush the soot out, carefully, and shovel it into plastic bags. It makes a mess. I clean the shelf as best I can. Still not clean. The soot seems to regenerate. Try harder and the grate area starts to improve. I'm trying not to get any on my clothes which I like to look old and frayed, but not dirty. Always like to feel clean. The rest of my bedroom is the same as usual. Dusty and untidy. Don't feel like it, but I'd better clean the whole room.

It's getting late. Nearly half eleven. It would be stupid to have a clean fireplace surrounded by dust and dirt everywhere else. At the moment, the hiding place shines out and I almost laugh out loud. When Mum came upstairs some time ago, she shouted to tell me to stop now and finish it tomorrow. But I can't leave it like this. With great care, I carry the bags of soot downstairs and take them out to the dustbin. Cover them with newspaper so they're not obvious. Can't leave them in the kitchen for Mum to see but I put the other bags of rubbish in the kitchen bin. I put the cleaning stuff back in the cupboards and heave a sigh of satisfaction. Finished.

I go back upstairs and sit at my little desk. I'm ready to start writing and it's only just gone midnight. But there's no way to type quietly and I daren't disturb her sleep twice in one day. I'll have to wait, but I'm pleased with myself and surely Jaffa will be back at school tomorrow.

***

Jaffa is not back the next day nor the day after that. As the days pass, my heart sinks lower and I don't feel like doing much, but I do carry on writing my diary. I write nearly every day and after I finish writing, I read through my diary pages and feel a sense of satisfaction, a little thrill.

Tuesday, March 27th 1979

The streets are empty now there's no Jaffa following me about. When I got home from school today, I saw VJ and he said hello and smiled at me. Can't believe that I used to fancy him. Not anymore. It's too late for him to smile at me now. I'm going to stay on my own. No Jaffa. No boyfriend. Wonder if VJ has the bedroom on the other side of the wall next to mine. If he does, he's very quiet. The most we hear of next door from his side is from the kitchen. And we can smell their curries. They smell better than ours but Mum's curries do taste nice.

Wonder what Steve is doing. He never rings during the week. He told me he was looking for a flat because there wasn't enough space at Paul's. I wonder where he'll go, and if it will be close to here. It would be nice to be able to walk there. That would be brilliant. I'm glad he's going to leave Paul's.

I'm going on fifteen now. Almost an adult, but Mum still treats me like a child. She's always giving me orders. Do this. Do that. Don't do something else. I bet Grandma didn't treat her like that when she was my age. But I have to admit that Mum can be very nice sometimes. Since my birthday, she's loosened up. It's since she's started seeing Darius again. She's started smiling. Almost like getting my old mum back, but I bet it won't last.

Thursday, March 29th 1979

Going to Steve's tomorrow. I want to see him, but I wish he didn't live so far away. It means I don't see Mandy at weekends because she has to do the Buddhist meetings on Sundays. And there's nowhere private to write my diary at Paul's. Not worth taking the typewriter.

Mum's still being nice. Perhaps she thinks I'll change my mind about Darius moving in, but I won't. It was me who was ratty today. Maybe because I got my period. It always makes me bad-tempered.

Saturday, March 31ˢᵗ, 1979

Oh God, here we go again. Mum's talking about asking Darius to move in! She's only been seeing him for a couple of weeks so what is wrong with her? I didn't even reply this time. Didn't trust myself. But there's no way I'm having him here. If he comes here, I'm leaving. I've told her and I mean it. Suzi's wrong. My mother really is a whore. She'd go with anyone.

35

It's the Easter holidays. Esme stretches out on the sofa but it's uncomfortable. She changes her mind and sits on the floor with her back against the sofa. That's better. At times she'd thought she would never make it to these holidays. There have been staff off sick all term and not enough supply teachers. The drama group fell apart with all kinds of quarrels between its members. Esme had wished she could give it up, but that would have been difficult. Instead, she has painstakingly sorted out one argument after another and put the group back together again. It's running smoothly once more but it has taken up masses of time. The term has seemed never-ending, and now, finally, she has a week to herself because Steve has taken Dani down to Summer Lane. Dani hadn't seemed very keen but wouldn't say why. They went down yesterday.

Esme's got a week to spend with Darius. Unfortunately, he isn't often available. He always seems to be working. Course work, she assumes. Or writing perhaps. Steve had wanted to spend two weeks in Summer Lane with Dani, but two weeks was the whole Easter holiday and this time, Dani refused. One week was enough she said so one week had been agreed. Esme is going down after Easter to spend a couple of days there before bringing Dani back. She's feeling a bit nervous about seeing her mother but it has to be faced. She will have to talk about Darius.

It's nice sitting by the fire but she can't seem to relax. What Esme needs is to properly wind down so she grabs her tobacco tin and sets off to go and see Suzi. When she gets there, Esme grasps the lion and bangs hard. She knows Dani likes the lion. It makes a huge noise and always seems to echo up and down the street. Strangely, it sounds quite tame heard from the inside of the house.

'Hello, Ess,' Suzi appears at the door. 'Haven't seen you for ages. Come in.'

'I could say the same,' Esme says and glances at the piles of stuff that have appeared in the porch. Suzi leads the way inside, asking her not to trip over a crate full of glass vases stacked just inside the doorway. 'What are all those?' Esme asks. 'What are you going to do with them?

'Spray paint them and give them as presents,' Suzi replies. 'Look,' she points at a vase that is drying on the draining board on top of sheets of newspaper. It looks stunning. Various shades of blue with runs and drips flowing into each other.

'Beautiful,' Ess says, 'but isn't it expensive to buy them in the first place?'

'No, they're cheap,' Suzi replies. 'Pete got the vases for just over a pound each. It's the paint that's expensive, but not too bad if you don't waste it.'

'You could do some for Christmas,' Esme suggests.

'I could. But it's only Easter,' Suzi says. 'And they'll all be gone by the end of the summer. Let me make a pot of coffee while you tell me what you've been doing. Has Dani gone yet?'

'Yes, she went after school yesterday. Steve picked her up and she just dropped in to collect her things. A big bag of clothes and her typewriter. Won't go anywhere without it.'

'Maybe she's started writing her life story?'

'She keeps at it long enough,' Esme says. 'Should have written it twice over by this time. She types every night. If I weren't so pleased that she was writing, I'd ask her not to do it after ten.'

'And she's doing well at school, isn't she?' Suzi says. 'I asked her last week how school was going, and she told me her last assignment was read out to the whole class.' Esme feels a stab of jealousy. Dani didn't tell her about it. 'But she still can't do the spelling tests,' Suzi adds. 'Same old problem of not being able to write the letters fast enough.'

'What about you?' Esme asks. 'What are you going to do this Easter?'

'Nothing,' Suzi replies. 'Glorious nothing.'

'Aren't you going down to Devon?' Esme asks. 'Or to Pete's parents?'

'No,' Suzi replies. 'Pete's going to see his parents by himself and I'm staying here.'

'We'll both be here then,' Esme replies. I'm going to fetch Dani back after Easter, but I'll be here over the weekend.'

'Don't suppose you'll be available much,' Suzi states with a grin. She knows that Esme has started seeing Darius.

'Hope not,' Esme agrees, 'but he works most of the time. He's got to finish the coursework assignments and then start on the dissertation.'

'What's it on?' Suzi asks.

'I'm not sure,' Esme admits. 'I haven't asked. We talk about other things.' They both light up, and Suzi puts Joni on. It is nearly always Joni. Suzi is looking cheerful and tells her that Pete seems to be behaving himself at least as far as she knows.

'He's even started talking about marriage,' Suzi confides.

'I thought Pete didn't believe in marriage,' Esme says.

'So did I,' Suzi agrees. 'But maybe it's me who doesn't like the idea.' Esme is surprised to hear this. She had always thought it was Pete who didn't want any formal arrangement.

'Maybe it's because of the babies,' Ess suggests.

'Babies?'

'Yes, the babies you're going to have together. Any news on that?' But Esme can see immediately that she shouldn't have asked. Suzi shakes her head and changes the subject. It's sod's law, Esme thinks. The women who end up getting pregnant often don't want to, and the women who want to, often don't.

'Do you want to try doing one?' Suzi asks.

'One what?'

'A vase,' she says. 'It's quite hard at first but very satisfying.'

'OK,' Esme says and Suzi hands her a long apron and fetches a new glass vase out of the carton. Suzi is always so calm, Ess thinks, no matter what she's dealing with. Esme can see that her friend is stressed about not getting pregnant, but Suzi puts it to one side and sprays vases. Or makes cakes. Gets on with life. Esme respects and admires her and even when she doesn't follow Suzi's advice, it isn't necessarily because she thinks the advice is wrong. More often, it is because Esme finds herself unable to follow it, unable to do the sensible thing.

'Watch,' Suzi tells her, and Esme watches how her friend holds the vase and uses the spray can, spraying near the neck so that some of the paint runs down the side. 'What colour do you want to start with?'

'Green,' Esme says without hesitation as she pulls on the rubber gloves and tries to copy what Suzi has just done but doesn't manage it very well.

'Don't be timid,' Suzi tells her and after that, the paint spurts gloriously and Esme alternates the green spray with silver. 'Stop,' Suzi says, 'or you'll spoil it.'

'What do you think?' Esme asks.

It's magnificent. Green and silver runs and swirls - as though each one was deliberate.

'Beginner's luck,' Suzi says and laughs. 'It will be dry in about an hour.' Esme goes back to the sofa.

'Would you like to meet Darius?' she asks. 'You still haven't met him.'

'OK,' Suzi agrees. 'If you're sure you're ready to introduce him. You haven't known him long.'

'I've known him several lifetimes,' Ess replies and notes Suzi's expression. What is it? Annoyance? Disapproval? 'I'll cook for us on Easter Sunday, and you can meet him then.' She is finding that whatever they talk about, her mind returns to Darius, and she keeps bringing him back into the conversation. Suzi looks faintly irritated that Esme keeps talking about him, but Ess can't help it.

Darius dominates her thoughts to a ridiculous degree, but she doesn't care. She keeps forgetting that she was going to be careful. How marvellous it is to find a kindred spirit. That's what Darius feels like. He feels familiar. The irony is that she doesn't know him. He feels like family but he's more alien than anyone she's ever met. As soon as Esme gets back to her house, she picks up the phone and dials Joe's number.

'Can I speak to Darius?' she asks, and a female voice answers. 'Is that Helen?'

'No, it's Geraldine,' comes the reply. 'It's Esme, isn't it?' Esme mutters an affirmative. 'I'm sorry,' Geraldine says, 'but he's out. I'll ask him to ring you when he gets back.' There is a pause. 'Can I take a message?'

'No, thanks, not really,' Esme says. 'I'll tell him when I speak to him.'

What can she do with her restlessness? She is on holiday but can't relax. What use is the holiday with Dani in Summer Lane if she can't spend time with Darius? This precious time shouldn't be wasted. Where is he? And what is he doing? And, oh dear she catches herself wondering, who is he with? The rest of the day stretches before her and Esme wonders what to do. She could read, she supposes. The chance to read is something she's been looking forward to for ages but she doesn't feel like it. After a few minutes, she decides to go and see Kate. Hasn't seen her for a long time. She could ask about John and whether or not he is back with Barbara.

It doesn't take long to walk down the ginnels. It's not raining but chilly and overcast. The English spring she thinks. When Esme arrives at Kate's, she finds the house full of people.

'What's going on?' Esme asks. 'Should I come another time?'

'Not at all,' Kate says. 'Come in. I haven't seen you for ages. Come in and see what we're doing,' then adds, 'we're planning a film.' Esme follows her into the house and is surprised to see Joe sitting on the sofa. Sprawled would be a better description. He is jammed in between two girls who seem to be quite happy to be jammed in next to him.

'Hello, Ess,' Joe says and grins at her. Kate goes around the room introducing everyone, but it's a waste of time. Esme tries to memorise the names as each person is introduced but ends up not being able to remember any of them. She sits down and listens to what is going on. One of the lads from the Youth Centre that Murray runs has written a play, and they've decided to turn it into a film.

This is the initial planning meeting to decide how many sets they'll need and whether or not they'll be able to film outside. The consensus is that filming on the street would be good for getting the local atmosphere, but there are several problems that would have to be overcome. Outdoor sets are difficult to control. And then there is the problem of the unreliable weather. The indoor scenes could be done at the Centre. They would be a lot easier. There is going to be another meeting for casting in a couple of days' time.

'What about you, Ess?' Joe asks. 'Why don't you join us? You could play one of the bit parts if you haven't got time to learn the words.' Esme is pleased to be asked, but she hasn't got time. It is true she has a few days off now, but she wants to keep every moment to spend with Darius.

'Thanks, Joe,' she said, 'but I don't have time. I'll come and watch it when it's finished.' It is pleasant sitting listening to the plans. Just being here makes her feel as though she's a part of it and it's a long time since she's done anything other than school work. She wonders if she could get her Thursday drama group involved. Or if they could make a film of their own.

The meeting is underway, but people are still arriving. They come into the room that had seemed full when she first arrived, but somehow they all find somewhere to sit down. Everyone is squashed but looking cheerful as they keep making room for newcomers. She turns to see John standing in the doorway.

'Hello Esme,' he says and stares at her in the same way that he always has done. 'How are you, girl?'

'I'm fine,' Esme replies. 'How are things with you?' John shrugs and looks for somewhere to sit down. Esme is relieved to see that there is nowhere available close to where she is sitting. She catches Joe giving her a knowing look and what appears to be a wink.

'You sure know all the boys, Ess,' he says and grins at her, but she doesn't reply. Doesn't know what to say. Who has been talking about her? Fortunately, the meeting is quickly resumed, and planning for the sets continues.

'We're going to need a motorbike,' somebody is saying, and Joe looks at Esme.

'You've got a bike, Ess,' he says. 'Will you lend it to us for an afternoon?' She hesitates.

'It's not insured for anyone else to ride,' she says, and suddenly feels a prickling in the back of her neck. She turns and sees Helen standing in the doorway and right behind her, Darius.

The rest of the meeting passes in a blur, and Esme leaves as soon as she can, saying she has to be somewhere else. Darius and Helen have both greeted her warmly and had then joined in with the meeting. What is wrong with her? Esme can hardly see properly. Can't bring herself to look at either Helen or Darius. For the first time in her life, she is thoroughly jealous. She has never thought that she would ever experience jealousy. Has scoffed about how stupid it is. Has gone on about not owning people. Has held others in contempt for their jealous behaviour. Has talked about freedom all her life. But look at her now. She is consumed by the very feelings she has always condemned. Her heart pounds, she can't breathe, and she can't get out of the house fast enough.

Back at home, Esme paces around trying to get her feelings under control. There is no reason why Darius and Helen shouldn't turn up at the meeting. No reason why they shouldn't arrive together. After all, they live in the same house so they are bound to see a lot of one another. But why didn't Darius ask *her* if she wanted to help with the film? Joe had. Darius could have told her about it before. And he could have asked her if she wanted to join them when he saw her there. But he didn't. And all he did when she left was to smile and say, 'See you soon.' He hadn't tried to get her to stay. Or offered to leave with her.

Esme knows that jealousy is an ugly emotion. She's said so often enough. She's seen what it did to Dani's father. At last, she starts to understand how Andreas must have felt the day he had found her in bed with another man and feels a renewed sense of guilt for the pain she caused him. Then she remembers that Darius said that he had to be free. That he is an artist. What kind of bullshit is that? And if he wants to be so free, why has he suggested that they could be together and so close that she would have to go back to Papua New Guinea with him? It doesn't make sense. She takes the tobacco tin out of her bag and slams it down on the table.

36

Esme makes a resolution and decides that she will say nothing to Darius about his appearance at the film meeting. Will not ask him how he is involved. Will not mention Helen. Even though this has involved her needing to glue her tongue to the roof of her mouth so that she stays mostly silent, she has, so far, managed to keep her resolution. She has seen Darius twice since the meeting, and he has been as attentive and intense with her as before. As though nothing has changed between them. But although she manages, with huge difficulty, to keep her mouth shut, Esme cannot shake off her feelings of jealousy. She finds that the more she doesn't speak about them, the worse they become. She is being unreasonable she tells herself, but logic doesn't help.

Today is Easter Sunday, and both Darius and Suzi are coming to dinner. Esme has spent all morning cleaning and all afternoon cooking. A waste of the day really. There was a call from Dani in the morning wishing her a Happy Easter. Her daughter had sounded polite rather than happy and Esme wonders again what's wrong. She's sure that there is something. Having a great time, Dani said but looking forward to getting back to Leeds again. She would have to say that while Grandma and Grandpa were there but she didn't sound as though she meant it. Esme is finely tuned to her daughter's states of happiness and hopes that it's nothing serious. She'll try to find out when she goes down to fetch her. Dani's call reminds her that there is only one more complete day to herself after today. To her shame, Esme hasn't thought much about Dani since her daughter has been gone. She's got Easter eggs waiting for her which she'd bought last week but apart from that, her mind has been almost totally on Darius.

Esme sits down. She needs a rest. Hadn't realised how much she'd let the housework slip, but the place is clean again now. She looks around and feels gratified at having done so much cleaning. Thinks about the bedroom where she's taken particular care. Clean sheets and pillowcases. Uncluttered surfaces, dust free for the first time in weeks. (Months?) Esme has swept all the clutter into drawers so that she could wipe the surfaces. She's cleaned everything with a damp cloth instead of a duster and smiles to think of her mother, who would be shocked at such slovenly ways. Her mother would say that wood needs dusting and polishing and Esme knows that she's right but it would take so much longer. Her mother has told her so very many times that wetting the wood will spoil it but she takes no notice on account of always being in a hurry. She's done the bathroom, too, and has put out clean towels.

The whole downstairs smells of the aromatic curry that Esme has been leaving to simmer but which she has now turned off. Curry was chosen so that she could prepare it in advance. Esme has a limited culinary repertoire but what she cooks, she does well and her food always tastes good. The curry will only need heating up when it is time to eat. They're cooking curry next door as well. You can always smell what they are cooking. It wafts in somewhere through their adjoining kitchens. Esme has to admit that the cooking smells from the Indian family next door are frequently heavenly.

One day, she will pluck up courage and go and ask for the recipes. Her own curry is always the same. Well, not identical of course, but similar. She varies the ingredients depending on what's available. To make it hot, Esme uses ginger and chillies but most of the curry taste comes from curry powder. Somebody once told her that proper curry is never made like that. But who cares? Her curry always tastes good and today's big pot tastes delicious.

Esme has decided to serve ice cream for dessert. Something sweet and easy so she doesn't have to spend time in the kitchen when her guests are here. It is cherry ice cream. Hers and Dani's favourite (and Steve's). Dani likes it because it tastes of almonds. Ess goes to the fridge to check the drinks. When she was buying the drinks, she had realised that she didn't know what Darius liked so she'd decided on Guinness and wine. She and Suzi would drink the wine.

There are crisps and nuts to eat as hors-d'oeuvres and a small jar of olives. Esme wasn't quite sure whether or not olives could precede curry but why not? The last thing to check was the music. She's been playing Billie Holiday all afternoon. Maybe it's time for a change. Esme looks through her tapes and chooses a jazz compilation. When it starts playing, it reminds her of the party where she'd first met Darius. *I've got you under my skin.... I've got you deep in the heart of me....* the pure tones of Ella.

Suzi arrives first, and Ess immediately opens the wine. By the time Darius arrives, she is beginning to feel mellow.

'Darius,' she greets him with open arms and a smile, 'Come and meet Suzi. I've told her all about you.' He walks in, hands Esme a bunch of yellow tulips and a bottle of wine and then goes to shake hands with Suzi. Esme watches as he greets her friend and notices that he seems to stare as intently at Suzi as he does at her. Maybe that is his way she thinks. Perhaps he looks intently at everyone he meets. Or is it only at women?

There is not much time for the nuts, crisps and olives because the main course is ready and Esme's curry is delicious. The food is repeatedly complimented by both Suzi and Darius. Even Esme thinks it tastes good and is sure that the fresh coriander (that she doesn't usually buy because it's expensive) has been worth it. The conversation flows easily which is a relief.

Suzi can be awkward and arrogant and has a tendency to be easily dismissive of people for all kinds of reasons. Never of children, Esme notes, but often of adults. It turns out that Darius knows quite a lot about the remedial reading area in which Suzi is interested, and he tells her about some new research that has recently been published. The wine Darius has brought is a red Esme notices, and it turns out that, he, too, prefers wine, so the Guinness is left for another time. Between the three of them, it doesn't take long to drink two bottles of wine.

After the ice cream, Suzi reaches for her pack of cigarettes and offers them round. Darius refuses and so does Esme, saying she prefers to roll one. She fetches her tobacco tin from the little table next to the sofa, and as she returns, watches Darius lean towards Suzi to offer her a light. Then Suzi glances across at her and Esme understands that her friend thinks that Darius is flirting with her and doesn't like it. After the cigarette, Suzi says she has to go. Both Esme and Darius press her to stay, but she insists, so at last, the two of them are alone. Esme stands up to clear the table, but Darius catches her arm. 'I've waited for this time,' Darius tells her and pauses. 'I've waited for you, Esme. Leave the washing up.'

Esme leads the way upstairs, and it is easy. They sit on the bed and laugh. Darius starts to undress her, and Esme lets him. The house is warm and soon they are lying naked on the bed.

'Let me look at you,' he says. And Esme feels his gaze linger on her body while all the while he seems still to be looking into her eyes. She looks up at him. His dark face is close now. His whole body is close, just above her, ready for her as she is ready for him. Yes, he is beautiful. She touches his skin feeling the muscles in his arms. Darius looks at her with the same intent gaze.

'Esme,' he says. 'Will you marry me?' She looks up in surprise but before she can answer, their bodies touch and they are wordless for a while. 'Will you?' he asks after a little while. 'Will you, Esme? Will you be my wife?'

'Yes,' she whispers.

'You are beautiful,' he says. She pauses for a minute and then laughs as she says, 'I am the good, the bad and the ugly.' Now where did that come from and why did she say that? It doesn't even make sense. The film is an old one but she saw it recently for the first time. Strange the words that rise unbidden to the mind's surface.

'You're the opposite of ugly and you're no use to me if you're bad,' Darius says, suddenly serious. 'I need you to be good, Esme,' and pauses, 'Will you be good for me?' Esme contemplates his question and wonders what to reply. 'Will you do that for me?' he asks again and smiles.

'Anything,' Esme replies. 'I'll do anything for you.' And the talking stops as they come together and roll into one.

'How was that?' she asks him.

'Not bad,' he replies. 'Not too bad. Quite good in fact.' And he laughs. What does he mean, she thinks, not too bad. Is he joking? Esme is quiet but after a while, she speaks again.

'And what will you do for me, Darius?' she asks. 'What will you do for me?'

'For you, my darling,' he replies, 'I will do anything in the world.'

37

On Tuesday morning, Esme is riding the bike down the motorway on her way to fetch Dani. It is monotonous driving along, especially as the bike is only 70cc and won't go very fast. It will manage almost seventy downhill but often falls below fifty on uphill stretches even on full throttle. It is lucky she has plenty to think about. The road seems endless.

Darius spent Sunday night and nearly all day yesterday with her, and they talked a great deal. At first, she wondered if he had meant it when he asked her to marry him. Or if he thought she wouldn't make love without an offer of marriage. She didn't think that Darius would propose marriage if he didn't mean it, but she was trying to be cautious and had kept reminding herself that she didn't know him. But yesterday he'd raised the subject again. He suggested they could get married at the beginning of the summer when the school holidays started. Yes, she agreed, that sounded all right, but it had felt like agreeing to go to see a film together or perhaps go on holiday. It didn't feel as though she were agreeing to a lifetime together at the other side of the world. Unreal. Despite a feeling of familiarity that might, after all, be an illusion, Darius was an unknown quantity. Esme was increasingly aware of this and was beginning to feel nervous.

Even as she whispered yes, Esme had wondered whether she was taking the right path. She doesn't know this stranger who comes from far away. Now again, as she sits on the bike, cold and uncomfortable, hunched over the handlebars staring at the road ahead and flinching every time one of the huge lorries overtakes her much too close, she asks herself the same question. Has she made the right decision? And what will it mean for Dani? It's not just herself she has to think about. She feels torn apart by the inner conflict. Half of her is sure that the decision is wrong and that the path she has chosen will lead to disaster, the other half pulls her to go with him, to go with Darius wherever he leads and however high the risk.

She needs a break. The next services are Woodall and she turns off and slows to a grateful stop. Gets off but is so stiff she can hardly walk. A heavily leathered man of possibly middle age parks his very large bike nearby and nods to her. Esme feels the familiar pleasure of being acknowledged by a fellow motorcyclist even though her bike is almost nothing in comparison to the large silver beast the leather-clad man is riding. She nods back and walks off towards the warmth of the interior where the space and bright lights of the food area combine to produce the usual impersonal atmosphere of every service station she's ever visited.

There aren't even any food or coffee smells. How do they manage that? Esme buys a coffee and sits at a table surveying the space. Not many travellers. Are the people who stop at service stations travellers? *Traveller* has the ring of someone with curiosity in their mind and adventure in their heart. Most people in here will be like her, just going from one familiar place to another. Not noticing much.

Esme takes in her surroundings with a quick glance and returns to her all-absorbing thoughts about Darius. Marriage. She's always said that she doesn't believe in it. For years. For most of her adult life, her opinion of marriage has remained the same. On several occasions, Steve had asked her to marry him, but she convinced him that marriage was an outdated institution. Not for her. When they had discussed it, Esme could hear echoes of her old self talking to Andreas. Yes, she had married Dani's father, but only to prevent the baby being made a ward of court in Germany. She hadn't wanted to get married and she had made that clear. To Steve, she always said that they could stay together without needing to be married. So why is she agreeing to marriage with Darius?

The coffee is not bad. At least it's strong. She can feel it warming her up and spiking her thoughts. The brain runs better on caffeine. Faster anyhow. Reaction times improved. Part of her decision to agree to marriage is to do with her trying to make sure of Darius. But only part of it. She wants to commit to him. Legally so that the statement of their union is public. Visible. She knows, of course, with her mind if not with her heart, that marrying someone does not make them yours. It is not possible to 'possess' another human being and she shouldn't want to. But she does. She does. She does want to.

There is already a conflict between what she believes she ought to think and what she actually does think. Between loving and giving which is what she ought to feel and loving and wanting to own exclusively which is what she does feel. Esme wants to tie the man to her as closely as possible. But another voice warns her to beware. It is all too fast. If only she could slow things down. But it isn't possible. Darius leaves in September.

They have discussed the wedding. There won't be enough time to arrange things she told him. She hasn't told her parents about him yet. Nor Dani. It doesn't matter, he replied. They can marry in secret to keep things simple. And tell everyone afterwards.

'No,' she said, 'I don't want to do it like that. Hiding away. I want our marriage to be public. Open and joyful.'

Oh, Esme,' Darius had replied, 'Our marriage will be public soon enough. And hopefully, always joyful.' The warning bells were sounding again.

'What do you mean,' she'd said, *Hopefully* always joyful? *Hopefully?*'

Darius had smiled. 'I'm always hopeful,' he said.

The coffee is finished and she could do with another. Feels hungry, but the sandwiches cost too much. Better to buy a bar of chocolate in the shop. The coffee's expensive, too, but worth it to keep her mind alert. Esme goes to get another coffee but this one is disappointing. Doesn't taste as good as the first so she gets up to leave. Buys some chocolate and eats it on the way back to the car park. Back to the motorway.

She had tried, yesterday, to carry on discussing the wedding but Darius had closed down and changed the subject. It bothers her. The prospect of getting married in secret. Another lorry pushes her sideways and she is beginning to ache. She's going to have to stop a second time. Her right leg feels as though she might get cramp. Eventually, she reaches Trowell Services where she has another break and more coffee.

257

At last, tired, stiff and cold, Esme arrives in Summer Lane. Dinner is waiting for her and afterwards, she sits in her mother's chair next to the fire. She stares into the flames and begins to feel her body relax in the warmth.

'Why don't you go and have a bath?' her mother says, 'So you can get properly warm.'

'I'm fine here,' Ess replies and then turns to Dani. 'I don't know how we're going to take your things back. We can get a small bag on the luggage rack. But it won't take your typewriter.'

'All sorted,' Dani replies. 'Steve's taken my things including the typewriter. He'll drop them off tomorrow night. I've got hardly anything left to carry.'

Later on, when Dani is in bed, Esme sits with her mother and chats. Her father is already in bed. He never stays up past ten, but she and her mother have often sat chatting after he has gone to bed when the house is quiet. Usually, Esme looks forward to these times alone with her mother but today she has been dreading it. She remembers the last time they talked. Remembers the phone conversation. She looks at her mother and knows that her mother, too, is nervous but she, too, knows that they will have to talk.

'How's Darius?' her mother says.

'I thought you'd never ask,' Esme grins at her, trying to lighten it. 'He's fine.' But then she becomes serious. 'I didn't like what you said about mixed race children, Mum.' She sees her mother pause and gather herself before she replies. Frances straightens in her chair and puts her knitting to one side. Esme can see that her mother has anticipated this moment, has prepared for it and doesn't find it easy.

'I knew you'd misunderstand,' she says. 'I'm not against black people, Esme. You know that. I should hope that you know that.' She pauses, and when she speaks again, it is with an effort and almost in a whisper. 'But I told you honestly how I feel. It seems to me that there are different cultures, and people belong in one group or the other. You can't stretch between them, and all of us need to belong somewhere. And to know where we belong.' Once again, she pauses. Frances doesn't usually make speeches. Actually, she never makes speeches. 'From what I've seen,' she goes on, 'mixed race children are accepted by neither black people nor white. They don't belong anywhere.'

Esme is growing angry.

'And how many mixed race children do you know?' she asks, her voice rising. 'What experience have you had with another culture? You're being racist. It's that newspaper that Uncle Ted brings for you to read. It's evil.' Esme can see that her mother is getting upset, but she can't stop. 'If he'll have me, I'll give Darius as many children as he wants.' There are tears in her mother's eyes and her mother never cries but Esme has hardened her heart and without another word, she gets up and goes upstairs to bed.

38

It's been three weeks since Jaffa told me we were finished. I thought we'd make it up straight away. I wrote him a note telling him I was sorry and carried it around with me day after day, but he wasn't in school. Mandy said he'd gone back to Hunslet to stay with his sister. Don't know how she manages to find out about everything that's going on. I never hear anything. After she told me, I spent the whole weekend trying to figure out how I was going to find him in Hunslet, but on Monday he was back in class.

Elation! Glory hallelujah! Jumping about with happiness to see him back. I put my note in a book and managed to put the book on his desk. He looked at me but didn't speak and I didn't speak either. Rushed off. I was sure things would be all right again between us but they weren't. Jaffa ignored me. Every day, it was as though I wasn't there and I got more and more miserable.

Home is not good either. Mum's been having violent mood swings. Up, up, up one minute and down at rock bottom the next. Grandma hasn't called much since Easter and I don't ring her. I don't like Grandma anymore but I love her and I miss her dreadfully. I know that doesn't make sense but it's how I feel. I've read that it's part of growing up when adults you once thought were perfect turn out not to be. Well, there are degrees of perfect. I can't believe that Grandma would write like that. Can't believe that she's a racist. And then I go one step further. I realise that Grandma doesn't think that writing as she has done is being racist.

The only comfort has been my writing. Who would have thought it? Who would ever have dreamed? I told Mandy that I was writing a diary but it was secret so I couldn't let her read it. I could tell that she just didn't believe me so I didn't say any more and don't know why I said anything in the first place. Just goes to show that I've got an ambivalent attitude towards keeping my writing secret. Can't make my mind up. I want her to know about it (and admire me) but I don't want her to see what I've written (which means that I've got no chance of her believing that I'm writing at all). Sod it. Serves me right for wanting to show off. At the end of the day. No. Cross that phrase out of my mind. It drives me mad. Everybody keeps saying it and I can't stand it. It's a cliche and cliches always end up being irritating. We had a lesson on cliches last week. What I wanted to say was that at the end of the day (I've given in), at least I've got my writing.

It's Sunday afternoon now and I'm standing just outside the park gates thinking about guess who. Well, of course. Who else would I be thinking about? I don't know if you can tell but I'm feeling bouncy again. It's because, at last, I've had a note from Jaffa. It's been three weeks since I last met him when he showed me the picture of his mother as she lay dead. I said I didn't like that picture and since then, it's been silence and misery between us. But at last, he's sent me a note. A typical Jaffa note. *Meet me in the park Sunday.* So I'm at the park gates. I had my hair cut yesterday. It's very short now. I've done my nails and they shine black with a hint of dark red when they catch the light. My jeans are full of holes in the right places. (I've got one pair that I tried to cut into holes but they went wrong and looked awful.) I wheel my bike slowly towards the bench that I've visited every week just to see if he came but he didn't. I can see him now. He looks better. Bigger. Not slumped. He smiles at me as I approach.

'Hi, Dani.'

'Hello, Jaff.' I sling my bike and sit down. 'Did you get my note?'

'Yes, thanks,' he says, 'did you get mine?' He knows I did or I wouldn't be here. We both know, just wanted to say something ordinary so we grin and sit quietly for a little while. 'Good match,' he says, nodding towards the empty court.

'Yes,' I agree. 'No idea who's going to win, have you?'

'Probably be a draw,' he says.

'They'll be at it forever then.'

'Is that what happens?' he asks. 'Does somebody always have to win?'

'Think so,' I say. 'Or they could both collapse simultaneously.' We look at each other and laugh. 'Jaffa....' He looks at me, waiting for me to go on. 'Can I have another look at your picture? Have you brought it?'

'Are you sure?' he asks. 'You didn't like it last time.'

'I was in a strange mood,' I tell him, 'and I didn't look properly.' Jaffa gets up and goes to his bike to get the folder. Like last time. Then he comes back and very slowly he opens it up to show me. I look at it for ages. 'Can I have a look at the first picture again?' I ask. Jaffa reaches into the very back of the folder and pulls it out. It's almost identical to the picture he first gave me of the young woman with the book on her lap. And now I understand.

I've been thinking about these pictures a lot. I point to the second picture, the one I didn't like before

'She's not dead, is she?' Jaffa doesn't speak. He sighs. I think he might cry but he doesn't. 'In the second picture, your mother is not dead.'

'No,' he agrees.

'And the young woman with the book is not your mother.' I pause and look at him as I say, 'The second picture is your mum. They're not the same person.' Jaffa looks at me and I can see the relief. He relaxes. His whole body relaxes 'I do like her, Jaffa. Your real mum. I do like her.' He leans towards me and I think he's going to kiss me but he turns away. I wait and he turns towards me again and leans forward. I can feel his breath and he pulls me close. Then he kisses me.

39

Only another few days to go until half term. Then I'm going to Summer Lane for a week. I roll the prospect around in my head and find that mostly, I don't want to go. I shall miss Mandy. Worse than that (I frown) I shall miss Jaffa. And, don't tell anybody but I like going to school. Unbelievable. The spelling tests are still dire, mainly because I haven't got my typewriter with me and because it's a test (but not a big test where I could sit in a separate room), I can't speak the letters into the little tape recorder I carry with me. With the spelling tests I fail as badly as ever but nobody minds. Nobody minds! Isn't that a miracle? Most of all, *I* don't mind.

I no longer think I'm stupid. I'm doing well in some of the subjects, especially English. For two of the big tests, I was allowed to dictate my answers onto a tape. I did it in the first aid room so I wouldn't disturb anybody and then I stayed in there and typed up my answers. School is frequently pleasurable, but my relationship with Mum isn't very good, and recently, it has got worse.

Our relationship varies depending on Esme's mood. I thought that I was supposed to be the moody one in the throes of adolescence and all that, but no, it's Mum. I'm never sure how she is going to react. In fact, everyone seems to be on edge. Even Grandma hasn't been as calm as usual. When we left after Easter, she seemed anxious and upset. Very unusual. And Mum, too. They looked at each other weirdly. I half tuned in to Mum's thoughts and realised that she'd found out that Grandma was worrying about her and Darius. Then I tried to tune into Grandma's thoughts. Hadn't done that for ages. My own thoughts have been more than I could manage and you get drawn in. Tuning in to people's thoughts is almost like starting to become the other person because you feel their point of view. It's exhausting so I stopped doing it. This time I didn't do it for long and I was out of practice but I found out that Grandma was worrying about me! She was worrying that Esme and Darius might take me to PNG!

Mum is frequently irritable and upset, but I have to admit that she's been worse than usual lately. Ever since Easter, Mum's mood seems to depend more on Darius than on anything else. In fact, Mum doesn't seem to care about anything or anybody else. If he is coming soon, she is happy. If he's just been, she is sometimes happy and sometimes not. If Darius is busy working and she isn't seeing him, she starts getting increasingly tense and irritable.

Actually. That's not a cliche but it is a word I use much too often. In my last English essay, I had *actually* crossed out seven times. Bad style my teacher said. Don't use it. Will have to try harder. Anyway, what I was going to say was that actually (ha ha - I'm not writing an essay at the moment), I half wish that I hadn't been so adamant about Darius not moving in. The more I see of him, the more I like him. He is good fun. It's Mum who is always so heavy-going. For instance, Darius was there when I got back from Steve's one Saturday. I'd come back early because I wanted to see Mandy, but Mum said it was too late for me to go out.

'It's only five o'clock,' I told her. 'There's all the evening left.'

'Where were you planning to go?' my mother asked.

'Gledhow Valley,' I told her. It was the first thing that popped into my head. We hadn't made any plans so I had no idea where we were going to go.

'What!' my mother screeched. 'Gledhow Valley at this time of night. No, you are not. It's not safe.' I looked at Darius who watched calmly. He was sitting at the table drinking tea and almost smiling.

'I could take you,' he suggested. 'I don't know Gledhow Valley. You and Mandy could show me around. I'd like to have a look.' I had noticed that he'd turned up in a car again and wondered if he was rich. Sometimes he comes in a car. Sometimes he doesn't. I thought students were supposed to be poor. But Darius isn't an ordinary student. He is a mature postgraduate student. Like Steve, I suppose. I thought about his offer but wasn't sure. If Darius came then my mother might want to come, too. I didn't want my mother coming with us to Gledhow. And I wasn't completely sure about Darius either. The places Mandy and I go to are private.

'No, thanks,' I told him. 'It's kind of you to offer, but I think we'll stay at Mandy's instead.' I saw that Darius was grinning at me. He wasn't surprised by my reply and he didn't mind but Mum was looking put out. Didn't know whether to be pleased or cross at Darius's offer, but the result was good. She changed her mind and said that I could go to Mandy's after all. Had to be back by eight. By the time I got back, Darius had gone.

Another time when Darius was there, I asked him if he played chess.

'Yes,' he said.

'Will you have a game with me?'

'He hasn't got time,' my mother interrupted. 'He's got to go and work on his dissertation.'

'Well, there might be time for one game,' Darius had replied and he smiled at Mum. So I played my first game of chess with Darius. He was the first person I'd played with apart from Steve. It felt odd at first, and I felt a bit nervous, but I didn't do too badly. Darius won, but it was enjoyable. I liked playing chess with him. When we finished, he got up and put on his coat. I could see that the pleasure on Mum's face when Darius sat down to play with me disappeared in an instant as soon as he got up to go.

'Are you leaving already?' Esme had said to him.

'Sorry,' Darius said. 'Got to get back to work.'

I've never seen my mother in a state quite like this. She swerves between super good moods where she sings and dances around the house to miserable lows. She's started chewing her nails. That is something Mum has never done before. She's also begun to drink more than she used to do. And she hasn't given up smoking. So much for those hundred promises. All in all, I think, my mother's relationship with Darius is not doing her much good.

On Tuesday, I arrive home from school before Mum, and the phone rings. I pick it up and speak.

'Leeds 453 692.'

'Is that Esme?' a voice asks. A man's voice. Deep, sort of gravelly. I don't know who it is.

'No,' I say. 'It's Dani. I'm her daughter. Can I take a message?'

'No,' the man says. 'No message. When will she be back?'

'Who's calling?' I ask. 'I need to tell her who called.'

'It's Jackson,' the gravelly voice says and then there's a silence. Oh my God, I think, it's him! I think that he's hung up but then he speaks again. 'Tell her that Jackson called.' Oh my God, I think again. What shall I do? It's the man who got Mum into trouble. I look at the phone and wonder what to do. Should I tell Mum when she comes home? If I tell her, what will she do? I remember all the stress and worry from last summer. I don't want my mother rushing off into danger and there is no Steve now. What on earth should I do? I'm still staring at the phone thinking about it when Mum arrives back from work. I decide to say nothing. Need to think.

'Hello Dani,' Mum says sounding cheerful. She must have had a good day. 'You look a bit washed out. Was school OK?'

'School was fine,' I reply and head off upstairs to sit in my room and decide what to do. After a while, I come to the conclusion that I need help with the situation. I think back to the summer. Jackson is dangerous. Mum got beaten up last time. I need to keep her safe. Steve is not in a position to do anything. I won't see him until Friday and whenever I ring, he is usually not in. Suzi is a possibility, but I can't imagine Suzi running after my mother into Chapeltown. No, it will have to be Darius. Can I trust him? I decide that I can. It is clear that Darius cares for Mum so I'm sure that he will help. I hesitate slightly when I remember that the last time I asked Darius for help he told me that it was none of his business. But things have changed. I hesitate again when I wonder whether Mum would want Darius to know about Jackson, but it should be all right. The problem with Jackson had been before Darius was around. I'm going to try him.

I consider how I can get in touch with him. Darius's phone number is in the little telephone book downstairs, but if I try to ring, my mother will hear. Could I get my mother out of the house somehow? I can't think of a way. Could I wait until tomorrow and get in touch with Darius as soon as I come home from school? No, I decide. That might be too late. Too dangerous to wait. I remember the last time when Steve and I had thought it was all over and that Mum was safe. But she hadn't been. Then I have an inspiration. I know what to do.

It doesn't take more than five minutes to nip downstairs and wait for my mother to go into the kitchen. Speedily I drop the little telephone book into my bag. Let's hope Mum won't notice that it has gone. I won't be out long.

'I'm going to Mandy's' I call to Mum. 'Back soon.'

'Half six,' Mum says. 'Make sure you're back by half six. I'll have dinner ready by then.'

Once outside, I set off and step behind a hedge to a place where Mum won't see me if she comes out of the house and looks down the street (not that she will, but just in case). Then I open the phone book to look for the address. Darius lives in Joe's house and it's somewhere in Chapeltown. I find it and recognise the street name immediately. I ride my bike round there. I know exactly where it is and it doesn't take me long to walk there. I ring the bell and wait. Hope Darius won't mind me dropping in. Luckily it is Joe who answers the door (not someone I don't know) and he doesn't even look surprised.

'Come in, Dani,' he says. 'How nice to see you.' He takes me into a large kitchen at the back of the house where his sister is cooking. Joe introduces her and says he'll go and get Darius from upstairs. I look around at the kitchen. Huge compared to our tiny little corridor affair. There are loads of saucepans and a couple of frying pans hanging on one wall. Shiny, not blackened like ours. Don't they use theirs?

Sheldine is the person cooking and she turns from the sink to chat with me. Think it must be chicken. Smells like it. It's warm and comfortable but I've hardly sat down when Darius appears so I go with him into the dining room. He, too, says that it's good to see me. We sit down at a huge table, and almost immediately, Joe's sister brings in two plates of food and two cups of tea.

'Thanks, Shelley,' Darius says.

'I'm sure you're hungry,' she says to me as she places the plates full of rice, black-eyed peas and chicken in front of us both. The food smells great and I'm suddenly ravenous.

'My mum's making my tea,' I try to refuse politely, but Joe's sister just laughs and says she is sure that I can eat two teas. Darius, too, encourages me, so I can't resist. We sit together and eat while I tell him what's happened.

'I hope you don't mind me coming,' I begin as Darius nods encouragingly. Then I tell him about the phone call, and how bad Jackson is. I tell him what happened in the summer before he came. I explain that my mother used to go dancing and I bend the truth a little when I tell him that Jackson caused her trouble. I don't tell him that it was Esme who went to see him. I'm deliberately vague about the details and emphasise that all my mother did was to go dancing. But people warned us that Jackson was dangerous and that eventually, Mum was beaten up.

'Was it Jackson who beat her up?' Darius asks.

'No,' I tell him. 'It was a woman, but it was Jackson who was behind it.'

'How was that?' he asks and I have to lie. I tell him that I'm not sure, but that I do know that Jackson is dangerous.

'And what did you think your mother would do when you told her?'

'I'm not sure,' I say, 'but she might go to Jackson's to try and sort things out. Steve helped last time but he's not here now and I wasn't sure that I could get in touch with him.'

'What would she have to sort out?' Darius asks. 'Does your mother still see Jackson?' I'm beginning to feel worried by this line of questioning. What is he thinking?

'I'm sure she doesn't,' I tell him. 'It happened a long time ago. It was before you came to Leeds, and I don't know how he's got our phone number. But I do feel worried.'

'How do you know Jackson is a bad man?' Darius asks.

'Oh, we all know,' I tell him. 'John came and told Steve about him.'

'Who's John?' Darius asks. Oh dear, this is turning out to involve saying much more than I had intended.

'He was somebody Mum went dancing with a long time ago,' I reply. I am beginning to feel that telling Darius has not been such a good idea. He seems to be asking an awful lot of questions and he doesn't look pleased. But suddenly he smiles and I feel relieved.

'Don't worry, Dani,' he says. 'I will make sure that your mother has nothing to fear from Jackson.'

'How will you do that?' I ask.

'I'll find his house and tell him,' Darius says. 'Don't worry. Your mother won't hear from Jackson again.' With that, I feel a renewed sense of relief. At least I don't have to worry about my mother anymore. I do need her to be safe.

'I'd better be off,' I tell him. 'I'm already late. I was supposed to be back by half six.'

'Wait a minute,' Darius says. 'I'll walk you back.'

'No need,' I reply.

'Yes, there is,' he insists. 'Have you forgotten about the Yorkshire Ripper? And there are other men, who might be dangerous.'

'I don't want her to know that I came to tell you,' I manage to tell him as we walk back, but Darius says it will be fine to tell her. He says that he doesn't want me to lie to my mother and doesn't want to keep our conversation a secret.

Darius comes back with me and stays late. When I go to sleep, he's still talking to Mum so it isn't until the next day that I get the chance to talk to Mum about it all. Well, bugger and shit. The heavens fall in. Darius was wrong. It was definitely not all right for me to have said anything to him. Anything at all. Esme is furious.

'How could you!' she yells at me. 'The trouble with Jackson was over a long time ago, and it is my private business. Nothing to do with anyone else.'

'I was worried about you,' I say. 'You got beaten up last time.'

'I am perfectly safe,' my mother almost spits at me, her voice full of anger modified by a restraint that looks as though it's killing her and what she really wants to do is to give me a good shake. Through gritted teeth, she says, 'And I'm perfectly competent. I don't need a fourteen-year-old girl to manage my affairs.'

'Well, I didn't think that I could manage your affairs,' I shoot back. 'That's why I went to see Darius.'

'It has nothing to do with Darius,' Mum replies. 'He has ended up misunderstanding everything you told him.'

'At least he'll keep you safe,' I yell at her but can believe that he might have misunderstood things here and there. 'He promised he would sort things out.'

'Well, I don't want him to sort things out,' my mother is shouting now. 'I'm an adult, and I'll fight my own battles. If there are any battles. Which there wouldn't have been.' She goes quiet for a moment and I wonder what's coming next. 'You're just a busybody, Dani. You need to remember that you're only fourteen. And it's time that you learned to do as you're told and not interfere in other people's affairs.'

40

Esme is shaking. Beside herself. To say that she is furious is an understatement. How dare Dani run off and tell Darius about the phone call instead of telling her that the man had called. Now Darius is treating her like a child. Says she is never to see Jackson again. Says she's been stupid.

'How could you have been so stupid.'

'What do you mean? Stupid?'

'Messing about with a man like that.'

'Who said I've been messing around with Jackson? And in any case, it's none of your business.'

Darius is angry. She's not seen him look like this before. Says he will go and sort things out. She should have known better. If he's going to behave like this, then she doesn't want to marry him. It's off! On no account is he to go to Jackson's and interfere in her affairs.

Darius looks at her and doesn't reply.

'Say something,' she shouts at him. 'You have to promise me that you will not interfere in my affairs.'

'You are my affair.'

'Promise me that you will not go and see Jackson.' No reply. 'You are NOT to go and see Jackson.'

Darius sits down and smiles. Smiles!

'Calm down.' He tells her to calm down... her anger boils over. What else can she say? She watches him fetch a beer from the fridge and sit down with it at the table.

Continues to ignore her until she stands in front of him and shouts.

'It's over. The marriage is off.' He looks at her. 'I mean it,' she says quietly. 'Now bugger off.' And he does. Esme watches as he picks up his jacket and leaves without a word. Closes the door softly and is gone. She follows him and pulls the door open. Shouts after him. 'Come back.' Sees him walking down the street. He doesn't turn round. Esme looks at his glass on the table. Still half full. What is wrong with him? He should have apologised. He should have stayed. She wants him back. Spends half the night awake.

And now it's morning and she has to go to work. She's told Dani what she thinks of her and her daughter has flounced off to school. This is a very bad day. And it is followed by another. And another.

Thursday is Dani's last day before Steve takes her down to Summer Lane. He's picking her up from school on Friday although she'll come back to pick up her things before they go. Mother and daughter have hardly spoken to each other since Ess told Dani that she shouldn't have interfered.

'Are you looking forward to going down to Grandma's?' Esme asks when Dani gets home from school. Dani shrugs.

'Not particularly,' she says and Esme is surprised.

'Why's that? I thought you liked seeing Grandma and spending time with Steve.'

'Not particularly,' Dani repeats and Esme sees that her daughter really doesn't look very happy. She goes to hug her and for a change, her daughter doesn't pull away.

'I'm sorry, Dani,' she says. 'What's changed?'

'I can't talk to Steve,' Dani says. 'He's distant. As though he's not there. Don't think he's interested in spending time with me anymore.' Esme bites back the instant contradiction that springs to her lips and waits to see if her daughter is going to continue. 'It's as though he's a copy of the Steve I used to know.' Dani hesitates. A clone of the real Steve.' Esme takes a breath before she replies.

'It's probably because he's still missing us,' Esme says. 'He might be taking antidepressants. I think they could have an effect like that.'

'I didn't think of that,' Dani says. 'I thought he didn't like me much anymore.'

'I'm sure that's not true,'

'And it's not just that. I'm going to miss Mandy. I don't really want to go away for the whole of half term.'

'Then don't go,' Esme says. 'You don't have to go, Dani. You can stay here with me.' She sees a hopeful look on her daughter's face but only for a second. It's immediately replaced by the dejection back again.

'Steve would be upset,' Dani says. 'I'll have to go. And Grandma and Grandpa would be upset, too.'

'Then why not go for a shorter time,' Esme suggests. 'I could come down on Monday and we could come back on Tuesday. Instead of leaving it until the weekend.' This time Dani's face does brighten.

'Are you sure, Mum?' Dani asks. 'That would be perfect.' Esme nods and goes into the kitchen to start the food. Dani follows her and asks if there's anything she can do.

'You can chop the veg,' Esme says. 'Onions, courgettes and a red pepper.'

'Did Jackson ring again?' Dani asks. It's the first time she's mentioned anything about him since the row about the phone call.

'No,' Esme says. 'He didn't ring again.'

'Suppose Darius must have sorted him out then,' Dani says while chopping the courgettes. Esme shrugs. Says she doesn't know. 'Where is Darius?' Dani asks. 'Is he working? He hasn't been around all week.'

'It's over, Dani' Esme tells her. She's been hoping all week that Darius would come back, but he hasn't. She tries to sound matter of fact but finds herself starting to cry so she turns away.

'Oh, Mum,' Dani says, putting the knife down and coming towards her. 'It can't be over. He loves you. Don't you love him anymore? What's happened?' Esme tells her a little about the row she had with Darius and why she told him to leave.

'But you didn't really want him to go, did you?'

Esme shakes her head.

'You'll have to get him back,' Dani continues.

'I can't do that,' Esme says. 'He was wrong to interfere in my life.'

'But he wants to interfere because he loves you,' she says. 'Like me,' she adds and Esme sees her daughter looking hopeful that at last Esme will understand why she went to Darius. Esme goes to give her a hug.

'Come here,' she says. 'I know you meant well, but I felt angry because I knew that Darius had misunderstood.' Dani hugs her back.

'You'll have to ask him to come back, Mum,' she says. 'And you'll have to put up with him interfering because that's the way he is. He loves you and he wants to keep you safe. Hasn't he rung you?' Esme shakes her head, 'It's his pride,' Dani says. 'You'll have to be the one to ring him.'

'I thought you didn't like him here,' Esme says. 'Replacing Steve.'

'Nobody can replace Steve,' Dani tells her. 'But I do like Darius. And I know he cares about you. He's got different ways. That's all. If you want Darius, you'll have to accept how he is.' Dani goes back to the chopping, then turns and grins. 'I'm beginning to sound like Mandy,' she says.

'I'll think about it,' Ess replies and turns towards her own chopping board. She's chopping garlic. Fiddly but worth it. This is her chance to choose a different path. Darius is dangerous territory. If he can't change his ways and she doesn't want to change hers, it doesn't bode well. His whole background is unknown. Probably everyone in PNG has attitudes like that and that's where she will have to live if she marries him. Dani, too. That's what she will have to accept. Limitations to her freedom.

Suddenly, Esme looks at her daughter and she knows who she is going to put first. She will ring Darius, but if they do get back together, there will be no question of moving to Papua New Guinea until she has discussed it with Dani and asked her what she wants. If Dani can't bear to leave Leeds and her grandparents in South Derbyshire, then that will be that. Her daughter's happiness has to come first. If Darius cares enough, he will still marry her and be willing to wait. Esme counts on her fingers - four years until Dani will have finished school and be ready to leave home. Would he wait that long? Esme has been selfish for too long and however much she wants this man, her daughter is more important.

***

On Saturday morning, Esme is ready to put her decision into practice. She makes a cup of coffee, lights a cigarette and picks up the phone.

41

'Now, there's a question,' Steve says, taking his eyes off the road for a minute and turning to look at me. 'Actually, I've got no idea.'

'*Actually* is redundant, actually,' I tell him. 'You don't need it at all. In fact, it's just bad style.'

'What!' he says, his cheeriness disappearing, replaced in an instant by irritation which he tries unsuccessfully to control or even to hide.

'We had a lesson on it,' I say. 'Actually, it wasn't just *actually*. It was bad style in general.' He doesn't say anything so I carry on, 'I got *actually* crossed out seven times in my essay. And I wasn't the only one.'

'Well, that's not from too much tv,' he says, clearly making an effort to remember Miss Smith's views on her pupils' use of English. Miss Smith thinks that almost all our inadequacies in use of language come from watching too much television.

'No,' I agree then change my mind. 'But it might be. They talk on tv, don't they? We might be writing like talking instead of writing like writing. They're different. Miss Smith says we don't know how to write anymore.'

'And why does she think that is?'

'Because we don't read enough. And she thinks that's caused by too much tv.' Aha, we've come full circle. 'We must be careful not to write as we speak,' I say. And Steve knows perfectly well that this is true, but he's obviously feeling irritable.

'Why not?' he asks.

'Because it doesn't work,' I say. 'It won't work because it's holey.'

'Holy? As in religious?'

'Don't be daft. I mean holey as in 'full of holes'. Spoken language has holes in it.' I smile. I'm enjoying this. Steve should try harder. He's not taking me seriously. He's a researcher into Russian history, a postgraduate student. He's perfectly aware of how writing is different from speaking, but I decide to remind him. 'We know what we're talking about when we're speaking to each other so we don't say everything. We don't need to explain our points of reference. But if it's written down like that, the reader often can't fill in the holes, doesn't know the context so the writing doesn't make sense.'

'Points of reference?' he asks half-heartedly. Then 'All right,' he says losing all interest in what I've been doing in class this afternoon when I thought it was interesting. 'But what's all this got to do with how pictures can communicate when they don't say a word?' Now we are back to the beginning. Back to what I was talking about before but he's not interested in anything I'm saying so I'm going to shut up and put some music on. Not much to choose from. Steve never seems to get any new music. I'm missing Jaffa.

***

In Summer Lane, the smell of baking fills the kitchen.

'Cheese scones,' George mutters as he takes off his boots and comes in for a cup of tea.

281

'They're too hot,' Frances tells him, 'Only just come out. You'll have to wait till they've cooled down.' She watches as he walks through the kitchen and goes to sit down. He is limping and wheezing as usual. Looking older, she thinks. More stooped than usual, but maybe it's because he is worried about Tom. George's elder brother was diagnosed with cancer a few months ago and he's going downhill fast. George is going to see him later on while Frances stays to finish the baking.

It's half term and Steve and Dani are due to arrive in a few hours' time. She is looking forward to seeing them although Esme rang and said that Dani wouldn't be staying for the whole week. Esme wants her daughter to spend some time at home in Leeds so she's fetching her back on Tuesday. Frances tries to push away the thoughts that plague her day after day. Why won't Esme go back to Steve? What's happening with her and Darius? She sighs.

'You've come in early,' Frances says. 'It's not dinner time yet.'

'I know,' George says. 'I've come in for a cup of tea and then I'm going to go and see Tom. Going early so I can go and get back.' Frances nods and goes to put the kettle on. She gets the biscuit tin out and smiles as she puts it on the table. George never has a biscuit with his morning tea, but she never fails to offer him one.

'Biscuit?'

'No thanks,' he says and grins at her, 'I'm waiting for the scones.' The kettle is boiling, so Frances goes to make the tea. She brings their cups in from the kitchen, the large white one that George always uses and her smaller cup with tiny pink roses. She sets the teapot on the stand in the middle of the table and waits for the tea to brew.

'I bought some grapes for you to take,' Frances tells him. George nods and fills his pipe. He never thought that he would outlive any of his siblings, but it looks as though Tom won't last much longer. Frances hasn't been with him since last Saturday, but George goes every day. He never offers much news after his visits, but Mary keeps her updated. Not long now she said.

After George gets back about five, they sit down to eat. No use in waiting for the travellers to arrive. No knowing when they'll turn up. George nods. They aren't expected before half-past seven at the earliest. They comment as usual on the Friday afternoon traffic and how heavy it always is. As usual, Frances reminds herself not to worry about them, and as usual, she fails.

'They'll be all right,' George says as he notices her glancing anxiously at the clock. 'Sit down and read the paper.' George hands it to her. He has already finished with it and is puffing away at his pipe. Little clouds of smoke rise towards the ceiling which is beginning to turn the familiar delicate shade of yellow that signals that it is time for a new coat of paint. They paint the ceiling every year usually at the beginning of the summer.

It's nearly eight before they finally hear the car draw up outside. Frances heaves a sigh of relief and goes into the front room to check that it's them. Yes, it is.

42

My heart always lurches just a little lurch whenever we turn into Summer Lane. And I feel happy. It's the same this time, but I know it won't last because I'm restless. I want to leave almost before I arrive. I won't see Jaffa on Sunday. I shall miss Jaffa.

'Here we are,' Steve says as we drive slowly down the lane. The house is at the bottom where the stile is and the public footpath. The road surface is rough so you have to drive slowly and you can hear the wheels on the gravelly bits as you drive down. I see Grandma appear at the gate before I've managed to get out. She must have been waiting for us.

'Hello Grandma,' I say and put down my bags to hug her. I'm thinking about the letter she wrote and what she said about Darius. But she's still Grandma. And I still love her.

'Hello, Frances,' Steve says as he follows me to the gate. 'Are we late again?'

'Not at all,' Grandma says and she tries to take one of the bags off my shoulder but I hang on to it.

'It's fine, Grandma,' I say. 'I'm fine. I can manage it easily.'

'Hey up, my duck,' Grandpa says as I go in. 'How long have you come for this time?'

'They've hardly got in the door, George,' Grandma says to him.

'I know,' he says and grins at me.

'Well, Steve's got to go back tomorrow night,' I tell him, 'but I'm here for a few days and then Mum's going to come down to get me. She said she'd ring and tell you'

'She did ring,' Grandma says and then turns to Steve. 'It's a shame you can't stay a bit longer. We've been looking forward to seeing you.'

'I'd like to,' Steve says, 'but a couple of unexpected jobs turned up, and I need the money. I'll stay longer next time.'

On Saturday afternoon, Steve insists on taking Grandpa to Uncle Tom's house. No need to catch the bus, he says, when there's a car available. Grandpa tries to refuse, but I can see that Grandma is glad when Steve insists. While they are gone, Grandma asks me if I'll help her to pick some blackcurrants.

'They taste nice, don't they' Grandma says, 'but they take ages to pick because they're so small. I'd be glad of your help.',

'No worries,' I tell her. 'I'm good at picking. Remember last year.' It is true. When I set my mind to something, I do it properly. Well, I suppose that's not always true. I used to set my mind to writing but for years I didn't succeed. But I know now why that was. Not my fault. Just think, all those years that I couldn't write and nobody knew I'd got dysgraphia. Grandma hands me a long blue apron which makes sense because blackcurrants stain easily. While we are picking, Grandma asks me how things are with us in Leeds.

'All right,' I say. 'Fine.' I know that what she wants to find out about is how things are with Darius, but she doesn't mention him and I don't say anything.

'And how's school?' Grandma asks.

'It's good,' I tell her and can't help smiling. I hesitate before I tell her my brilliant news. 'I came top in an English test. It's never happened before.' Grandma stops picking, straightens up and comes over to hug me.

'That's wonderful,' she says. 'That's fantastic news. Why didn't you tell us before? Your Grandpa will be so proud of you.'

'Well, I don't want Steve to know,' I say. 'And I haven't told Mum.'

'Why ever not?' Grandma asks. I can see that she's taken aback. Can't imagine why I haven't been shouting it from the rooftops. (That's another cliche I think as the thought flies past in my brain. I'm going to have to ignore what I've learned in school or I won't be able to talk at all. Or think.) 'Why ever not?' Grandma says again. 'They'd both be thrilled.'

'I know,' I say and wonder how I can explain. I'll have to say something. 'But it's boasting. Isn't it? And it was only a mid-term test.'

'Not at all,' Grandma replies. 'It's telling your family and letting them share your good news.' I see Grandma looking at me. She looks concerned.

'But Steve's not my family anymore, is he?'

'Well, strictly speaking, he's not your family,' Grandma replies slowly. 'But I'm sure he'll always love you and that's nearly the same as being family.' I consider what she's said but I don't reply. Steve doesn't feel like my family now. He's separate. Not like my dad anymore however much I want it not to be like that. 'And why haven't you told your mum?' I turn away.

'I don't know if she'd be pleased,' I say although it isn't true. I do know that she'd be pleased so I don't know why I haven't told her. I think I want to hurt her. 'I never know what she's going to say these days. Or how she's going to react,' I say to Grandma who stops and looks at me and thinks for a minute before she replies.

'Well, maybe she's got a lot to think about at the moment. Perhaps your Mum's life isn't as easy as it looks,' Grandma says and I'm surprised. I thought Grandma was annoyed with Mum because of Darius. I say nothing and start picking again. The blackcurrants really are very small. Fiddly little things. 'But I'm sure that she loves you, and she'll be hurt if she finds out about your good marks from someone else,' Grandma says. Then she adds, 'I'm not going to say a word to anyone until you've told her.'

'Are you sure?' I ask.

'About what?'

'That she still loves me?' Whoops. I didn't mean to say that. Grandma puts down her bowl and walks over to where I'm picking.

'Look at me,' she says and I do. 'I'm absolutely, totally and utterly sure that your mother loves you more than you can imagine. And she always will.'

'How long is always?' I ask. 'Mum said she loved Steve for always.' Grandma sighs.

'Oh, Dani,' she says, 'I'm sorry about Steve. But a partner or a husband is never the same as a child. A child is forever.'

'And a husband?' I ask.

'Not always,' Grandma says.

After Steve has gone, I settle down into the slow pace of life at Summer Lane. I spend quite a lot of time in the front room typing, and Grandma tells me about all the hours that Mum spent in there when she was young. Says it seems like only yesterday. I sigh. I've heard it all before.

'Can I go with you, Grandpa?' I ask on Sunday as George prepares to set off to see Tom.

'I don't know,' Grandpa says. 'He's very ill.'

'I know,' I say. 'Grandma told me. But I'll sit quietly. I won't disturb him.'

'Why do you want to go?'

'I like him,' I reply. 'He used to buy me ice cream soda. And he told me jokes.' Grandpa looks at Grandma and she nods so that's a yes and I set off with Grandpa. She watches us go and I wonder for a minute how she sees us. Grandpa. An old man with his cap pulled well down at the front, even in the warmish summer weather. And me. A young girl with a blonde spiky haircut. I stand out down here with my frayed jeans and Doc Martens. And my black nail varnish. I like my look. I think I look older than fourteen. I think of Jaffa. He likes my look.

Grandma tried to talk to me about Darius this morning and I didn't know what to say. I didn't want to tell her that Mum had a row with him and he hasn't been back all week. I feel loyal towards Darius but don't know why because it's Steve I love, not him. Maybe it's because of the horrible things Grandma wrote about him although as she talks I begin to understand a little bit about how she feels. I think that it's not so much the fact that he's black. It's more the fear that he'll take us away and she won't see us anymore. Grandma seems sure that it's serious between Mum and

Darius. Secretly, I agree with her but don't admit it. I wonder how Grandma can have picked that up in such a short time. She only saw them together once. On my birthday.

We talked for ages. I could see Grandma's face brighten when I told her that Darius hadn't moved in with us. She hadn't known that. And I could almost see her working out how long it was until he's due to leave although she knows Mum better than anybody. Knows she's capable of ditching everything and just taking off. Leaving the job, the house. Everything. I catch myself with that little fear again. Will leaving everything include me? Would she leave me behind with Grandma? It would be awful having to go to Papua New Guinea, but it would be worse if she left me behind. In either case, I'd lose Jaffa so my future doesn't look that bright. Can't bear the thought of losing Jaff. Or Steve, or Grandma, or Mandy. But mostly, Jaff.

It's a good visit to Great Uncle Tom. It's a relief to be somewhere different and he's good fun even though he's so ill. When we get back, Grandpa and I are still laughing.

'I thought you'd just been to see Tom,' Grandma says looking slightly surprised.

'Yes, we have,' I say, 'and he's very poorly.'

'But not too poorly to tell jokes,' Grandpa says. 'He kept telling one after another all afternoon. His voice sounded weak, and we kept telling him to rest, but he wouldn't stop. He laughed and coughed at the same time.' Grandpa sits down. 'I think Dani did him good. It's the first time I've seen him smile this week.' He grins at me and then turns back to Frances, 'Maybe he's getting better. Perhaps the doctors have got it wrong.'

289

***

Later on after tea, Frances goes up the garden with George. They leave Dani typing away in the front room.

'I can't stop worrying,' Frances tells him as she pushes the watering can under the water butt and turns on the tap.

'What about?'

'Esme and Darius,' she says. Frances stands waiting for the can to fill up. It always takes ages. 'I've never seen Esme behave like this before. She's my daughter. I saw how she was with Dani's father. I've seen how she was with Steve. I'm sure she loved them, but this is different. She's besotted.' She stoops to turn off the tap but leaves the watering can where it is. 'I talked to Dani this morning and he hasn't moved in with them, but I'm not reassured. I know it's serious and I can tell that Dani thinks so, too.' Frances looks at George and manages to say the thing that frightens her most. 'What shall we do if Esme marries him and they go to Papua New Guinea? And take Dani.'

'We'll be all right,' George says surprising her, 'and they'll be all right, too. You'll write to them, and after a while, they'll come back. If they go, I'm sure they'll come back. Dunna you worry.' He looks at Frances and walks over to put his arm around her. It is something he never does. 'Come on, Frankie,' he says. 'It's her life, and we can't live it for her. We can't stand in the way.'

'But he's black,' Frances says.

'I know,' George replies.

'Look at that man who got killed recently when he was standing up for black people. What was his name?'

'Do you mean Blair Peach?'

'Yes, that's the one,' Frances says. 'He got killed, and Esme's like him. She believes in the same things, and she's just as hot-headed. I'm worried that something awful will happen to her.'

'She'll go her own way,' George says. 'We canna stop her, Frankie.'

43

Esme sits with the phone in her hand for about five minutes thinking about Darius. Then she puts it down again. If he cared about her, he would have got in touch. Why does it always have to be her? Why does she always have to make the running? A small internal voice reminds her that it was she who told him it was over. That the marriage was off. It is Saturday. Dani's gone to Summer Lane with Steve and Esme is going to fetch her back at the beginning of the week. These days of freedom are precious and they are being wasted.

No, she thinks, these days are not being wasted. They are precious times for stopping to think. In her mind, there is a conviction that she can be with Darius if she wants to, marry him if she wants to. She's sure that he wants her, but under what conditions? How would he react if Dani wasn't ready to go to PNG? Maybe she should just forget about him.

Esme hasn't said a word to Dani (or anyone else) about getting married despite the fact that they've set the wedding date. Will Darius have cancelled the arrangements since she told him the marriage was off? She needs to talk to him and she needs to talk Dani. It's the haste and the secrecy that is driving her crazy. But what will she do if Dani says she won't go to PNG? And what will she do if Darius says that he can't marry her if she won't go with him straightaway? Ess gets up and walks backwards and forwards in the small living room. She decides that they can't go if Dani is not ready to leave. But Dani might be willing. She was surprisingly understanding on Thursday night when they talked about Darius. It was Dani who had said she should ring him.

So, no, Esme thinks again, these days are not being wasted. She is thinking things through and beginning to see more clearly than she did when she was merely hurtling forward blindly. At least, she thinks she's beginning to see more clearly. These days are like a holiday, a little time out from the inevitable life track that she is bound to rejoin. But now Esme is no longer sure which track it will be. Time to go for a walk. She will separate herself at least from the telephone. From sitting next to it waiting for it to ring. Or from being tempted to pick it up and ring the man herself.

Nearly the whole weekend is spent tramping around. Up to Roundhay Park. Back home. Down to Gledhow Valley. Up the wooded hillside and out on the other side. Ess calls on an old friend who lives up there with his partner. They look surprised to see her standing on their doorstep but don't actually ask her what she's come for. She goes in. Makes some polite chat. Drinks their coffee. Leaves.

Can't stop herself rushing to the phone each time she arrives home but there's nothing. No messages. No-one has rung. Not even her mother or Dani. On Sunday evening, there's a knock on the door and her heart jumps.

'Suzi,' she says. 'Come in.' She sees that Suzi has brought a bottle of wine. Good. And there's one in the kitchen. Both Merlots. Maybe they'll be able to manage two. What a good idea.

'Where've you been, Ess? I've been round three times. Was beginning to think that Darius had run off with you.' Esme fetches glasses and a packet of nuts as a gesture towards hangover prevention and they sit down at the table. She tells Suzi what has happened and where she's been all weekend.

'It's Howard's cure,' Esme tells her.

What is?'

'Walking.'

'Cure for what?' Suzi asks. Esme almost says the summertime blues but the frivolous response dies before it is spoken.

'Depression. Indecision. Confusion and misery,' she replies more accurately. Suzi raises her eyebrows. 'And what about you? Any baby news? Has Pete been talking about marriage again?' Esme has told Suzi nearly everything but hasn't breathed a word about Darius's proposal. And worse. His suggestion that they get married secretly. Her mind is back on Darius before Suzi has even had a chance to reply.

'No baby news,' Suzi tells her. 'It's depressing. And yes, Pete mentions marriage from time to time, but we don't get any further.'

'Are you going to?' Esme asks.

'Yes, I think so,' Suzi says. 'It will please the parents and be good for the baby. If a baby ever comes. And Pete says there are tax advantages.' Esme starts to frown at this last piece of information, but Suzi pre-empts whatever she's about to say. 'Don't scoff, Ess. It's not sensible to turn down money for no good reason.'

'I suppose,' Ess replies.

'So what are you going to do about Darius?'

Esme shrugs and sips her drink, rolls a cigarette and lights up.

'Nothing I can do, is there? He's gone.'

'Only because you told him to go. Is that what you want?'

'I don't know,' Esme replies. 'I love him, Suze. I can't stop thinking about him. But it's not sensible.'

'No,' Suzi agrees. 'You're right. It is not sensible.' She finishes the first glass and pours another. The nuts are sitting untouched. Esme notices that Suzi is drinking a lot. More than usual anyhow. 'But you'll regret it if you let him go, won't you?'

'I suppose so, but I'm angry. How could he even consider going to see Jackson? Interfering in my life without consulting me. I'm not a child.'

'No, but he considers himself responsible for you,' Suzi says.

'Yes, it's his foreign ways.'

'Bullshit!' Suzi says. 'What do you mean? Foreign! It's exactly as most men here would behave. It's old fashioned. They think they're being gallant. It's unenlightened. But not foreign. And it's well-intended,' she adds. 'He's trying to look after you.' When Esme doesn't reply, Suzi adds, 'It's how your father would probably behave towards your mother.' Esme concedes that Suzi is probably right, but she doesn't like the thought of being the one to ring Darius. Doesn't like the thought of giving in and apologising. But she knows she's going to have to. Darius seems to be as stubborn as she is. It doesn't look as though he's going to beg to come back. Nor even apologise.

'He asked me to marry him,' Esme finds herself saying. 'And I said yes. That was before we argued about Jackson and I told him it was over.' There is a pause before Suzi replies.

'Did you tell Dani?'

'No,' Esme says and starts to roll another cigarette. 'I didn't tell anyone.'

'Do you still want to marry him?'

'Yes,' Esme admits, the word spoken before all the hesitations, reservations, sensible conclusions get a chance to appear.

'Then ring him, get him back and go ahead,' Suzi says.

'But what about Dani?'

'You will have to tell her. And she will have to accept it.'

'It would mean going to Papua New Guinea.'

'She'll cope,' Suzi replies.

'But she might not like it...'

'No, she might not like it,' Suzi agrees. Esme goes to make another cup of tea. Suzi wanted a change from coffee she said.

'I had sort of made a decision,' Ess says and relights the cigarette she'd put out a few minutes ago.

'Go on.'

'I am going to let Dani decide when she's ready to go. It's not fair to drag her to the other side of the world away from her family and her friends, the places she knows. That is if Darius agrees to wait for me until Dani is ready.' Esme looks at Suzi and waits for her response.

'That's stupid,' Suzi says. 'You can't be serious. You can't put such a huge responsibility on to Dani. It's not fair.'

'What do you mean?'

'She's a young girl. You can't give her the responsibility of whether or not you commit to Darius and go to live in PNG.'

'She wouldn't have that responsibility. I'd marry him anyway so long as he was prepared to wait until Dani was ready to go to PNG. If he wouldn't wait, then that would be that.'

'No,' Suzi pronounces with conviction. 'You should go ahead with your life and do what you think is best. She's not old enough to make such decisions. At least if you decide to go and she hates it, she can be angry with you. It won't be her fault.'

'I'll think about it,' Esme says. She hadn't looked at it from that point of view. She draws on the cigarette. Very short now. She's almost burning her fingers. 'I'm going down to Summer Lane tomorrow.'

'Then you'd better hurry up with that phone call,' Suzi says.

By the time Suzi leaves, they are both drunk. They haven't managed two bottles but one and a half have disappeared. And no nuts.

'Are you all right, Suze?' Esme asks as her friend is getting ready to leave. Suzi doesn't usually drink this much and they've spent all the time talking about Esme and her problems. Nothing about Suzi.

'I'm fine,' she says in the tone of voice that tells Esme that she definitely is not. 'I'll tell you another time. Goodnight, Ess. Don't forget to call Darius.'

It's nearly eleven pm but Esme is drunk so she picks up the phone and calls.

'Hi, Joe,' she says. 'Can you give Darius a message? Can you tell him that I'd like to talk to him?'

Twenty minutes later, Darius appears at her door and they fall into each other's arms. There is no talking for ages and he stays all night. It is only the second time that Esme has spent the night with him and this time she hasn't organised the bedroom or put fresh towels in the bathroom. It is good, even better than last time and eventually, they start to talk. They have a slow, lazy breakfast before Esme sets off down the motorway. The wedding is on again, but Esme still hasn't decided what to do about Dani.

44

Mum came to get me as promised and I had hardly anything to carry. I was going to say that it was lucky but it wasn't lucky, it was properly planned because very little will fit into the box on the back of the bike. Steve had taken the typewriter back like last time. He's going to drop it off on Friday so I'll have to manage without it until then. I'd been so busy thinking about Jaffa and missing my Sunday with him that I didn't think about Steve until after he'd gone. It was then that I realised that I hadn't felt bad when he left. For the first time, it was all right. And I don't think he'd felt bad either. I could see that I'd often irritated him this weekend. As though I'd changed from somebody bathed in a golden glow, somebody who could do no wrong and who had to be pampered and handled carefully into an ordinary kid, who at times, annoyed him so much that he had to be careful not to snap. What a nice change. It felt so much better.

I'm back home now and Darius is back, too. Not moved in, but here a lot. I keep asking myself how I feel about that but I think it's OK. If he starts to look after me or tries to boss me about, it will not be all right. I don't want another Dad. Steve is the one. I will always think of him as my dad. I told him that and I think he was pleased. I told Darius, too, and he seemed to understand which was a relief. Not long until Sunday. I'm counting the days but I'm going to stay with Steve before then. Off with him on Friday and back Saturday as usual.

'Do you feel like chopping some veg?' Mum shouts from the kitchen. I don't mind. I get a chopping board and we sit at the table and chop together. The vegetables look bright and beautiful against the wooden boards. Chopped and ready for the pan. Colourful, fresh and moist. I make patterns. Almost too pretty to eat.

'How was Steve?' Mum asks me. 'Is he still distant with you?'

'No,' I reply. 'I think he's back to normal.' I go into the kitchen to get the other knife. The little one with the serrated edge that I like best. She's given me the wrong one. 'He nearly got cross with me.' Mum laughs.

'That sounds like a good sign,' she says and then, after a minute or two. 'And how about Darius?' A small tentative question.

'I like him,' I say. 'I'm glad he's around again.' And I hear Mum sigh with relief. Then I ask what's happening with her and Darius. Mum continues to chop courgettes then stops and stares into space. Puts the knife down.

'I don't know,' she says. 'I think I want to stay with him, Dani. I think I want to marry him, but I'm worried about you. What do you think?'

I think about it for a minute and summon up my courage.

'If you stay with him, will you go to PNG?'

'Yes,' Mum says. 'I probably will.'

'And what about me?'

'Well, you would have to come, too,' she says. 'But if you don't want to go, it's OK. We'll stay here and Darius can go back by himself. He'll have to wait for me.' She stops talking and puts her knife down. Looks at me. 'It's up to you, Dani. We could wait until you were ready. You are the most important person. Not Darius.'

My whole body relaxes. Hadn't known that I'd been so tense. Can't believe what Mum's just said. Don't quite believe her because it sounds too good to be true. I don't want to go, of course. But I sure as hell, don't want to get left behind if she does go. And I don't want Mum to get left behind by Darius. She'd be impossible to bear. I don't say a word.

'How would you feel about it if it happened? If I married Darius?' she asks, picking up the knife and resuming the chopping. 'And how would you feel about going to PNG?'

'Don't know,' I say but I do know. Of course, I know. 'I'd miss Grandma and Grandpa and Steve and Mandy,' I tell her. And Jaffa. But I don't say his name. 'Wouldn't you miss everyone?'

'Yes,' Mum says. 'I would.'

'But it might be all right,' I say. 'To go over there for a little while.'

'It wouldn't be for a little while,' Mum says. 'It would be for a long time, Dani.'

'Couldn't we come back to visit?' I ask.

'Yes, of course,' Mum says, 'but not often.'

I think about this and don't like the idea.

'Then I don't think so,' I say. 'I'd rather we stayed here.' But then I see Mum's face and I understand what she's doing. She's offering to give up Darius for me. Does she mean that? 'Can I think about it?' I ask. 'I don't think so, but can I think about it?' Mum comes and hugs me and her face is wet with the tears that she is trying hard to control.

But now I know or at least, I think I know. Mum does love me.

'Dear Dani,' she says and goes to get some kitchen roll. 'I'm fine,' and she laughs and blows her nose. Smiles at me. 'We'll stay here if that's what you want.' Then she hesitates and asks, 'Would a year be long enough for you to be ready?'

'Probably,' I say.

***

Mandy comes round after we've eaten and we go down to the cellar. I'm about halfway through building her bike. It's taking a long time. Much longer than the first one. I've had problem after problem with it. We sit down to chat but there are no crisps or biscuits.

'Shall I fetch some from our house?' Mandy asks me. 'Haven't you got any at all? None left over somewhere in a tin?' I shake my head. We never have any left over. We always eat them all in one go. 'I'm going to fetch some,' she says. 'Can't think properly without a biscuit. Back in a minute.' When she comes back, she asks me about Jaffa.

'What do you mean,' I say.

'I mean, how's Jaff?' she says and giggles. 'Everybody knows, you know. You've been seen!' I feel myself blushing and try to stop but my face just gets hotter.

'Don't know what you mean,' I say, playing for time and hoping that she's bluffing. I don't want anybody to know about me and Jaff.

'He kissed you,' Mandy says. 'Margaret Jones saw you. She said you were in the park near the tennis courts.' She giggles again and waits for me to say something. 'You didn't tell me, Dani,' and then asks, 'What's he like?' I find that I don't want to talk about Jaffa. Don't want the kids talking about him or us. Our friendship is private. But it's too late.

'I like him,' I say. 'We're friends.'

'Friends!' Mandy almost screeches. 'Margaret Jones said that you were a lot more than friends. Said you kissed for ages and she walked past but you didn't see her.'

'She shouldn't have been snooping about,' I say, feeling angry. 'What we do is none of her business.'

'She wasn't snooping about,' Mandy says. 'She lives up there. Her house is in that terrace that runs down the side of the park.' Mandy stops to get another biscuit. 'Down by the allotments. She was going home when she saw you.' Mandy offers me one. Gingernuts this time. Not our favourites but better than nothing. I go upstairs to make us a drink so we can dunk them.

'Tea or coffee?' I ask.

'Tea,' she says. 'They'll taste better with tea.' When I get back with the tea, Mandy asks me why I don't want anybody to know about me and Jaffa and I shake my head.

'Don't know really. It's just that it feels private. Don't want anybody to know.'

'Do you like him?' she asks. I nod. 'Do you love him?'

'Course not,' I say but it might not be true. I try to change the subject and ask her about all sorts of stuff but she keeps coming back to me and Jaff.

'You're lucky, Dani,' she says. 'He's fab.' I blush some more and turn away to dunk my biscuits. The steam from the tea mixes with the heat in my cheeks.

'What about you?' I ask her. 'Who are you seeing, Mandy?'

'Nobody,' she says. 'I quite like Morgan Thompson,' she volunteers, 'but I'm not sure.'

'The one in the sixth form,' I say. 'He must be eighteen.'

'Yes,' she says. 'That's him.'

I can't concentrate on what she's saying. I keep thinking about everybody knowing about me and Jaffa. Will he want to keep on seeing me? I've got the feeling that Jaffa might be like me. He might want us to be private.

***

'I missed you,' Jaffa says when I arrive on Sunday and sit next to him on the bench.

'Me, too,' I say.

'How was Summer Lane?'

'OK,' I say.

'And Steve?' Jaffa knows how important Steve is to me.

'Steve was fine this time. I think he's getting better. It was easier. More normal.' Not very well explained but I can see that Jaffa understands. 'What about you? How's your dad?'

'He's gone again,' Jaffa says, 'but nobody's noticed so I haven't been sent back to Hunslet.'

'So who's looking after you?'

'I am,' he points at himself and grins.

'What about meals?'

'I can cook,' he says. 'It's finding money to go shopping that's hard, but Annie gives me some. I tell her that I have to do the shopping and Dad doesn't give me any. It's true, anyway, but she hasn't got much herself.' I immediately wish that I'd got some money to give him, or at least some biscuits but I haven't got either. 'It's all right,' he says. 'I'm managing fine. Don't look so worried, Dan.' I notice the 'Dan' like the 'Dani girl'. Nobody else calls me those names. It feels intimate. Gives me a warm feeling when Jaffa talks to me like that. I realise that I'll have to tell him about Margaret Jones.

'There's something I've got to tell you,' I say before we go any further.

'What's that?' he asks catching my serious tone and beginning to look concerned.

'Everybody knows about us,' I say in a rush and wait for his response.

'What do you mean?'

'Margaret Jones saw us here last week. She walked past and we didn't see her. She's told everybody.'

'Do you mean she saw us kissing?' he asks and I nod. He laughs and pulls me close to him. 'Then we'd better do it again, Dani girl. In case she's still around and thinks that we've fallen out with each other.' And Jaffa kisses me again and my words disappear. I don't think. I just feel. When we stop, we look at each other and smile. Without thinking I start to tell him about Darius.

'There's something I'm worried about,' I say and he nods at me to carry on.

'We might be going overseas,' I tell him and my stomach tenses even to say it.

'What? On holiday?'

'No,' I say. 'If Mum gets together with Darius, we might go with him to PNG.' Jaffa looks shocked at this piece of information, but not as shocked as I feel to have actually said it out loud. 'It might not happen,' I say. 'But it's a possibility. We'd have to leave Leeds.'

'Forever?' he asks and I nod.

'I think so.'

45

Now they're back together, the marriage is on again and Esme's wedding day is drawing closer, but still, no-one knows. Suze and Dani both know that Ess has been thinking about marriage but even they don't know how things have progressed and that the wedding is now imminent. The date was set weeks ago to coincide with the beginning of the summer holidays. Esme was sure that Darius would change his mind about keeping it secret. She had thought that all he needed was time, but it seems not.

The second half of the term has flown by and she is feeling increasingly uneasy. She half-mentioned to him about her decision to wait until Dani was ready to go with her to Papua New Guinea but she doesn't think he even heard what she said.

'Do you want to cancel, Esme?' Darius asks whenever she brings up anything to do with the marriage. 'You don't have to go through with it, you know. You can always change your mind.' But no, she doesn't want to cancel, but she doesn't want it to be secret. She's giving up so much for him but there's no point in reminding him of that. Darius knows and tells her over and over again that she can change her mind.

'There's something I need to tell you,' she says feeling a wave of fear that she hadn't expected sweep through her body.

'What's that, Ess?' She can see that Darius is beginning to look apprehensive because of her serious tone.

'I do want to marry you,' she says again and he waits for her to go on. 'But I'm not going to come to Papua New Guinea until Dani is ready to go with me. It's not fair to her.' There she's managed to say it. Darius gets up from the table where he's been sitting with a book and walks towards her. Takes her in his arms and kisses her.

'Of course,' he says. 'I can wait, Ess. I don't want to, but I can wait.' It's going to be all right, Esme thinks, it is going to be all right. Darius will wait. I thought he wouldn't, but he will. He does love me. A feeling of happiness flows through her. 'Do you want to postpone the marriage?' he asks.

'No,' she says.

'Are you sure?'

'Yes,' she replies. 'But I don't want it to be secret.' Darius shakes his head at her.

'Everyone will know soon enough,' he says.

After he has gone, Esme can't stop thinking about the prospect of getting married and how uneasy she feels to be doing it secretly. The whole point about marriage, surely, is to make a public statement. The days whizz past and soon there is less than a week before the wedding date. She doesn't want to change her mind but over and over again she thinks of her parents and what their reaction will be. She ought to tell them. And there's Dani. She, more than anyone, ought to be told. Esme still can't quite understand why Darius wants it to be kept secret. Nor why she feels so terribly scared of telling her family. But she does know. It's because she remembers what her mother said and how much they would miss her and Dani if they went to PNG.

'Are you ashamed of me?' she has asked several times and Darius has given her a look that says such a question doesn't deserve an answer.

The days and weeks have passed and Esme hasn't seen nearly as much of Darius as she would have liked because he seems to spend his life working. At least that's what he says. No choice, he keeps telling her. He has to pass. Has to do more than pass, he has to complete his master's degree with honours. His university is paying for him to do this. It's important.

So it's still a secret. Only a few days left until next Saturday when she will marry, but the closer it gets, the worse she feels. She loves Darius more than she has ever thought it possible to love a man, but it is also true that she hardly knows him. She knows that everyone will think her crazy. They will condemn her for marrying him. Esme cannot even understand herself. After years of saying that she would never get married, never wanted to and couldn't see the point, she now wants more than anything to make a public statement that she loves this man. And wants to stay with him forever.

And what about Dani? Even her beloved daughter has not been told. Nor her parents. Esme tries to face the fact that the thing she most wants, this marriage to Darius, will not be able to count as a public statement if she is too afraid even to tell her parents. The secret act will cause misery. She draws on her cigarette and makes a decision. No, it will not happen like that. The marriage will have to be announced.

Every time Esme and Darius have disagreed, Esme has been the one who has given in and has accepted what he wanted. She has gone along with him even when she has wanted things to be done differently. With a superhuman effort, she has not moaned about his long hours of work or about his going off with Joe and Helen sometimes. She has even put up with his anger after Dani told him about Jackson.

That was their biggest argument. The one over Jackson. Darius had called her stupid and said that her behaviour had to change. She was furious and accused him of treating her like a child. Esme told him she was a woman, not a girl, and capable of making her own decisions whatever the consequences. If that's how women were treated in Papua New Guinea, she told him, then he would have to learn that it was different with her, but he had refused to listen. Darius had been angrier than she'd ever seen him and so was she. She had told him to go and he'd gone. When she had finally asked him to come back, he had assured her that she would never hear from Jackson again and Esme had to accept that. What had happened she asked? He wouldn't say.

The one person they had never argued about was Dani. Darius accepted that Esme was Dani's mother and even when Esme could see that he would have treated Dani differently or would have made a different decision, he had not said a word. And he liked Dani. If it had not been so, it would have been the one reason that Esme would have left him. She is glad that the two of them had got to know each other through the writing sessions when Esme was not involved. At the time, she had wished it otherwise, but in the end, it had made life easier.

Darius accepts that Steve is important to her daughter and is supportive of her seeing him. Funny, Esme thinks to herself. The one thing that could have kept them apart was Dani. If Darius hadn't liked her, for instance. Or if he had tried to interfere or if he hadn't understood how important her daughter was to her, then however painful it might have been, the relationship would have had to end. It's ironic, Esme thinks. The only way there was any chance of Darius becoming Dani's third father was for him to renounce the role in advance.

But this matter of the marriage would have to be thrashed out. Darius's insistence on secrecy was wrong. She remembers her first marriage to Dani's father. She was heavily pregnant and reluctant to marry but it had been necessary. She hadn't even invited her parents, although they had been told about the wedding. For the first time, she wonders if they would have wanted to come. But this marriage is different. This is the real one. The one she dreamed of as a young girl. She is not going to have this marriage spoiled. And if her daughter and her parents are not there, it will be spoiled and there will be no going back.

Esme thinks about it while she cleans the stairs. The whole house needs cleaning. She's left the housework for much too long thinking she could catch up with it at the end of term. But it's nearly the end of term already and time is running out. Esme is cleaning the stairs with a brush and dustpan in preparation for going back over the uncarpeted parts with a damp cloth. The pan is already full of dust.

Reluctantly, she faces up to the reasons she has not argued with Darius about marrying secretly. It's because she is afraid, no, terrified, of their reactions. Dani still loves Steve, and Esme remembers what she had said just after Easter about Darius moving in. Dani had spoken a firm and horrified no. No way her daughter had said. It wasn't that long ago. Dani has softened towards Darius since then and Esme is afraid of spoiling the hard-won harmony. But she will have to.

She finishes with the brush and dustpan and gets the cloth and a bucket. Goes back up to the top where Dani's bedroom and Steve's old workroom is. As Esme cleans, she considers her mother's reaction to Darius. Her mother has always seemed to be aware of her feelings, although she doesn't always get it quite right. In the past, even when her mother didn't agree with her, and Esme knows this happened often, Frances didn't comment. Her mother had never before ventured to interfere in her life. Until this time. Until Darius. Esme realises how strongly her mother feels and how much she has wished for Esme not to get involved with him.

Gradually, Ess understands that her mother has known from the start that her love for Darius would mean that she and Dani would eventually leave. They would go to Papua New Guinea. Esme stops for a moment to consider how her parents might feel at the prospect of both their daughter and granddaughter moving so far away. Ess remembers the night they had argued about mixed race children and she had seen her mother cry. Next day when Mum had tried to apologise and explain, Esme had turned away. No, Esme thinks. She has been a coward. If they refuse to accept her marriage, she will go ahead anyway, but she will have to invite them. They are her beloved parents.

46

When Darius arrives to have lunch with her, Esme tells him what she wants.

'Why does it have to be secret?' she asks. 'You have kept saying that our engagement and wedding have to be kept secret, but you have never said why. Tell me.' Darius looks at her, and she can feel her eyes flashing. She is angry. It seems to take forever before he speaks.

'It's because I've been afraid,' he says, and Esme can't believe her ears. Darius afraid? She has never seen him afraid of anything. In the months she has known him, he has been fearless. Self-confident and assured. 'Yes,' he says quietly in answer to her refusal to believe him, 'I'm telling you the truth.' He pauses and then continues, 'I was afraid of losing you. I thought that if we told Dani, she would convince you to change your mind.' He sits down. 'And then there is the problem of my family. I have been afraid to tell them because I thought they would disapprove.' He pauses and looks at her. 'And I thought that your parents would never let you marry me. My country is on the other side of the world. It's natural that they wouldn't want you to go so far away.'

Esme doesn't speak. Doesn't know what to say. Is amazed to hear Darius talk like this.

'But I was selfish,' Darius goes on, 'I wanted you despite my awareness of what it would mean to others. Or the sacrifice it would cost you and your daughter.' Darius takes a deep breath and looks at her intently, 'You have no idea,

Esme, how hard it will be for you in Papua New Guinea, but I have. I know. And still, I couldn't stop. Despite myself, I wanted you at any cost.' He stops again and the time stretches. She still does not speak. 'I did try, Esme. In the beginning, I tried so hard to avoid you.' Another pause. 'But in the end ....' His voice trails off.

Esme hugs him and holds him tight. She has never seen him vulnerable before, and it makes her love him more. Suddenly, the song that was playing when they first met springs into her mind ... *I've got you ... under my skin....*

'I'm going to marry you anyway,' she informs him. 'But I'm going to tell Dani and my parents and invite them to the wedding.' It is her turn to pause. She looks in the tin for a cigarette, but she hasn't rolled one. 'And I'm going to tell them this afternoon,' Esme says. 'We'll be travelling to see my parents tomorrow, so you'd better go and get ready.' Ess speaks with a lot more confidence than she feels. She is not sure what will happen when she tells Dani and her parents about the wedding, but there is no point in confiding these fears.

Darius leaves after lunch to go back to Joe's house to sort out his work and collect his things. He has said that he'll be back later. Esme takes a deep breath, rolls three cigarettes, lights the first one and dials her parents' number.

'Hello, Mum,' she says. 'It's me. Can I speak to Dani?'

'I'll get her for you,' her mother replies. Is she imagining things, Esme wonders, or does her mother sound more relaxed than before?

'Hi, Dani,' Ess says as her daughter comes on the line.

'Hi, Mum,' Dani says. 'I've got something to tell you.' Pre-empted, Esme thinks to herself. Things never go quite as planned, but her daughter sounds happy so it must be something good.

'What's that then?' Esme asks.

'I came top in English,' Dani says and waits. 'For the second time, Mum. The first time was in a small test just before half term. But now I've done it again in the end of term exams.' Esme does a double-take wondering why Dani hasn't mentioned it before but feels that now is not the time to ask.

'Well, that's wonderful,' Esme says. 'Just wonderful! I always knew you were the most brilliant girl. It was only a matter of time until you showed the rest of the world.'

'Do you mean it, Mum?' her daughter asks.

'Mean what?' Esme asks, baffled.

'About me being a brilliant girl?'

'Well, of course, I do,' Esme says. 'We've always known you were a brilliant girl.'

'I thought for so long that I was stupid,' Dani says. 'Mrs Richards always said that I was lazy. And I'm sure she meant stupid.' Her daughter hesitates. 'And I thought you and Steve thought so, too. I thought you were just being kind when you said encouraging things.' Esme can hardly believe what she is hearing. 'And then after Darius diagnosed my dysgraphia, I stopped thinking I was stupid. But I wasn't sure what you thought. Sometimes I still thought you were being kind and that you still thought I was stupid.'

'Not in a million years,' Esme says. She is amazed. 'How could you ever have thought such a thing?' Esme hears a happy sigh at the other end of the line. 'And now I've got some news to tell you.'

'What is it?' Dani asks.

'I'm going to marry Darius on Saturday, and we want to come and fetch you so you can be chief bridesmaid.' There's a silence and Esme waits for Dani to speak.

'But you said you'd wait for me,' Dani says. 'Until I was ready to go.' Then she's silent again.

'And I meant it, Dani,' Esme tells her. 'We are going to wait until you are ready to go. No matter how long it takes. But Darius and I are going to get married.'

'Even if we don't go back with him?' Dani asks. 'Does he know?'

'Yes, of course, he knows. I told him after we talked about it and he said he understood and that he'd wait for us.'

'I can't believe it,' Dani says and Esme hears a sort of splutter at the end of the phone. 'I can't believe it, Mum.'

'So how about it, Dani? Will you be my bridesmaid?'

'Why didn't you tell me before, Mum? Saturday's only four days away.'

'I know,' Esme says. 'I'm sorry, Dani. I should have told you before. And Grandma and Grandpa, too.'

'So why didn't you?'

'I was scared,' Esme says and there's another silence at the end of the line. 'So how about it, Dani? Are you going to be our chief bridesmaid?'

'Chief bridesmaid?' asks Dani. 'Who are the others?'

'Well, actually,' Esme confesses, 'there aren't any others. Would you mind being the only one?' There's another silence on the line and Esme wonders this time if the line has gone dead. 'Are you still there?' she asks.

'There's something I have to ask,' Dani says after the longest pause.

'Ask away,' Esme says, drawing heavily on her cigarette and wondering what is coming.

'Will you still want me after you're married?' she asks. 'Will there be a place for me?'

'Oh Dani,' Esme says. 'My dearest daughter,' and she stifles the sob that rises unbidden. 'How can you ask such a thing? How can you ever ever ask such a thing? You are my number one girl, my most precious one. More precious even than Darius,' she says, 'and nothing in the world will ever change that.'

'Not anything?' Dani asks.

'Not anything.' Esme confirms.

'Not ever?' her daughter presses.

'Not ever,' Esme repeats.

'Then you'd better come down quickly because I'll have to find a bridesmaid's dress before Saturday.' They are both weeping now and Esme feels her whole soul rock with relief. What an amazing daughter Dani is.

'We'll be down tomorrow,' she says. 'Now can you get Grandma for me? I want to tell her, too.'

To Esme's amazement, when she manages, at last, to give her mother the news, her mother sounds pleased for her.

'I knew,' she tells Esme. 'And I told your father.'

'What did he say?' Esme asks feeling nervous all over again.

'He said that it was all as it should be,' she replies.

47

Saturday dawns with a clear blue sky. It is Esme's wedding day and the sun is shining but it is the windiest day you can imagine. Esme can't see for the hair that keeps blowing into her eyes, and the long cream satin wedding dress (that Suzi has made for her) wraps itself around her legs. Darius, too, battles the wind and so does Dani as they get out of the taxi and walk the short distance to the registry office. They laugh in the wind, but once inside there is a sudden calm. The three of them stand together and Esme looks in amazement at the crowd of friends who have come to wish them well.

Instead of just the two of them with a couple of witnesses picked up from passers-by as they had originally planned, the place is full of family and friends. Esme is overwhelmed. There is Dani, her beloved Dani looking beautiful. Like Esme, she is wearing a satin dress (pink) and a crown of flowers. Esme has tea roses. Dani has rosebuds. Grandpa has made their crowns with flowers that have thornless stems that he has twisted expertly together. Dani's are pink, and Esme's are red. Dani is a young girl, not a child anymore. Grandpa thinks of her as a young lady.

And there they are, Esme's parents, standing at the front, looking proud. Esme and Dani are carrying bouquets of roses and ferns, a large bouquet for the bride, a smaller one for the bridesmaid. Grandpa again. He has provided all the flowers. Even with such short notice, he has managed to produce magnificent bouquets that no-one will ever forget. By the end of the day, Grandpa's satisfaction at the compliments that flow from all sides on the beauty of both his flowers and his daughter and granddaughter makes him almost talkative. He doesn't stop smiling. And the roses are the old-fashioned scented ones.

Esme's memories of the day are drenched in the scent of roses provided by her father. She will never forget. The flowers are from the garden in Summer Lane. They are the roses she'd told Darius about on their first date together when they had sat in the park and looked at the single rose. The rose of peace. Esme looks through tears of happiness at all her friends. Mandy and Marsha, Pete and Suzi, Kate and Murray, Joe and all of his family and Dani's friends, too. Her daughter has invited some friends from her class that Esme has not met before. Who would have thought it she whispers to Darius? Who would have thought it? And she sees that although he is not close to tears as she is, he is moved.

After the ceremony, they all go back to Joe's house where the reception is to be held. It's true that the house is large but Esme would never have believed that so many people would fit into it. It has elastic sides Joe says and grins. The house is full of music, food and drink and the happy chatter of wedding guests. How did they prepare it all so quickly she thinks? It's almost like magic.

'What about your family?' she asks Darius. 'Don't you miss them?'

'Of course,' he replies, 'but eventually we shall be in Papua New Guinea and you will meet them then.' Esme has hardly thought about leaving England and has only occasionally thought about Darius's family and what life will be like in PNG. Esme is beginning to think that Dani might not keep them waiting for too long.

Darius has told Esme that she will be able to continue her teaching career in Papua New Guinea and she smiled about that. It had never occurred to her that she had what you would call a career, but she does want to carry on working. Earning her own money, being independent, finding satisfaction in work are all so important to her that she takes those things for granted. She has always worked. It has never occurred to her that her life could be otherwise. But it will be different there. Darius has warned her that it will be different.

When her daughter is ready, Esme will give in her notice, but that might not be for a year. Two years? It doesn't matter. She can wait. Esme looks over to where her parents are sitting and starts to think about how much she will miss them. And realises just a little of how much they will miss her and Dani.

'When we live in PNG, we'll come back to visit, won't we?' Esme asks him.

'Of course,' Darius replies. 'We'll try to come back every couple of years.' Esme swallows and tries to push the *try* out of her mind. It is a special day. No time for thoughts of future sorrow. She sees Joe coming towards them, grinning broadly.

'There's a phone call,' he says. 'For you, Darius.' Darius gets up and goes to the phone. In a few minutes, he comes back and asks Esme to go with him.

'It's my brother,' he tells her. 'He wants to speak to you.'

'Is that Esme?' a voice asks, a voice that sounds surprisingly similar to Darius's voice.

'Yes,' she replies.

'Welcome to the family,' he says. 'We're looking forward to meeting you.' Voices on the phone usually sound close, but Darius's brother sounds distant, very far away. His name is Michael.

'Me, too,' Esme says. 'And thank you.'

***

At last the evening is over. Esme's parents are staying at Joe's, so in the end, it is just the three of them going back to Potter Terrace. When they get in, Darius asks Dani to make a pot of tea for them all while he takes her mother upstairs.

'I have to do something,' he explains. He takes Esme's hand and leads her up the stairs. 'No,' he instructs as she reaches the bedroom door. 'Stop there.' Esme stops and looks at him. He opens the door, then picks her up and carries her inside. Just about makes it as far as the bed where he drops her and laughs.

'I thought you were supposed to carry me in from outside,' she says. He looks at her and grins. 'Well,' Ess goes on, 'We've done it. It's finished.'

'Not a bit of it,' he replies. 'We've only just started,' and Esme looks at him. There is a sudden shout from below.

'Tea's ready,' Dani calls.

'Coming,' they reply and go back down.

48

'Are you definitely going then?' Jaffa asks as I dismount and throw my bike against the bush. I see that he is looking at me in that way that makes me feel strange all over. 'You looked fantastic yesterday, Dani,' he says. 'I shall always remember you looking like that.'

'But not today?' I ask, laughing.

'Of course,' he replies, and adds,' but yesterday was special. You glowed, Dani girl. You glowed.'

'Thank you,' I say. 'You looked pretty good yourself.' And now it's Jaffa's turn to look pleased.

'I've still got the rose,' he says. 'It's coming out.' When we went out to talk in the garden at Joe's yesterday, I gave him one of the rose buds out of my bouquet.

'I've sketched it already,' he says. 'I'll paint it today. It still smells.' Jaffa's one of the few people to whom I could give a rose. On second thoughts, maybe he's the only person.

'I'm glad you brought Granville,' I say. 'I've met him at last. But he doesn't look much like you.'

'No,' Jaffa agrees. 'He looks more like Annie. I don't seem to look like anybody.'

'That's true,' I say.

'And who do you look like?' he asks. 'Your Mum doesn't look as though she's even related to you. She's small and dark and you're tall and blonde.'

'Mum says that I look like my father,' I tell him,' and I've seen photos but I can't see it myself. Except for the hair.'

'What was he like, Dani? Can you remember him? Was he really like the man in your dream?'

'I can't remember,' I tell him. 'Sometimes I think I can. I feel sure that I can. But then they tell me that I was too small. I must be remembering what other people have told me about him.'

'And what do you think?'

'I'm not sure,' I say and I'm hesitating because I remember the day when we had the row. It was the day I told him about my dream and he said that finding out what happened wasn't important. I decide to try one last time so once more I tell Jaffa about the dream and about both Grandma and then Mum telling me they think that it might be a memory.

'I want to find out what happened that day,' I say. 'I need to find out whether my father really did try to kill me.'

'I can understand that,' he says and I heave a sigh of relief. 'Do you think you're any nearer?' I move closer to him and he puts his arm around me. 'You keep thinking about it and the dream keeps coming but do you think you know any more than you did?'

I think about it and shake my head. The dream comes in phases. Sometimes it happens a lot and then it's as though I have a break before it comes back again. Just as powerful. Just as frightening. Knowing that it might be a memory doesn't seem to make it any less frightening. I don't remind Jaffa of what he said the first time. I'm just relieved that I can talk about it again. I turn to look at him and watch him go to his bike. He comes back with his tobacco tin.

'I need a smoke,' he says and I smell that it's weed he's smoking. 'Do you want some?'

I shake my head and he grins at me, the special Jaffa smile. We sit there in companionable silence until I start to giggle.

'There's still nobody playing tennis.'

'I think there is,' he says and I watch him move his head from side to side as though he's watching a match. We hear a noise and look to one side and see an old man sitting on the bench next to us. He looks in amazement as I start to move my head in time with Jaffa as we watch the match together and can't stop laughing. After a while, the old guy gets up and walks past us, turning from time to time to peer at the court.

'Have you gone a bit doolally?' he asks us as he walks past.

'Probably,' Jaffa replies and we laugh again.

'Has your dad come back yet?' I ask and Jaffa sobers up a bit.

'Yes, he's back,' he says.

'Well, that's a good thing, isn't it?' I ask but Jaffa says he isn't sure.

'What about PNG then?' he asks again. 'Will you definitely be going?'

'Yes,' I say. 'But not for a long time. We've got the whole summer first. We're not going until I'm ready. Like I told you.' Jaffa reaches for my hand. 'What did you think of Darius?' I ask him after a while.

'I hate him,' Jaffa says with a lazy smile, 'because he's taking you away from me. What do *you* think of him?'

'I like him,' I say. 'although I don't want to go to PNG.' I pause. 'But I'll have to eventually.' I stop speaking and look directly at him. 'It's like Mandy says. I can't change it, so I'll have to roll with it.'

'It's a long way to have to roll,' Jaffa says.

THE END

Acknowledgements

Many thanks to all my beta readers especially to Jill Tennison, Elaine Segura, Caroline Timus and James Gallaugher.

I thank my family in Australia.

For keeping me going, I thank Zoltan Patai-Szabo and Greg Savva.

For unfailing encouragement and technical help, I am grateful to Francis Booth.

For endless patience and helpful feedback, I thank Paul Way-Rider.

Novels by angela j. phillip

Daniela Hoffman's Family Matters - series

This series (each novel complete in itself) tells the story of Daniela and her family through her teenage years to adulthood. It's the story of the bonds between daughter and mother - both doing their best to cope with overwhelming needs that frequently conflict. Fathers come and go but are more important than they seem and their influence remains. The family configuration changes but at its core Esme and Daniela, mother and daughter, slowly work out their relationship. The outside world is ever present and new experiences form turning points in each of their lives until finally Daniela is a woman. She has come of age.

Daniela Hoffman is Not Stupid (Book 1)

Her mother loves her but needs some space. She doesn't know that teenage Daniela has a secret that she can't confide. Dani can't cope at school and tries to hide it. She's clever and has taught herself to be tough, but things go from bad to worse until she fears she will be thrown out. Dani has nowhere to turn. She sees her respectable mother going off the rails while the family falls apart and she struggles to

328

stop it happening. Mother and daughter love and misunderstand each other until a crisis is reached and slowly new understandings emerge. This is a gripping family drama with a feel-good ending.

The Third Father (Book 2)

Daniela doesn't understand what happened with her first father but she still dreams about him. Daddy number two was kind and she loved him, but he's gone. Her family is falling apart and now there's the prospect of yet another father figure. Dani's mother is besotted with a man from overseas, but Dani has little sympathy. She is determined there will be no Daddy number three. Her mother is torn between the man she loves and the needs of her daughter. A family drama with the needs of a daughter for her father at its heart and her fear of change that is gradually overcome.

Respectful request
Please will you write a review? Feedback is the most precious thing and helpful for the author as well as for other readers. Even if it is only one or two lines, it would be very much appreciated.

For more information and to sign up for the newsletter, please go to:
https://angelajphillip.com.

Printed in Great Britain
by Amazon